The same frustration from before—hell, from forever—darkened his gaze once more but other than a small sneer, he held his frustration. "That's not what I meant. This is dangerous. You have no idea what you're dealing with."

"Which is why I've been trained. It's my job."

His hand fell away and Tate took a few steps back. The physical withdrawal was mimicked by the way his gaze shuttered and his mouth firmed into a straight line. "The job. Just like always."

Belle wanted to argue. She wanted to rant and rail and give him the litany of reasons why she was not only good at her job, but called to it. But the day had begun too early. And the pain of seeing him again, so up close and personal, always left her slightly empty and more than a bit bruised emotionally. So she skipped the ready defense and nodded instead.

"Just like always."

* * *

We hope you enjoy the Midnight Pass, Texas miniseries.

* * *

If you're on Twitter, tell us what you think of Harlequin Romantic Suspense! #harlequinromsuspense

Dear Reader,

Welcome to Midnight Pass, Texas. Nestled along the banks of the Rio Grande, the Pass is home to several ranching families and some of the hardest-working police teams in the Lone Star State.

Tate Reynolds is the middle son of one of those ranching families. Along with his siblings, he's worked hard to return Reynolds Station to its former glory and he's horrified to discover a body on their property early one spring morning. His upset quickly takes on a new direction when the detective assigned to the case is his old flame, Belle Granger.

Belle hasn't fully gotten over her relationship with Tate, which ended because of his unwillingness to accept her job choice. Their decade-long feud has always churned up a fair amount of gossip in the Pass on account of the sparks that still fly whenever the two of them get within striking distance. But when town gossip shifts to a new subject—a serial killer on the loose—Belle has to work with Tate and his family to uncover what evil lurks at the edges of the ranch.

When she uncovers a threat that's far closer than anyone could have suspected, Tate will need to make a decision. Will he keep his distance from the woman he let go of all those years ago? Or will he hold her close and try to protect her from a dangerous killer?

I hope you enjoy *The Cowboy's Deadly Mission*, the first in my new Midnight Pass series. Tate's siblings, Hoyt, Ace and Arden, have their own stories still to come and I hope you'll love the Reynolds family as much as I do.

Best,

Addison Fox

THE COWBOY'S DEADLY MISSION

Addison Fox

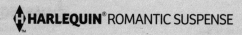
HARLEQUIN® ROMANTIC SUSPENSE

Recycling programs
for this product may
not exist in your area.

ISBN-13: 978-1-335-45653-3

The Cowboy's Deadly Mission

Copyright © 2018 by Frances Karkosak

Printed in U.S.A.

Addison Fox is a lifelong romance reader, addicted to happy-ever-afters. After discovering she found as much joy writing about romance as she did reading it, she's never looked back. Addison lives in New York with an apartment full of books, a laptop that's rarely out of sight and a wily beagle who keeps her running. You can find her at her home on the web at www.addisonfox.com or on Facebook (Facebook.com/addisonfoxauthor) and Twitter (@addisonfox).

Books by Addison Fox

Harlequin Romantic Suspense

Midnight Pass, Texas

The Cowboy's Deadly Mission

The Coltons of Red Ridge

Colton's Deadly Engagement

The Coltons of Shadow Creek

Cold Case Colton

The Coltons of Texas

Colton's Surprise Heir

Harlequin Intrigue

The Coltons of Shadow Creek

Colton K-9 Cop

Visit the Author Profile page at Harlequin.com.

For Grant

Sweetness and light and giggles and love.
How wonderful it will be to watch you grow.

I'm so lucky to be your aunt.

And, in the immortal words of Monica Geller,
"I will always have gum."

Chapter 1

Midnight Pass, Texas, had exactly three things to recommend it: the finest pool hall in all the state; thick, rich, foamy beer brewed off the waters of the Rio Grande; and the Reynolds boys, who had grown into the finest-looking cowboys in the entire Southwest.

Annabelle Granger was well aware she'd been born with the gift of keen observation and a tendency to exaggerate what she saw, but there was nothing exaggerated about the swagger that gripped Ace Reynolds's hips when he walked. The firm grip of Hoyt Reynolds's long, thick fingers on his Stetson. Or Tate Reynolds's wicked smile that had removed the panties of more than a few lucky women.

Belle, sadly, had been one of them.

Tamping down on the old feelings that had no place in a criminal investigation, she ignored the cocky grin

Tate shot her across the wide expanse of damaged fence she'd been sent out to investigate.

"Thanks for coming, ma'am."

"It's Detective."

"Of course." He nodded. "Detective Ma'am."

Tate wasn't remorseful—the infuriating man didn't do contrite. And she was convinced he'd never used the word "sorry" in his life. Yet try as she might, she couldn't quite work up the degree of anger required to squelch the demon bats that dive-bombed her stomach every time they got within thirty feet of each other.

"'Detective Granger' will be just fine. Or have you managed to forget my name after thirteen years of school, one miserable year as biology lab partners and a rather ill-advised date to the Sadie Hawkins dance senior year?"

She avoided mentioning the six glorious weeks they'd been as wild and carefree as mustangs, falling into each other's arms every moment they could.

"I know your name."

She risked a stare straight into those vivid green eyes. "So you're threatened by my authority, then?"

"Yep. That's it."

Belle ignored the sarcasm and dropped to her knee. It gave her a break from staring at those broad shoulders, lean hips and his thick brown hair streaked blond from the sun. The fence had been cut clean through, the work likely as swift and efficient as it looked. "You lose any of your cattle?"

"No. I found the breach early enough to manage and the herd's grazing on a different sector. This stretch hasn't been tried before and I don't have cameras out here."

Belle filed that information away, the likelihood this was a well-planned—*illegal*—use of private property increasing exponentially. "Notice anything or anyone suspicious lately?"

"Other than a twenty-foot section of barbed wire cut clean through? No."

A few of Tate's ranch hands worked in the distance, preparing the stretch of fence for repair by removing what was cut. Their hands were coated in thick gloves but even with the barrier, they worked quickly.

"I'm here to help you."

The eyes that usually flashed with easygoing humor clouded, transforming into a hard, cold emerald. "You'll have to forgive me if I don't take comfort in that. You're the third member of our esteemed police force out here in the past six months and no one seems able to fix the little intrusion problem I seem to have developed on my land. That fence isn't cutting itself."

Belle chafed at the suggestion her department wasn't doing enough, but she damn well knew problems along the border had grown nigh impossible to contain. Between drug trafficking and illegal immigration, the local cops had their hands as full as the Feds.

And both problems were only growing worse.

She got to her feet, her gaze roaming over the dry footprints that were barely visible in the scrub grass that surrounded the fence. They'd likely never even be visible if it hadn't been for the spring rains that had softened up the land. "You put the patrol on like the chief asked you to?"

"So now it's my problem?"

"It's all our problems, Tate. I'm asking if you've done your part."

Tate's shoulders hunched before he turned back to the men cutting wire. Stubble still coated the firm jaw that was hardening in anger. "We all take turns. I've got extra patrols on each night. Added several men on top of that and I let the Feds roam around here with all that Yankee finesse they're known for. Doesn't change the fact that it's a hell of a lot of acreage to cover over every night after a long day of work."

"And people looking for a way in observe patterns. Weak spots. The Pass has more than most."

While she refrained from saying much to the contrary at work, she wasn't going to sugarcoat it for Tate. Midnight Pass had gotten its name for the deep ravines and many hiding places that ran along a small tributary of the Rio Grande. That tributary—and the larger river a half mile away—made up a stretch of Texas-Mexico border that was a challenge to patrol.

The rich, fertile land was home to the three largest ranching clans in the county. The Reynolds, Vasquez and Crown families had built massive cattle operations over the lush earth. And for the past decade, their land had increasingly become the conduit to a drug trade that was far more lucrative than cattle.

"You think anyone on your team's letting them in?"

"Ace, Hoyt and I have a zero tolerance policy and make that known. Our older guys keep an eye out, as well. Best I can say is we watch out for it."

"Fair enough."

Tate moved in, his fingers snaking out to toy with several strands of hair that had come loose at her ear. The 6:00 a.m. wake-up call ordering her out to Reynolds Station hadn't allowed for much prep time and putting her hair in a hasty bun and some slapdash makeup was all the armor she'd had time for. "Why are you here, Belly? You know this is a dangerous job."

The whispered endearment only increased the flapping wings of the demon bats and she slapped at his hand. "You know how I feel about that name."

"Which is why I use it."

"And you know how I feel about my job, dangerous or otherwise. You have no say in the matter."

"I never did."

Tate stared at the only woman who had the ability to wrap him in knots and dropped the curl winding around his finger. Annabelle Granger had been his nemesis since the first grade and little had changed in the ensuing quarter century. Trite as it was—he'd pulled her pigtails then and had been proverbially doing so ever since—he couldn't remember a single moment of his life that Belle Granger hadn't occupied space in his head. The amount of real estate changed pending how recently they'd seen each other, but she was always there.

His Belle.

With her blond curls that made his fingers itch. Vivid blue eyes with a gaze as sharp as her tongue. And the small dent in her chin that fascinated him as much at thirty-two as it had at six. There'd even been a time—a short, gloriously wonderful time—when he'd run his tongue over that little dent while his hands roamed over—

On a hard, mental curse, Tate shut down that unproductive line of thought and focused on his problem. Once again, Reynolds Station had been used for trafficking—either drugs or illegal immigrants. He was committed to finding a solution to the poor souls who gave everything they had to come across the border, no matter the cost, a stance that didn't make him incredibly popular with the locals. He had no time for the abuse so many of those individuals suffered in the process and made his feelings known as a voting member of the town council.

The drugs, on the other hand, had gone positively nuclear. What had been an irritating problem had mushroomed over the past decade into an all-out war. And there were far too many days Tate believed he and his brothers were losing. Every time they found a cut line of fence or line of footprints tracking over their land, it was another skirmish they'd fought and lost.

And no amount of manpower seemed to be helping.

"When did you discover this? I got the dispatch around six."

"About five." When she only stared at him, he added, "I was out early."

Her gaze narrowed, that sharp blue spiking even sharper points. "You're not sleeping?"

Her lack of response over his barb about her choices, coupled with the sudden focus and attention on his lack of sleep, had Tate sliding back into the familiar comfort of their usual sparring. "Just because you'd gladly hug your pillow until noon doesn't mean some of us aren't early risers."

"Sun's not even up at five this time of year."

"I took a flashlight."

Tate had no idea what had pulled him out to this end of the property but he'd had the urge and had pushed Tot this direction on their early morning ride. Good thing he had because they were planning on rotating the herd to this section later this week.

Belle dropped to her knee again, her gaze roaming over the ground. Clear signs of feet were stamped into the earth, but unlike that volume of prints he'd expect from a border crossing, there seemed to be far too few for a group of people spirited across the border. The coyotes—those guides who led those desperate for opportunity or freedom from poverty over the border—had increasingly been replaced of late with drug smugglers. Criminals who saw the border crossing as an opportunity to use their charges as drug mules, all while promising them freedom.

Even with that change, there should have been more variance in the footprints.

Her gaze remained focused on the ground as she duckwalked, stopping every few feet to assess from a new angle. She was an observer—had been one since she was in those pigtails—but it always fascinated him to watch her work. He might not like her professional choices but he couldn't argue she was damn good at her job. Dedicated, too.

And hadn't that been the problem?

"You see this?"

Her question pulled him from his musings and Tate crossed the distance, crouching down when she gestured once more to the depressed earth. "Here. There are a few sets of footprints, then this depression, rounded out like someone set down something heavy."

"You can see that?"

The depression she spoke of was nothing more than a soft bending of grass, but now that he looked, he could see the rounded outline of a heavier shape.

"It looks like a heavy bag or weight was set down. Could be a bag of drugs, set down out of the way."

Tate scanned the length of fence. "They did all this for one duffel bag full? It hardly seems worth it." She shot him one lone raised eyebrow and he pressed on. "I'm not condoning anything. I'm suggesting if I were planning an illegal border crossing with drugs, I'd look to move a hell of a lot more to make it worth the risk."

"I don't disagree."

"You think it's something else?" Knowledge flashed in the cool blue of her eyes—a sure and recognizable sign Belle had already formed an opinion—and Tate moved closer, curious. "What?"

"I'm thinking it's the payoff."

Her words hovered there, the brisk air swirling around them in a rush like an exclamation point. Before he could even muster up a response, she had her phone out, snapping several quick pictures from a variety of angles. She then pulled a packet of bright yellow tape out of her pocket. "Let me mark this. I'll get Julio out to review the area and give his impressions."

"He's been training you well."

"He's patient with me. He'd have seen this the moment he walked up but that's okay. I'm learning."

Learning? He'd say she was doing a damn fine job, spotting a small patch of earth he'd have missed after fifty tries. Add on the implication that someone he and his brothers trusted let the problem onto Reynolds land and Tate struggled under the weight of her suspicions.

"What about my fence? Can the guys get started on it?"

"Can you hold them off a few hours? Keep them

and anyone else out of this area to leave the tracks as clean as possible."

"Sure."

The urge to bait her was strong but the frustration at more lost hours of work was stronger. How much damn time were they expected to give in to this BS? Every few months, he and his brothers dealt with another attempt to breach their land. In the past year alone they'd dealt with six such issues, never in the same place twice and always done with maximum precision.

"Tate, come on. I know it's an inconvenience but it'll only be a few hours."

"Then Tot and I will wait."

He glanced back at his horse, the bay mustang standing quietly as Tate finished his business. Tot had been one of the feral horses he and his brothers took in through a partnership program with the Department of the Interior. Tot had been found in a precarious position, struggling against the tight lassos of a pair of bumbling assholes who wanted the horse for meat. The department had arrested them before they could see their heinous practices through, and then worked on finding a home for Tot.

Something about the pretty bay had tugged at him the moment the horse had arrived at Reynolds Station and Tate set about building a relationship with him. It had taken several long months of working together and training together before Tot had been ready to roam Reynolds Station with him, but patience and persistence had done the trick to build trust and what became a deep friendship. Ever since, they'd been inseparable.

"He's a beauty." Annabelle extended a hand, then waited patiently for the horse to acknowledge her. Once he did, she offered up warm strokes to his cheeks before following the affection with an apple from her pocket.

For the briefest moment, Tate was jealous of his horse as he imagined the gentle slide of Belle's fingers over his own face. The smooth press of skin against skin, a sweet gesture that simply was.

There was a time he'd believed they could have that. Could be that free and easy with each other. How wrong he'd been.

She gave Tot space to munch the apple before turning to give Tate a steady stare. "This is the horse that was rescued from that pair of jerks in Arizona who've been roaming free for the past year?"

Tate couldn't help but be impressed that she'd done her homework. "Same."

"Good riddance," she muttered.

Tot nudged her hand where it sat perched on her hip, seeking another treat, and she laughed before stroking his face and neck again. "He's lucky you found him."

"I'm lucky I found Tot."

"I thought that's what you said. Tot is his name?"

The briefest acknowledgment flitted across her face before it vanished. It was a surprise, Tate mused, to realize he'd wanted to see something more.

When she gave no further acknowledgment, Tate shook it off, burying the small stab of pain beneath a cocky smile. "Ace has called me Tater for years. It fit."

Annabelle's gaze roamed over the horse. "Yes, it does."

It was only a name. A dumb, stupid name for a dumb, stupid horse. That was all. Only the horse was far from dumb or stupid if the innate intelligence that flashed in his deep brown eyes was any indication.

Nor was it only a name and they both knew it.

She'd suggested Tot would be a good horse's name ten years ago, the idea taking root after a particularly rowdy night out with Ace and Veronica Torres, then a Midnight Pass newcomer and the woman Tate's brother been dating at the time. She and Ace had paired up for a game of pool against Veronica and Tate and had beaten them soundly, Ace's repeated taunts of "Tater" at his younger brother, adding frustration to the sound thrashing.

Tate's sullen frown on the drive home hadn't faded so she'd pushed and pressed, teasing him until she managed to pull one of those lazy smiles that tripped up her heart. He wasn't a man to stay angry for long and that lazy smile had quickly turned to laughter, the storm clouds passing as fast as they'd arrived.

"You upset about losing the game?"

Tate turned his gaze from the rutted road that led out of town, his eyes wide. "The game was good fun. Ace just pissed me off with the name."

"You don't like 'Tater'?"

"Not particularly." He glanced across the expanse of his truck's cab. "Would you?"

"He's been doing it for years and it's done with affection. Especially when he's not goosing you about your pool skills."

"It's annoying."

"It's family."

She hadn't given much thought to her response until his hand slipped over hers, his fingers wrapping tightly around hers. "I guess it is."

A wash of emotion clogged her throat with a tight fist, the tears sort of stuck there in a lump, not quite making it to her eyes. How was it thoughts of her mother and the empty liquor bottles that always filled the trash could intrude so quickly? And so completely?

And how was it that Tate understood when her thoughts shifted?

He'd always understood, even at their worst when their conversations seemed to consist of nothing but teasing and jovial taunts. He accepted her circumstances and all the reasons she got quiet every now and again.

She was coming to see how much that meant, in ways she'd never expected when they'd started their relationship. For a guy who seemed so easygoing and carefree, he had surprising depths. He missed nothing and in quiet moments found ways to show he understood.

Annabelle managed to swallow back the tears, unwilling to ruin a fun evening with a discussion about her mom. Things never changed there and a bout of tears would only ruin a perfectly good evening. As they receded, an odd, silly thought took their place.

"Next horse you get, you should name Tot."

"Tot?"

"As in Tater Tot. Get it?"

His sharp bark of laughter filled the cab and it was enough to quell the somber thoughts that had threatened to take her over. Her mom wasn't getting any better, but for the moment, she was here with Tate.

And when she was with him, all the rest faded away.

She hadn't thought about that night in a long time, the silly conversation in the car or the suggestion for naming his horse replaced by the more painful memories of what had come after.

On a soft sigh, Annabelle pulled into the police station, willing away the maudlin thoughts. She had a job to do and it didn't matter if Tate Reynolds still tied her up in knots. His property had become increasingly overrun by those coming up through the Rio Grande Valley out of Mexico and she'd taken an oath to battle that problem, determined to prosecute coyotes or drug lords to the maximum extent of the law.

The large, black SUVs the Feds habitually drove took up three spaces behind the precinct house, a sight that had become all too familiar in the past year. Their presence only reinforced the reality of what she'd observed on the far west end of the Reynolds property that very morning. The drug trade flourished in Midnight Pass and there were days she wondered if they could ever erase the poisonous blight that had descended over their small slice of heaven.

Chapter 2

"Heard Belle was out visiting this morning."

Tate stilled, the unfurled length of barbed wire heavy against his thickly gloved hands as his brother's voice drifted over his back. He loved his brother but Ace had developed a way of nagging him over the years about Belle that was about as subtle as a cold sore at the prom.

Which, Tate figured, was sort of the point.

"She was the one lucky enough to pull duty this morning at six a.m. when I called in the breach."

"Breach?" Ace pulled on his own pair of thick gloves. "That's what we're calling it now?"

"You have a better name?"

"Invasion. Attack. Infection. Take your pick."

Anger and frustration layered Ace's words and Tate stilled, giving himself a moment to really look at his brother. The weight of the ranch sat heavily on all of them—as welcome a burden as it was challenging—but Ace's load carried a bit more freight. As the eldest son, he carried the weightiness of expectation along with all the other requirements of running one of the largest cattle ranches in southwest Texas.

Streaks of gray lined Ace's temples, visible through the military-short cut of his hair. Lines fanned out from the Reynolds green eyes Tate and his brothers carried like a matched set of luggage, but it was the stiffness in his brother's shoulders that told the real story. Where Tate and Hoyt carried a linebacker's bulk, Ace had inherited their mother's slimmer genes. The man was tall and wiry, his lean frame belying the sheer strength he bore in every bone and sinew.

Anyone who thought Ace Reynolds might be an easy mark quickly learned their mistake. Raw strength and power were the man's hallmarks, his body as unyielding as his honor and approach to life.

"So what did Belle say?"

"She did some rudimentary tracking. Will be back out in a bit with Julio Bautista to look at the site. After they look at everything, we can repair the fence." Tate let his gaze drift over the clean-cut hole before refocusing on Ace. "I sent the hands on to other tasks. Told them to come back around noon."

"Should be enough time."

"You don't have to wait with me. I'm sure you've got better things to do with your time."

Ace quirked one eyebrow. "Trying to get rid of me?"

"No. Just figured you had better things to do."

"I consider this better."

Waiting for no further invitation, Ace hunched down

and tugged at the bale of wire, smoothing over the edge Tate had already cut. "I'll put this back on the truck."

They worked in silence for a few minutes. Tate lined up the pieces they'd replace while Ace puttered around the back of the truck he'd driven out from the main house. Although he knew his brother would find out eventually, some small voice had Tate holding back his suspicions.

The light depression in the dirt. Belle's suggestion of a lone bag of drugs or the suspicion of a cash payoff. *Hell.*

He didn't need any help reading between the lines. And if she shared her concerns, they'd have Feds crawling the property before the afternoon was out. He ran a working ranch, not a damn forensics lab.

"You always were a crappy liar. Ready to tell me what's going on?" Ace slapped the thick gloves against his thigh. "And before you argue with me, omission's a lie."

It briefly crossed his mind to argue, but Tate held his tongue. Ace had a right to know. Even as he knew he'd only add to the weight that already rode his brother's shoulders.

"There's yellow police tape over there. Belle thinks the shape left in the grass looks like a single bag of drugs."

"One bag?" The words were barely out before Ace shook his head. "A payoff?"

"That's what I think."

"Son of a bitch."

"Come take a look." Tate led the way to the small marked area. The yellow tape was visible in the grass as they got closer. "I don't know how she even saw it."

"Because it's her job."

More truth. Raw and unsettling, but the truth all the same. Even more unsettling, Tate knew what it had cost her. What it had cost both of them. Belle took her job seriously, both the work she did and her reputation. Yet she'd still shared her initial impressions, even if she should have saved them for her colleagues.

Ace dropped into a hunch once more, his attention fully focused on the marked area. Tate moved closer, the bright, mid-morning sun seeming to throw a spotlight on the small area. With the additional light, it was easier to see the outline—easier to envision the heavy duffel bag that would have made the mark.

"One of our own." Ace added a string of curses that matched Tate's thoughts from the past two hours before their attention was pulled toward the bump of tires about five hundred yards away.

"Belle's back." Tate could see Julio Bautista in the passenger seat, his grizzled features a contrast to Belle's smooth skin and eager visage.

Ace shaded his eyes before his hard stare swung toward Tate. "Looks like she is."

Julio Bautista was one of the best trackers in south Texas and had worked as a field expert for the county for what had to be forty years. The man could tell you everything from the shoe size on a partial footprint to the age of animal scat to what types of scrub grass grew in the region. His senses were so refined the man predicted the weather better than any ten TV meteorologists.

While she admired it all, Belle loved him because he was the gentlest of teachers, more than willing to impart his knowledge and understanding of how living beings left their impressions on the earth.

"That the place you marked?" Julio pointed through the windshield to the area where she'd laid yellow police tape earlier that morning, his wizened face scrunched up against the glare of the morning sun.

"That's the one. Tate Reynolds found the cut fence early this morning and called it in. I almost missed the small depression but saw it at the last minute."

"Reynolds being cooperative?"

"Of course he is."

The words spilled out too quickly and Belle winced inwardly as Julio's solemn gaze shifted from his view through the windshield to her. "You sure?"

"Yes. Oh, he was a bit surprised to see it was me who arrived to take his statement, but he got over it. He understands the force is stretched thin. Understands I'm a member of that force."

He understands the implications, too, she mused, considering what a possible payoff on his land would mean in regards to his staff.

Julio snorted at the "stretched thin" comment but said nothing, opening his door and hopping out of the SUV. The man's services had been stretched thin of late, too. And although he worked for the county, he'd spent more than a disproportionate time in Midnight Pass over the past few years. He waved to Tate and Ace Reynolds before crossing to the two men and shaking their hands.

"Bella says you had a problem last night."

Tate shot her the slightest raised eyebrow at Julio's affectionate name for her before pointing toward the fence. "Not the first one we've had."

"Likely won't be the last." Julio puttered toward the fence line, careful to steer clear of the area she'd marked off with tape. His gaze never left the ground, his steps careful in the event she'd missed other key clues depressed into the earth. Belle left him to his work, well aware he needed to get a sense of place before he'd be ready to speak with them again.

"Julio's the best."

"Word around town is that you're his protégée." Ace's smile was warm and encouraging, a decisive counterpoint to the scowl that painted Tate's face.

The two men might be brothers—might love each other fiercely—but they rarely saw eye to eye on anything. Her career choice was likely another item on that very long list of disagreements.

Which only served to rub salt in the wound. How could the man's brother see her as a competent professional and Tate couldn't? Since that line of thought only served to add to her simmering frustration, she offered up a smile instead.

"Julio's been kind enough to take me on and train me. He's plenty busy so I'm grateful for the help."

Tate let out a loud snort. "The way I hear it, you more than pull your own weight."

The comment was as surprising as the idea that Tate kept up with her career. Annabelle wanted to press him on his comment, but Julio had already begun working his way back to them, his shout and hand wave effectively ending anything else she might have said.

"Come see this." Her mentor stopped near the taped off area and dropped to his knees. Belle was careful to watch her footsteps before dropping to her haunches beside Julio, Ace and Tate following suit. Once they

were all in place, Julio traced an outline into the air.
"You see here? This part Bella marked."

"Of course."

"I do think she's right. It has the weight and shape
of a heavy duffel. It also matches a light depression I
found on the other side of the fence."

"I missed it?"

Julio's smile was broad. "I'm not quite ready for you
to put me out of business, Bella. And the mark was
faint and easy to miss. I saw it because I knew what I
was looking for."

Belle appreciated the encouragement but couldn't
hide the sting to her pride. She'd been careful this
morning, but she was well aware her focus had been
divided between the work and Tate. If Ace or Hoyt had
greeted her, she suspected she'd not have missed the
second depression Julio discovered.

But Ace and Hoyt hadn't made the call to the precinct.

Tate had.

She risked a glance in his direction, only to be
greeted by a quick flash of humor. The wholly unpro-
fessional urge to stick her tongue out at him rippled
through her before she tamped it down.

How did he do this to her?

They weren't on the school playground and she'd
given up the pigtails he'd loved to pull as kids. Yet even
now, after all this time, she couldn't help seeking him
out. Was it for approval? Or worse, was she seeking
the agreement she knew she'd never get? Because they
didn't agree. And they hadn't seen eye to eye on anything except the sexual awareness and attraction that

always flared sky-high when they were within fifty feet of each other.

Tate Reynolds had claimed he wanted her. He'd claimed a lot of things during the time they'd spent together, freely giving of themselves to one another.

But he hadn't held up his side of the bargain.

Worse, he'd asked her to choose between the one thing in her life—except for him—that gave her purpose. Fulfillment. Joy.

And every time they looked at each other, she saw the reality of that choice reflecting back at her.

Tate didn't want to be impressed. He didn't want to be fascinated. He didn't want to be awed. But despite every attempt to squelch those impressions, he was all those things and more. The girl who'd intrigued him in ways he hadn't understood had grown into a woman who still had the ability to trip him up.

He was a simple guy. He liked ranching and a good night out at the rodeo, cold beer and a rousing evening of pool. And he liked women. Tall women, short women, curvy and slender—he appreciated them all. Enjoyed them all. But he didn't love any of them.

Because none of them were Annabelle Granger.

The damned truth of his life lived in that lone, miserable fact.

"Come see what I marked over here." Julio's command penetrated the unsettling rush of thoughts and Tate followed, pleased to get out of his head for a few minutes. They followed the old tracker from the initial area Belle roped off and on over to the impressions he'd discovered by the fence. Belle kept up a steady line of questions as they walked, from size of the imprint to the relatively few marks in the dirt, sharing her theories with Julio.

"Do you think it's the work of a coyote? They're paid to help people cross the border. This would be as good a spot as any and it could be their payment or a payment the coyote made to whomever helped him cross."

"It's a good theory, but this is the work of few, especially since there aren't a lot of footprints. A coyote would take more people, Bella."

Tate saw her subtle frown and suspected the question was for his and Ace's benefit. It was a long shot question, designed to stave off the inevitable, and there was no way Belle really thought a late-night crossing on his land was the work of illegal immigrants. While they did have border crossings through Midnight Pass, the town's core problem was drugs. The trade had flourished over the past decade, a stark reminder of what troubles lurked beneath the quiet facade of the Pass.

Businesses on Main Street prospered right alongside the marijuana, cocaine and heroin trafficking that followed in the dark of night. She and her fellow officers worked tirelessly to keep up with it, along with the increasing cadre of federal agents who'd set up shop in town, but they'd had relatively little success in stopping it.

Other than his time on the town council, Tate had diligently avoided the politics of life in the Pass, but he wasn't blind or deaf. Hell, he'd had a conversation three days ago at the feed store about the same thing, and a few days before, Tabasco Burns had been bitching about a low-level dealer he'd tossed out of his pool hall.

Drugs and all their associated evils were a blight on

their town and, like a greasy oil slick, they continued to spread. Two overdoses the year before and twenty across the county. And that was just what had hit close to home. He knew damn well what crossed through the Pass fanned out across the state and farther.

"So you do think it's a drug run?" The words were sour on his tongue, but Tate had never been afraid of a fight. Nor would he tolerate the abuse of his land—of his home—like that.

Julio's dark gaze ran over the fence line once more before he rewarded them with his full attention. "How much do you trust your team?"

"Up until a few minutes ago, I'd have said implicitly." Ace's comment matched his thoughts and Tate's mind already whirled with the possibilities. Who could it be?

Ranger McBride was fairly new. The incidents hadn't started until after he'd been hired on. Or maybe Tris Bradshaw? He had smelled whiskey on the guy's breath a few weeks ago and sent him back to the house to get some coffee. Even as his mind whirled through reasons both men should be suspects, something in his gut didn't sit right.

A few impressions in the dirt and he was ready to go on a witch hunt of his men? Was that how it was going to be now?

If Ace sensed Tate's rising frustration, he said nothing, instead focusing on the physical ravages. "You good with us doing our repairs?"

"*Sí, sí.*" Julio nodded. "I've got my camera in the car. Let Bella and I take a few pictures and then you can fix things."

"I'll alert Trey Vasquez and Harrison Crown in the meantime. See if they've had any incidents."

"We can do that, Ace." Belle was quick to jump in. "You don't have to spend your time warning everyone."

"Somehow I think his conversation will be a bit different than yours." Although the comment was meant to get under Belle's skin, Tate knew his point remained true. If there was a problem with the hands at Reynolds Station, the two other ranches that dominated the county needed to know. They all had a silent agreement not to poach off each other, but a man had a right to move around and make his own living and the Vasquez and Crown families fished in the same employment pool as Tate, Ace and Hoyt did.

Belle's gaze swung to his, challenge sparking in that pretty blue color. "Oh?"

"You'll focus on the problem. Tell him how hard the police are working to manage the situation. You'll likely even offer to drive out and visit their ranches, do a quick swing around the fences that line their properties."

Belle stared at him, confusion crinkling soft lines into her forehead. "What's wrong with that?"

"Nothing."

"So why does it sound like a mocking indictment of the Midnight Pass police force?"

"I'd never mock such a superior institution."

The words hit their mark, just as he'd intended. *Parry, thrust, jab, jab, jab.* The strategy had worked for twenty years; why should he stop now?

"Yet somehow you are."

"Don't be so sensitive."

That jab was harder than the others and Tate was

surprised to feel the kickback in his own stomach. Why did he always manage to take it a bit too far?

"Then what's your point?"

"You're waving at the problem with your badge. We're a bit more subtle than that."

Belle's hands flew to her hips, the fingers on her right hand resting comfortably against her service weapon. Too comfortably, he realized with a hard, solid punch to his stomach. Belle Granger was all cop as she stared at him. "Subtle?"

"Sure. You think the badge is the deterrent."

"And you don't?"

"Not at all."

Of anything he could have said, it was that statement that proved just how far apart the two of them truly were.

"If you think the police are ineffective, then what do you propose, Tate? Vigilante justice? You angling to become the law and order of the land?"

"Bella—" Julio's voice was quiet yet firm as he returned from the SUV, camera in hand, and Tate innately sensed the older man knew far more about Belle and Tate's long-standing feud than he let on.

For reasons he couldn't name—even to himself—it bothered him that Belle might have confided their personal business to Julio and his voice became sharper than the roll of barbed wire he'd just cut. "All I want is to fix this. Crime's at an all-time high in the Pass and now innocent people have drug runners roaming their land."

Tate had no interest in becoming a vigilante, but he did want the problems to stop. He and his brothers had struggled to bring the ranch back from the brink from their father's illegal business practices that nearly shut them down. It had taken considerable hard work and a ton of sweat equity but they'd done it. Because he recognized the value of hard work, it burned him to think there were those whose "work" consisted of transporting a truck full of drugs that went on to ruin thousands of lives.

"And we don't want to fix it?" Belle's retort shot back at him without a moment's hesitation.

Whether it was the stubborn pride that had fueled him his entire life or the small shot of pity he saw in Julio's eyes, Tate had no idea. Or maybe he was beyond caring.

"I don't think you can fix it. Unless you'd prefer the more commonly accepted explanation."

"Which is?"

"Most law-abiding people in town think the Midnight Pass police force couldn't find justice with both hands and a flashlight."

Belle held her tongue, even as her jaw nearly cramped with the effort. How *dare* he?

The idea of the Reynolds brothers taking the law into their own hands was a stark reminder of just how far apart she and Tate remained on the subject of law enforcement. But it was Tate's sheer disdain of the police force that had claws. Brutally sharp and far more lethal than she'd have expected, especially after all these years.

He'd made no secret of the fact he found her ambition misguided, but she'd believed he would come around, especially once they'd given in to the feelings both had fought for so long. She'd traipsed right past the warning bells that clanged in her head, convinced if she could only make him understand how important being a cop was to her—how *essential*—they could find their way.

Oh, how she'd believed that once.

Until her world had come crashing down when Tate abruptly walked away.

Even in the nearly ten years since, she'd not been able to fully understand his decision. She'd made no secret of her interest and intent to join the force. The law was her passion—anyone who'd known her for any length of time understood that.

And Tate had known her better than most.

Yet he'd still walked away.

Even after all this time, that simple little fact hurt like a gaping wound. Would it ever heal?

That question might linger, but she knew the answer in all its stark reality. So long as the two of them still called Midnight Pass home, there was little chance of fully putting Tate Reynolds out of her mind.

Or her heart.

And since it didn't appear as if either of them were leaving anytime soon, there was nothing to be done for it. Fastening her emotional armor, Belle stood at her full height. Her heart might continue to do battle with her mind, but in this her mind would win.

She would not back down.

"Obviously you and your family are welcome to handle employment matters as you see fit. I will, however, be setting up this afternoon at the bunkhouse and I expect that every member of your staff will be available to talk to me. This is now an open investigation."

Before Tate could argue, Ace stepped in. "We will

cooperate fully with the Midnight Pass police force. The staff will be there at the assigned time."

Julio had already drifted away to take his photos—probably afraid of stray bullets, Belle thought—and she turned to follow the older man. "Thank you, Ace."

Tate remained stubborn and stoic, his gaze flashing fire in the early morning sun.

Since there wasn't anything else to say, Belle headed over to join Julio. She diligently avoided looking back at the two men she'd known most of her life and instead focused on putting one foot in front of the other. And if her hands shook, well, they were clenched so hard at her sides there was no way anyone could see it.

Damn that fool man and his vigilante justice and his piss-poor attitude about the police and his conjecture their town was no longer safe.

Damn him.

Belle unfisted her hand before she reached her mentor. Julio already saw too much and she refused to let her personal life—or lack thereof—cloud her ability to do her job. She was determined to be a brilliant cop. It was the only thing she'd ever wanted, a feeling that had only built as she watched her mother succumb to a lifetime of addiction.

Which was the stubborn lie she'd told herself for years. If given the choice, there were actually two things she wanted. But Tate had taken that choice away from her.

Julio had started with the first area she'd found, inside the fence line. He waved her over. "Bella. Come here." The sudden urgency in his voice banished thoughts of her relationship with Tate.

"What is it?"

"Look at this. Walk over there, please." She was careful to follow the way Julio pointed out to her, a curving path instead of a direct walk to his side.

"What is it?"

"Here. Crouch down and look."

The man was nearly seventy, but he had a quick mind and a small, spry form. He duckwalked back a few steps so she could take his place. "What am I looking for? Did you find another depression? Another bag?"

"Just look and tell me what you see."

Belle scanned the area, taking it in like he'd taught her. A broad look to see if anything was out of place, then careful quadrants as she mentally cataloged everything she saw.

Blades of grass, intermittently broken up by rocky scrub.

A small patch of Indian paintbrush doing its best to bloom in the early April weather that had been unusually cold.

A dry, patchy area of dirt where even the scrub wasn't growing, spattered with—

"Julio?" She whirled, coming to her feet in an instant. "Is that blood?"

"It looks like it." He got to his feet.

"There's a lot of it. Not just someone who might have gotten cut on the wire fence. And it looks like it continues into the brush beside it."

"I know, Bella." She nearly moved toward it when Julio laid a hand on her arm. "Let's get a few more things from the car."

Their field kits.

As Belle trudged behind Julio, a heavy pit cratered

her stomach. That sinking feeling only grew harsher when she looked up to see Ace and Tate watching from a distance. Whatever frustration rode them, it was nothing compared to the news she and Julio needed to share.

If her instincts—and Julio's somber gaze—were any indication, Reynolds Station had been home to a murder.

Chapter 3

"Smooth."

"Bite me." Tate spat out the words before slapping the thick gloves he needed to repair the barbed wire on his thigh. They needed to get that line of fence back up and he needed to get back to work. Lollygagging out here all day hadn't been on the agenda.

"Belle looks good." Ace's gaze never even drifted Tate's way as he watched Belle and Julio do their work. "She's a fine representative of the Midnight Pass police force. And wow, is she easy on the eyes. 'Course, she always was."

The simmer in his blood rolled on toward a slow boil at the evident appreciation in Ace's voice. Belle was a gorgeous woman and he'd never known a police uniform—pants, a button-down shirt—and a badge could look so damned sexy when covering high, firm breasts and a slim waist that begged for the span of a man's hands.

As vivid images of curling his fingers against that warm flesh consumed him, Tate fought the urge to slug his brother. They weren't kids any longer and he was well able to take him in a fight.

Which was further proof of just how badly Annabelle Marie Granger got under his freaking skin.

The woman was a poison. A lethal one, like something that came out of an exotic flower. Only instead of death, this one drove a man into a sort of ever-loving madness.

They saw a lot less of each other than in the past, but she was still *around*. An off-hour trip to the feed store might produce her walking down Main Street, a sexy swing to her walk as she worked the beat. Or a stop off for a cup of coffee in downtown Midnight Pass at the Drop-In Diner might turn her up at a front table, having lunch with a fellow officer. Hell, he'd actually had times where he'd seen her and gone the other direction, not willing to live with the emotions she managed to churn up for days.

"Keep your eyes off Belle."

"I don't take orders from you, little brother." Although the threat was real, Tate didn't miss the humor that threaded through the words. "No matter how badly you want me to."

Tate was about to reply, determined to keep up the line of stubborn, verbal territory-marking when Belle and Julio abruptly stood and headed in his and Ace's direction.

"That was fast," Ace murmured.

"Too fast." Tate watched them march closer, their

matched looks of concern pushing thoughts of punching his brother out of his mind.

"You find something?" Tate asked.

Belle nodded. "I'm afraid we did."

Tate moved to walk toward the patch of scrub Belle had been bent over when she laid a hand on his arm. "I need you to stay here."

"This is my land."

"Right now it's my crime scene. And I need to ask you a few questions."

Ace had remained quiet, but moved to stand beside Tate. "What's this about?"

Annabelle's voice was quiet but strong in the light breeze that whipped tendrils of hair around her cheeks. "What brought you out here this morning, Tate?"

"I told you. I couldn't sleep and Tot and I headed out."

"Do you normally go out this early?"

"No." Something hard hit the bottom of his stomach. "What's with the questions? You gonna read me my Miranda rights?"

The question was legitimate, but the taunt underneath scraped at her nerves. How was it the man managed to toss her profession at her at every turn? It was yet one more example of how little respect he had for her.

Or how little had changed in their war of wills.

She knew she walked a dangerous line, but she'd never been very good at backing down from that challenge. The urge to pull out the small, laminated card she'd carried on her since graduating from the academy dogged her, but she kept her focus on Tate.

"Do I need to?" If she had to take him into custody, she'd be required to read him his rights, but he wasn't a suspect.

Or damn it, he shouldn't be.

But standing there, staring at Tate Reynolds, she wasn't sure what to think. The man wasn't a killer, that was for certain. And since the hardest thing she'd ever seen him touch was a lone tequila chaser along with a beer at Tabasco's place, she didn't think drugs when she thought of him. So how did blood end up on his property and how was it Tate was the one to kick that discovery off with a cut fence?

"You think I did something?" Something dark and cold settled in the depths of his green eyes. "What the hell is going on?"

She ignored the heavy feeling that made her feet feel like they were cased in concrete, rooting her to the spot before him. "I'm trying to find out. Part of that is asking a few questions."

"I know my rights," Tate bellowed, the sound surprisingly similar to his father's. "This is my land and my home. I have a right to roam it whenever I damn well please."

Ace stepped in. While the move didn't stem the storm clouds in Tate's eyes, it did have him moving back a few steps. "What's this about?"

Belle hated the necessary distance that had her stiffening up. She'd known all of them since she was small and didn't truly believe any of them were guilty. But she had to do her job. Assumptions and innuendos didn't make cases, nor did they set the basis for good cop work.

She had to keep her focus and she had to be above reproach.

"We need to call in a team."

"A team for what?"

Ace ignored Tate's question and continued with his patient, calm questions. "We already agreed to having you talk to the staff. We'll set you up at the house."

"This takes priority."

"What takes priority?" Ace's gaze, so like his brother's, shifted to the area where she and Julio found the blood.

"There's blood on the ground." Julio spoke first. "The sort of blood that spills when there's death. Bella and I need to close this off and call in help."

"You think someone was murdered here?" All notes of belligerence faded from Tate's voice, replaced by sheer disbelief. He sat down hard on the open gate of Ace's truck, the slapping of the thick work gloves he carried beating a steady tattoo against his leg. "On our property?"

Belle wanted to go to him. In a moment that should be about comfort, all her presence did was cause more pain. But she held her ground. Whatever Tate felt, it was nothing compared to the terror and horror the victim would have felt.

"The amount of blood and the apparent pattern suggests that someone, if not dead, is in bad shape. We need to get this area cordoned off and the lab out here and we need to do our best to find them. Fast."

Ace nodded at her words before stepping back. "Do what you need to do."

She eyed Tate, banishing her emotions to a place

she rarely visited. "I still need to question you but your reputation in the community works in your favor."

"Thanks." His response was drier than land in a drought—a surprising match for the bleak disappointment in her chest.

She was a cop. A good one. But she never expected something like this would blight Reynolds land. Or would come so close to people she cared about.

Three hours later, Belle finally found a moment to sit in her SUV and sip a cup of coffee from her thermos. The morning had unfurled pretty much as she expected—with half of the Midnight Pass police force descending on Reynolds Station.

The chief had arrived within fifteen minutes of Julio's call into the precinct. His arrival was followed shortly thereafter by several of her fellow officers and then two of the Feds assigned to the Pass. Their jurisdiction was drug and human trafficking, but until they knew what they were dealing with, the Chief had decided to play nice and proactively bring them in.

Not for the first time, Belle considered Chief Hayes Corden. A big man, he'd worked in both Houston and Dallas in the early days of his career before coming to the Pass in his midforties. He'd been their chief for the past ten years and he ran a tight ship. He respected his cops. He let them do their work. And he played well with the Feds, who spent an increasing amount of time focused on the border.

It had chafed at first, these interlopers who believed they knew better than the locals. She'd complained about them over beers with her fellow officers and shot them the stink eye whenever she could. And then Belle had gotten fully enmeshed in the work that needed to get done in the Pass and had finally accepted the fact that their help went a long way.

When had things changed so much?

She'd lived in Midnight Pass her whole life and couldn't imagine making her home anywhere else. But recently, she had to admit to herself, things had begun to seem overwhelming.

And now they might have to add murder to the growing list of sins?

She was a cop—she knew people made bad choices—and they'd dealt with homicides before. But something about this seemed different. Darker.

It was a sense more than a confirmed fact, but something about the blood spatter on the ground—and Julio's somber features—had her instincts quivering.

In addition to the blood and cut fence, there were those weird depressions in the earth. The more she turned it over in her mind, the more those disparate facts didn't sit well with her. What made the depressions?

A bag full of drugs? Or full of something else? Tools to commit murder?

The tap on her window had her turning toward the chief. His large frame towered over the top of the car and she quickly climbed out, not wanting to seem as if she were slacking on the job.

"Chief Corden."

"Officer." The chief nodded, his dark eyes warm. "No rush. You took an early call on this. You're entitled to a cup of coffee."

"Thank you, sir."

"What are your impressions?"

Relaxing under the kind words, she focused on the scene that spread out before them. To the untrained eye, it looked as if people ebbed and flowed over the land like mindless ants, but like those same ants, there was an underlying symphony to their movements.

Photos of the crime scene. Forensics samples. And as of five minutes ago, a couple of K-9 handlers from El Paso to fan out over the surrounding land. Each person on-site had a job to do and they were hard at work in trying to both secure the scene and find usable information.

"The Reynolds family has been cooperative. They're more than willing to let us interview their employees."

"You think this was an inside job?"

"It's too early to tell, but it can't be ruled out."

"First impressions?" Chief Corden's gaze roamed the crime scene and beyond.

"Initially, I suspected drugs. The depression I pointed out to Julio suggested a drop and we know the Pass has seen its fair share of trafficking."

"And now?"

"The blood, sir—" She broke off, hesitating. "It's concerning."

"Drug deal gone bad?"

The chief's question was a fair one, his tone level as he asked the question. Yet even she knew there was more that lay beneath.

"It's easy. Neat."

"But?"

She turned to the chief. "Except it's too easy."

"How?"

"There's more than enough violence in the warring

drug cartels. We know that. But to commit violence like that at a drop point? It's messy."

"What else?"

"Drug traffickers want to get in and out. This property and any others they use are a means to an end. No one's looking to spend time here and risk getting caught."

"Random violence happens."

"Yes, it does."

Once again, Belle struggled to explain why her gut churned so hard on this one. Yet for reasons she couldn't fully define, ever since Julio pointed out the blood, she'd had a deeper, darker sense that something evil happened here.

Something worse than the drugs. Worse than the greed.

"Heard you and Julio questioned a few of the Reynolds boys this morning. Tate Reynolds in particular. Do we need to keep an eye there?"

Annabelle nearly bobbled what was left of her coffee. "No, sir. I don't think—"

The chief raised a hand, effectively quieting her alarm. "I'm not questioning how you do your job, Detective Granger. Is Mr. Reynolds a person of interest?"

"No, I don't believe so."

"So there wasn't some sort of misunderstanding before over his rights?"

"Mr. Reynolds asked if I was going to read him his rights. I felt his tone and manner were meant to tease me instead of to truly ask a question."

"So it was just a misunderstanding?"

"Yes, sir." The sheer alarm that someone might have been killed on Reynolds land was a big one, but loss of the family's cooperation wouldn't put the Midnight Pass police force in the best place as they tried to investigate. "Tate Reynolds is a good man."

"Good men can do bad things. He's known to be a bit of a hothead from time to time."

"He is. But—" She broke off again, the truth of her earlier exchange with Tate coming back to bite her. "The fault is mine, sir. I let personal feelings get in the way. I'll ask Mr. Reynolds the same questions I ask his staff, but I don't believe he's done anything."

Corden shrugged. "Discussion of rights never hurt anyone."

"Yes, but they tend to alarm people."

The chief pulled his gaze from the group of people fanned out around them, his dark eyes tinged with a bleak edge she'd never seen before. "Maybe it's time people got a bit alarmed, Detective Granger. Alarm makes people careful."

"You think the Reynolds family needs to be careful?"

"I think we all do."

He patted her shoulder before taking off back into the melee. His first stop: the FBI's lead field agent that managed the Bureau's work in the Pass.

The remaining coffee in her thermos lid had gone cold and she tossed it on the ground. On a sigh, her break at an end, she resolved to follow her chief back into the teeming throng that worked in and around the fence line. Tate and Ace had kept their distance, leaving to talk to their staff after the chief had arrived. The large black truck that bumped over the uneven land in the distance indicated they were back.

The sight of the brothers filled her with mixed emotions. Tate left her with any number of disparate feelings, but her world was always better when he was in view. It was ridiculous and stupid—and a horrific curse to bear—but it didn't make it any less true. Yet something about this scene, and the swirling sense of menace, had every instinct she possessed screaming for him to get away. Hell, the man would probably hang around just to make her mad.

And she didn't want him here.

She'd studied blood spatters in college and something about the patterns on the ground haunted her. It suggested the use of a knife with powerful force. She'd leave the specifics to the forensics experts but it didn't sit well.

Could it be an animal?

Even as the wishful thought hit her, she knew the truth. Someone had been harmed terribly on Reynolds land. And with the obvious pain and suffering they'd have sustained, she couldn't honestly say if the person was better off dead or alive.

Tate couldn't tear his gaze off the view through Ace's front windshield. "It looks like a war zone or some creepy movie set."

"I think before this is over we're going to be wishing it was make-believe," Ace said.

He couldn't argue with his brother's statement, or the increasingly disturbing sense that something was very, very wrong. He and Ace had given their employees a lowdown of the high points—namely the concern someone had run drugs through Reynolds land—but had pointedly kept any mention of violence or possible death from their comments at the Chief's request.

Then they'd gone into the house and filled in Hoyt and their baby sister, Arden, sparing neither the full details of the morning.

He and his siblings managed to get on pretty well in the sprawling confines of the ranch house, but they also knew how to get under each other's skin. There were times Tate wondered what they were all doing now that they were full-grown, living under the same roof, yet he couldn't imagine it any other way. After their parents had died, they'd somehow found the ability to move on, all while doing it at Reynolds Station.

And at a time like this, he appreciated the benefit of all of them being together.

Arden could take as good a care of herself as Hoyt and Ace, but Tate couldn't deny the overwhelming need to keep an eye on her. And he felt better knowing it was his family doing the protecting.

"Do you think they found anything yet?" Tate asked.

"Hard to say." Ace pulled up behind a line of government-issued cars and put the truck in park. He made no move to get out.

Fingers tapping against his thigh, Tate fought the nagging weight of idleness. He preferred action to sitting, and allowing strangers to mill over his land was the equivalent of being stung to death by bees. Nerveracking and painful.

"I'll be damned if I'm going to sit around here all day waiting for something to happen."

"Then let's go. We don't need to be here. Belle will call if—" The rest of Ace's words were lost in the heavy shouts and loud barking that rumbled in through the open windows.

Tate was out and headed for the group of people, uncaring what he might find. He was done sitting around and done imagining what might have taken place on his family's land.

His land. More, his home.

The shouts continued as the assembled cops tumbled through the cut fence and into the ravines that peppered this part of the Pass. Another bark went up, followed by the heavy cries of a dog on the scent, and Tate kept pace behind them, Ace on his heels.

Was it possible they'd found something? He'd been out here early this morning all on his own. Had he been that close to such violence? Worse, was it possible he interrupted something?

He and Tot were generally in sync with each other. And even though he worked with the horse regularly, Tot's feral upbringing ensured a keen awareness of his surroundings.

Was it even possible they both could have missed something early this morning?

Questions without answers kept pace with Tate's heavy trudge over scrub grass and into the rocky slide of one of the ravines. He nearly stumbled on a loose bed of rocks but caught himself, arms windmilling to stay upright.

Tate had barely righted himself when everyone in front of him came to a hard stop behind the K-9 unit. The team had canvassed the ground as a pair, but the dog had come to a quick stop, dropping to his haunches. His handler was already praising his partner's skills as the rest of the police team closed in around them.

The steady hum of conversation that filled the air ceased. The dog's panting was the only sound floating on the morning breeze until Belle gasped. Tate's gaze shot to her first until he saw how her attention was focused on something near the dog.

It was only then that he saw the body that lay nestled in a ravine, its throat slit.

Chapter 4

Belle fought the urge to avert her eyes as she took in the dead body. The poor man was horribly mutilated, the slash across his neck the most obvious wound but not the only one. His hands were badly bruised and she could see two of his fingernails had been torn from their beds.

Tamping down on the rising slick of illness that threatened her empty stomach, she forced herself to think of her job. And the oath she'd taken to protect others.

And knew, beyond a doubt, she and her fellow officers had failed to uphold that collective promise with this man.

With the same precision she and Julio had reviewed the edge of the Reynolds property, Belle began the slow perusal of the site. She took in the broader swath of land, then worked her way determinedly through those quadrants, looking for clues. Unlike the lone patch of blood spatter, this area had dozens of points of interest. Spilled blood. Dirt covering a good portion of the body. And a clear trail of where the dead man had been dragged to the ravine.

Who had done this?

Her earlier conversation with Tate whispered through her mind. The assumption drugs were to blame for the cut fence seemed like an obvious answer, but was it? Drugs brought untold violence—she'd seen her fair share of it—but this was brutal.

Savage.

And a sight that would haunt her nightmares for a good long while.

She felt him before he spoke, the large presence at her side coupled with the masculine scent of man, earth and horse that was distinctly Tate. "This happened on my land? Near my family and my home and my men?"

"It appears so."

"Because of drugs running through the Pass like an out-of-control virus." The words dripped with derision and disdain, a clear continuation of what Tate had leveled at her earlier.

Most law-abiding people in town think the Midnight Pass police force couldn't find justice with both hands and a flashlight.

"Despite the feelings you've made abundantly clear regarding the capabilities of the Midnight Pass police force, you should get back and let everyone do their job."

"This happened on my property."

"We're no longer on your property. This is border-land."

"Belle—"

She whirled on him. "No. You're not giving orders here and you're not in charge. Let us do our job and figure out what happened."

Once more, she felt him before he moved. His hand closed around her upper arm to pull her closer, their faces practically touching. His grip was firm, yet retained a core of gentleness that only reinforced what she already knew.

Tate Reynolds wasn't a killer. He wasn't a drug dealer or a criminal either. He might be the monumental pain in the ass of her life, but he was a good man. A caring man.

And right now he was processing the fact that his home had been breached and violated in one of the worst ways possible.

"This isn't about you and me arguing on the playground, Belle. Someone died. And by all accounts, they were killed on my land."

"I know." She laid a hand over his forearm and took strength from the solid muscle beneath her palm. "Which is why you need to let us do our job."

Although conversation had restarted among the assembled officers, the sounds were muted as people spoke in quiet whispers. She kept her voice comparable, not wanting anyone to overhear them. "You need to trust that we will handle this. Regardless of your feelings."

"That was—" He broke off. "I'm not suggesting you won't do right by this person."

Tate's gaze shifted to the body, still untouched in

the ravine. His hand tightened on her shoulder before he seemed to make up his mind, turning firmly away from the gruesome sight. "I know you'll do your job. But please be careful."

"I will."

"Something's wrong here. This isn't a drug deal gone bad or dishonor among thieves."

She wanted to believe otherwise, but couldn't in the face of his certainty—or her own. "No. I don't think it is."

"You need to be careful."

"Right back at ya."

The same frustration from before—hell, from forever—darkened his gaze once more but other than a small sneer, he held his frustration. "That's not what I meant. This is dangerous. You have no idea what you're dealing with."

"Which is why I've been trained. It's my job."

His hand fell away and Tate took a few steps back. The physical withdrawal was mimicked in the way his gaze shuttered and his mouth firmed into a straight line. "The job. Just like always."

Belle wanted to argue. She wanted to rant and rail and give him the litany of reasons why she was not only good at her job but called to it. But the day had begun too early. And the pain of seeing him again, so up close and personal, always left her slightly empty and more than a bit bruised emotionally. So she skipped the ready defense and nodded instead.

"Just like always."

"Will the police still be setting up here in the kitchen?" Arden asked. She'd changed out of the pajamas she'd worn earlier when he and Ace had told her what was going on at the edge of their property into a pair of yoga pants and a top in vivid neon. She was busy fixing enough food to feed ten police stations, evidenced by the heavy scent of blueberries that rose into the air as she pulled a tray of muffins out of the oven.

She looks like Mom.

The thought wasn't a new one, Tate admitted, but as she puttered around the kitchen, he saw the clear resemblance between his sister and his mother. Well, minus the eye-boring neon.

Both were petite, but where Betsy Reynolds had seemed to fade into herself later in life, Arden was as bright and vibrant as her outfit. The yoga ensemble belied a strong, fit woman and despite her size—or maybe in spite of it—he'd dare any man on the ranch to attempt a head-to-head battle with her.

Arden was fierce.

She was also in danger, if the discovery at the edge of the property was any indication.

"I think you should consider rescheduling your classes this week. Stick close to home instead of heading in and out of town."

Arden glanced over from where she placed the muffins on a cooling rack. "Why's that?"

"We need to be careful until the police know what they're dealing with."

"And we will be. That's what locks are for. And making plans to meet up with others and stay in groups. All of which I will take full advantage of. But I'm not canceling my classes."

"It's a few yoga classes, Arden. They'll keep."

The subtle smile never left her lips, but the glint in

her blue eyes—also so like their mother's—grew decidedly flinty. "Perhaps you didn't hear me the first time. I'm not canceling anything. To put a finer point on it, neither am I holing up in this house like a prisoner."

"You're not a prisoner."

"Then get the warden act out of your thoughts."

Damn, but what was wrong with the women in his life? When had he become the bad guy because he didn't want them anywhere near the unsavory aspects of life? "It's wrong to worry about you?"

She drifted over from the stove, the scent of blueberries mixing with the pot of coffee she carried with her. "Worry is okay. Telling me what to do isn't."

Tate grabbed the sugar bowl off the center of the table and dumped a few teaspoons into his coffee. Arden pointedly ignored the liberal dosing of sweets and poured her own cup before sitting down.

"How do you drink that without anything in it?"

"How do you drink that," she pointed at his mug, "with the equivalent of a cotton candy bender in it?"

He shot her a dark look over his mug. "Yet another impasse this morning."

"You're in a mood." Arden got up and walked to the counter. She placed a few muffins on a plate, her attention seemingly focused on her task. "Would that have anything to do with Annabelle Granger showing up at our ranch bright and early this morning?"

What was with his family? First Ace grilled him and now Arden? He could only thank the heavens Hoyt was a man of few words. His youngest brother would sooner cut off a finger than question Tate about something personal.

"Belle has nothing to do with anything."

"You sure?" Arden carried over the plate of fresh muffins. Tate could still see steam rising off the top as he reached for one and imagined the top of his head likely looked similar.

"Positive."

"Then you won't care if I set her up in here. I'll make sure she's got enough coffee and snacks, but you or Ace or Hoyt will need to see to it that she's got what she needs when the men come in to talk to her."

Tate dragged the wrapper off his muffin, tossing his breakfast from hand to hand to cool it off. "Aren't you efficient today?"

"I'm always efficient. And prepared. I'm just glad I bought the extra blueberries in town yesterday. I figured I could use them for something."

His sister was a mystery to him. Clichéd as it was, she was truly tough as nails, her upbringing as the youngest in a family full of boys ensuring she could hold her own. Yet even with the edge that never quite went away, she seemed to revel in her yoga and cooking from scratch and feeding the chickens they kept in their coops.

He had no objection to independence in a woman and he'd never bought into the concept of a weaker sex. Strength came in a variety of ways and the emotional support his baby sister gave their family wasn't something to underestimate. But the yoga and the earth mother routine did confuse him. She could be anything she wanted, yet she seemed stuck in the Pass, communing with nature.

None of which was really his business. She seemed happy enough. Balanced, even.

So why did it still nag at him?

Arden reached for a muffin of her own. "So how is Belle doing? Presumably you two had a civil conversation."

Strains of their argument came back to him, including his kidney punch of criticism at the effectiveness of the Midnight Pass police force.

Smooth, Reynolds. Real smooth.

"Belle and I don't do civil all that well."

Arden waved her butter knife at him. "Belle does civil just fine. You're the stubborn one who can't keep your mouth shut."

"Sort of like you?"

"Chalk it up to a family trait." Arden grinned. "But you know what I mean. You two should just jump each other and move on. It would make life a heck of a lot easier for the rest of us."

"Amen to that," Hoyt muttered as he came into the kitchen. Dust covered the back of his shirt and Arden was already yelling at him to go straight to the mudroom.

Tate wanted to believe he'd have been quicker on the response if Arden's comment didn't surprise him so or his brother hadn't interrupted, reinforcing her suggestion. Later, he'd tell himself that was the reason. When he was out on Tot, rechecking the property, or enjoying a beer watching the night's Astros game or brushing his teeth before bed, he'd maybe convince himself she'd simply caught him off guard.

But right now, he'd be lying if he didn't admit, at least to himself, that he was scared.

He didn't recognize the body in the ravine, but that didn't mean much. Midnight Pass was a small town, but still big enough for there to be a few strangers. Add in the number of people who traveled through and it wasn't a complete surprise the man was a stranger.

And yet…

It clawed at him. He'd lived here his whole life. He might have had his ups and down, but this was home. And now they were dealing with a possible killer on the loose?

Hoyt ambled back into the kitchen, his work shirt gone and an old high school football jersey in its place. He shot Arden a dark look as he reached for a muffin. "Happy now?"

"Yes." She smiled, her expression prim. "I already cleaned up in here for the police and I don't want you messing up things."

Hoyt's mouth firmed into a straight line and he laid his half-peeled muffin back on his plate. "They found something?"

Tate nodded. "A body. Down in one of the ravines before you hit the border."

"Our ranch?"

"No." Tate shook his head. "There's blood on our property but the body was found in part of the borderlands."

Tate filled in Hoyt on the few details he had, recounting the search as well as the findings of the K-9 team.

The Reynolds family had ranched in Midnight Pass for five generations. They'd worked the land and raised their cattle and been a part of the community. The land itself—as well as that of the Crown and the Vasquez families—was close to the US-Mexico border, but no one's property line ran straight up to the border. The

US government had seen to it that they kept a small strip to manage as its own.

Was it a coincidence that the body was discovered there? A sign, maybe?

"What do you make of it?" Hoyt asked around a bite of his muffin. "Seems odd the actual crime was committed on our property and yet the body was moved. Like a screw you to the Border Patrol?"

Tate turned the idea over in his mind. As theories went, it was as good as any. What it didn't explain was why anything had happened on their land in the first place. "So why the cut fence?"

Hoyt shrugged. "A mystery for the cops to solve."

The heavy knock on the back door interrupted their conversation before Belle peeked her head inside. "Okay if I come in?"

Hoyt smiled, his normally gruff demeanor nowhere in evidence for Belle. "We were just talking about you."

"Oh?"

"All good things." Arden was already up, waving her in. The two women exchanged quick hugs before Arden gestured her to the table. "Come on in and take a seat."

In moments, Arden had a fresh mug of coffee and a plate in front of Belle before she rejoined them at the table. "Any updates?"

"Not many."

"Do they know who it is?"

"Not yet, but it's only a matter of time." Belle took a sip of her coffee—black, just like Arden's—and pointed to the sink. "I'm just going to wash up."

Tate allowed his gaze to linger, the snug fit of her outfit outlining each and every curve of her body. She was thinner than he remembered. Leaner. Which was a surprise. She'd never been a heavy woman, but she'd always had a fair amount of curves. While he could still see the arch of her hips and the firm outline of her breasts when she turned back toward them, there was a decided leanness to her frame.

One more thing cop work had taken away from her.

And she also looks strong, Reynolds. Strong and lethal. And more than capable of protecting herself.

Damn it.

Just like his sister, he admired Belle's desire to make her way in the world on her own terms and under her own steam. It just burned him that the woman couldn't see the danger she subjected herself to by being a part of the police force.

Since he'd been battling the same thoughts for more than a decade now, Tate pushed them away. He and Belle didn't see eye to eye and nothing was going to change that. "Why do you still want to question the men?"

"We need to talk to everyone. That includes all of you."

Tate leaned back in his chair. "Brace yourselves. Belle's gonna pull out her Miranda rights."

"If I did do that, it would be for your protection," she snapped back, that ire that he'd been poking for nearly his entire life sparking in her eyes. It was an old, familiar routine. It had also grown tired.

Even with the emotional exhaustion, he couldn't resist one more jab. It also gave him the ability to let her know he understood far more about her work than he let on. "Reading me those rights would also mean I was in custody. You putting handcuffs on me, Belly?"

He knew the moment his taunt hit her and re-bounded straight back to him. Like an uncontrollable Harry Potter curse, it swung back at him with unbelievable force. An image of Belle in handcuffs—and little else—filled his mind's eye and every cell in his body stood up and took notice.

"I like having rights," Arden interjected, effectively ignoring his innuendo and dragging him out of the moment. "I thought you did, too."

Belle nodded, her own anger seeming to fade as she shifted her attention to Arden. "For the record, I didn't read him anything. And if we get to a point where it's needed, it's done for legal protection. Same goes for your men."

"Yet you still want to question them?" Hoyt leaned forward and reached for another muffin. "You worried about any of them?"

"I want to talk to them, nothing more. People see things and often don't even realize the implications of what they've seen."

"You don't think it's drugs anymore?" Tate had wondered at that, but his earlier questions about his staff still nagged at him. Ranger and Tris had come to mind first, but what did he really know about his men?

"We're not ruling anything out yet."

Unbidden, an image of the man with the slit throat filled his mind's eye. He'd known Belle long enough to know the image haunted her, as well.

He just hoped she'd find the killer before they had a chance to act again.

He hefted the large duffel bag from the front entrance of his hidey-hole out at the edge of the Pass.

Since it was small town USA, no one had even been around to pay him any attention as he drove through town early that morning, and they'd likely have paid him no mind, even if someone had.

Heading for the small kitchen, he placed the duffel on the counter and got to work.

Blood had dried on the knife, a stark reminder of the job he'd completed in the wee hours of this morning. A blight and a pestilence. That's what drugs had become in Midnight Pass.

And like any good landowner knew, you handled pests with force. One or two, you'd swat at and forget about them.

But an infestation needed swift and active punishment.

The police, then the Feds, had tried. But the enemy had only become craftier. The technology designed to find the drug runners had been used against the cops, identifying the trails each night that were open and unmanned.

And where technology wasn't a viable solution, good, old-fashioned recruitment had done the job.

How many of Midnight Pass's sons and daughters had been consumed by the blight? Lured into addiction, the promise of another fix more than enough incentive to mule for the kingpins who grew rich off their misery.

He'd watched it all. First from a distance, and then later, when the need to act grew and grew until it consumed him. When it would be a personal sin to ignore the monstrous proportions of the plague that now hung over the Pass.

So he'd acted.

He'd practiced and waited and then practiced some

more. The low-level drug runner based in Juarez had been first. He'd intended to use the gun he'd bought off the streets, but had been inspired at the last minute by the man's extensive collection of knives.

The smooth stroke of metal on flesh had been intoxicating.

And it was then that he'd known. Had understood.

Society needed riddance from its dregs and he had a mission. A purpose.

More, he now had a calling.

Chapter 5

Belle settled herself at the table in the pretty, peach-colored kitchen and ignored the flood of memories that threatened to consume her. She had a job to do and dithering over the night she and Tate had made love on the floor after a midnight craving for vanilla cake batter wasn't going to get it done.

But oh, what a sweet memory it was—and for far more than just the batter.

She pushed the image of a naked Tate—moving over her, around her, inside of her—out of her mind and fully focused on her job.

And murder.

Although the crime scene still required full analysis, there was no way the outcome would be classified as anything but murder, no matter how badly the chief might wish otherwise. The Pass struggled enough with the drug trade—and kept his officers busy year-round—but up to now they'd kept things together. They continued making arrests and even caught a few of the bigger fish over the past year. The chief's leadership had a lot to do with that, but so did the force's collective, stubborn refusal to let the Feds get their hooks in too deeply.

But murder took things to a whole different dimension. Especially something as grisly and dark as the sight she witnessed this morning.

The issue, to her mind, was how to action her way through it all and keep focus. She was a good cop. She loved what she did and she was dedicated and devoted to the work. The fact she now had to do that work in close proximity to Tate Reynolds couldn't deter her from the job at hand. Even with the shift in attention from concerns over drug running to hunting for a murderer in the Pass, she still needed to question Tate's employees.

She'd already set up her work laptop on the long, Texas pine table that dominated the big kitchen and had taken up residence on the end of the cushioned bench seat on one side. Reynolds Station might have stood on that very spot for decades, but the storied history of the ranch hadn't kept the Reynolds family from securing the latest technology. She was hooked up to a lightning-fast internet connection that rivaled what the Feds had brought with them when they set up shop in town. And it outpaced by a mile the molasses-in-winter one she typically experienced during the middle of the day when everyone was at work.

Or a terabyte, as it may be.

The quiet of the kitchen was a nice break from the early morning battle with Tate and the discovery of all that had come after, and Belle used the time to her advantage. She set up her notes for the interviews, then went to work on her report of the early morning call to the ranch. She hit Save on the draft—she'd add in Julio's notes to her own back at the precinct—and stood to refill her coffee mug. The sound of the opening door had her turning, the light breeze that spilled in sparking with the scents of spring. Her smile of welcome faded as Tate stomped his way into the house.

"The first group of men will be in to see you around three. Sorry we've kept you waiting but spring calving season is in high gear and you can't stop Mother Nature."

She glanced at the clock over the sink. "I've had plenty to do. And I can wait. I understand this is a working ranch."

"Good."

He stood there, the jacket he'd worn that morning gone in favor of the warming weather. His broad shoulders were shown off to perfection in a dust-covered Henley and his slim waist was encased in a pair of well-worn jeans. If she didn't have a firm enough grasp on her tongue it would likely be hanging out.

With that image fresh in her mind, Belle turned back to the counter and the pot of coffee, willing her hands to still. "You want a cup?"

"I'll switch to water. Too much caffeine makes me twitchy."

"Okay."

"How many is that for you?"

She turned around, her battle armor fully intact. "Cups? I don't keep count."

"You should. All that coffee'll stunt your growth."

As if to punctuate his point, his gaze roamed from the top of her head down to the bottom of her toes, then worked its way back up.

"I'm fully grown."

"Yes, you are."

Just like the earlier innuendo with the handcuffs, something dark and twisty unfurled lower in her belly. Oh, the man did things to her. Dark and wicked things. It was the whole reason she kept her distance. And she'd been doing it so long, she'd be damned if she'd consider it cowardly or weak.

It was one hundred percent self-preservation.

She avoided looking at the curve of that delectable backside when he bent to get a water out of the fridge. "It will be up to the men if you can stay here when they're interviewed."

Tate stopped mid-pull on his bottle of water. "Telling me what to do in my own house?"

"People aren't comfortable talking about private matters in front of their boss." Even if she hadn't observed this very behavior after interviewing thousands of people over the past ten years, Belle had lived it. She'd always hated talking of her mother's alcoholism—that went double for talking about it with a superior.

"I'd wager they're less comfortable saying it to the police."

"Yes, well, you don't know what might come up. Delinquent childcare payments or illness or any number of personal matters can be the cause of odd behavior. Whatever it is, it's not for you to hear."

"I feel the need to repeat, this is my house."

"Then I'll just have to remove myself from this lovely kitchen and have all your men come into town.

It'd be an awful shame to waste everyone's precious time during such a busy season for something as simple as a spot of privacy, but that's how we'll handle things."

Tate hesitated, something flickering behind his eyes before he seemed to give in. "Fine."

She expected him to turn on his heel and leave, so it was a surprise when he took a spot opposite her at the table. The heavy drag of the wooden bench seat over the slate tile floor scraped and creaked slightly when he settled himself onto the bench. "What are you going to ask them?"

"Police busin—" The words weren't even out when he had her computer in hand, snaked back across the table.

"Tate! That's work."

The telltale laughter lines that normally crinkled around his eyes—especially when he was at his jerky, cocky best—faded as he scanned the screen. "This is the report you've written up. About this morning?"

"Yes."

"You're recommending a police patrol here on my land and stakeouts down in the ravines."

"Yes."

"You're also proposing that you run the op down in the ravine?"

"Yes again."

"Then you're a bigger fool than I ever thought."

The words stung with all the evil ire of a mound of fire ants. Worse, it hurt that he still had the power to hurt her at all.

He'd never liked her decision to go into police work, but an incident late one night when they were dating, when she'd gone on a ride along with a couple of officers, had sealed his ire. A domestic incident that had become violent had resulted in her getting kicked in the thigh.

As injuries went, it was minor and hadn't deterred her much, but Tate had latched onto it as if it proved him right somehow. That police work was dangerous and not something she should be involved in.

What if the husband had wielded a knife or a gun instead of his leg? The arguments had started there and steamrolled as his imagination got the better of him.

An imagination that, ultimately, got the better of their relationship, too.

"And there we go again, Tate. Right back to the same spot we've been in for almost ten years."

He handled the laptop back, setting it so the screen faced her once again. "We keep hitting that spot because you stubbornly refuse to understand the danger you choose each and every day."

"No!" She pushed back on the bench seat, the hard scrape of wood over tile a harsh punctuation to the eruption of emotion. "You don't understand. You seem to think that I'm some sort of punching bag for your ego."

He was on his feet, his chest heaving, his fighting stance a match for hers. "My ego? What's that supposed to mean?"

"If you really cared at all about me, you'd understand that I need to do this."

"Now whose ego are we talking about, Belle?"

The question tripped her up, pushing the air from her lungs as she fought to find the right words. Fought to explain this need she barely understood herself.

She'd given up everything—*everything*—to be a

cop. And standing in his kitchen, staring at Tate, that truth came back to her full force. So she did what she always did.

She protected herself.

"You can't stand that I'm here. You can't stand that I'm the one who was called out to the ranch this morning to help you. And you really can't stand that I am making a life for myself."

"Make a life. Make whatever the hell you want. It doesn't mean I have to sit around and watch you put yourself in harm's way and act like I'm okay with it or not have an opinion on it."

"It's smothering. Even your attitude about the ranch hands. They're grown men. They can choose what they're going to say to me without you hanging over their heads like some den mother."

"I'm not—"

"And it's not just me or the ranch hands either. You do it to Arden. How fast did you hightail it back here this morning to tell her to lock herself in her room? Meanwhile you went out to the ends of the ranch at five a.m., still in the dark, without a care for your own safety."

The barb clearly hit its mark as his gaze went a cold, hard green. "You stick to what you know. You've made your decisions more than clear, but I don't need you interfering with me or my family."

"I'm not interfering."

"You have no idea what my family means to me."

"Of course I do."

"You haven't been around for ten years, so no, you really don't."

She knew he was fast—she'd watched him win more

than a few high school football games as a wide re-
ceiver because of his long legs and speed. She'd experienced a different sort of speed in the length of time it
took him to get her out of her panties in the back seat
of his car when both of them were in a frenzied rush to
make love. She'd even seen him race across the town
square to corral a puppy who'd lost his way at the annual Memorial Day picnic before he headed straight
into Main Street.

But none of them compared to the speed of how fast
she tumbled into his arms.

One moment she was standing beside the long table
and the next she was in his arms, pulled tight against
that impressive chest.

And it was even better than she remembered.

The firm contours of his pecs were harder than the
ones she pressed against in her mind's eye. The strong
lines of his shoulders were broader than the ones she
traced in the dreams that woke her in a fever. And the
firm lips that pressed against hers were far softer—
and far more adept—than any she'd recreated in her
most vivid fantasies.

Belle knew she should fight him—should pull away
and avoid going down a path fraught with memories
and pain and sadness—but heaven help her, she could
no sooner stop kissing Tate Reynolds than she could
stop breathing.

He held her close, his lips tinged with the subtle
cues of desperation. Somewhere in the hard press of
his mouth and the glorious exploration of his tongue,
she felt it.

Fear.

It hummed beneath his skin, subtle yet insistent.

And it added depth and dimension to the harsh words and dismissive tone he'd used earlier.

Hadn't that been the root of all their problems? He was so convinced she'd come to a bad end as a cop that he refused to see her competence. Her strength. Or her ability to train and plan for the work.

If only—

"Cops cleared us. Time to mend the fence line." Ace's voice boomed into the kitchen in advance of him, but it was enough to pull them apart and out of the electrifying kiss. Belle whirled from where she stood pressed against Tate to see Ace stomp into the kitchen, his move reminiscent of his brother's.

She nearly stumbled back into the bench seat until Tate held her steady, his large, capable grip strong on her biceps.

"You okay?"

"Fine." She pressed her hands on his forearms to fully steady herself before pulling back. "I'm fine."

Ace was smart enough to keep his mouth shut as he tromped over to the coffeepot. "Rex Hudson will be in shortly. He's just cleaning up after that last calving and will head in."

"Thank you." Belle picked up her notebook and pen and scratched down Rex's name. She knew the man— had seen him around town and had even hung out with him and his girlfriend one night at Tabasco's—but the notes gave her something to do.

And it kept her from looking at Tate and the curious way his dark gaze seemed directed toward her.

Ace turned from the coffee maker, his attention on Tate. "You ready to go fix the fence?"

"Sure."

"Then let's go." Ace doffed his hat in her direction, then shot a pointed stare at his brother that spoke more than any words. "We'll see you later, Belle."

"Please don't rush. If you're not back by the time I'm done, I'll just let myself out."

"We'll be back," Tate said. His words held an ominous sort of promise and she wasn't sure if she should be worried or aroused.

Since her stomach still quivered with butterflies and her mouth practically trembled from the heavy imprint of Tate Reynolds's lips, she decided worry was the better choice.

Arousal held far too much risk.

Tate dragged on the thick gloves needed to finish installing the line of fence. Their hands had been prepared to do the job earlier, but when the cops took over their investigation, he and Ace had sent them into more productive work instead of waiting around to be cleared.

He'd have preferred to be out here by himself. Or would have gladly dragged Hoyt out with him. His younger brother knew when a man wanted to keep things to himself. He respected that. Understood that.

Not Ace.

Tate glanced over to find his brother dragging on his own gloves, as if he had all the time in the world. Yet one more thing to chap at Tate's ass, but he knew arguing with his older brother would only make the man move slower.

Which took the low-simmering anger that had burned beneath his skin all morning and turned up the heat a few notches. And while it was unfair to lay all that heat at Ace's feet—Belle had done a damn fine job of upping his ire all on her own—it would do no good to use Ace as his personal punching bag. His older brother hit back.

Hard.

"I said it this morning and I'll say it again. Belle looks good." Just like with his coffee refill in the kitchen, Ace never even looked at him as he bent down to pick up his end of the barbed wire they'd already pulled out of the truck bed.

Since he knew exactly what Belle looked like—and smelled like and tasted like, for that matter—Tate said nothing and walked to the opposite end of the length of fence. He bent to snag his end of the wire and nearly tumbled over himself when he miscalculated his grip. His thick gloves swiped the barbs instead of gripping them and he quickly hopped in his boots to right himself. As if sensing his overcompensation, Ace pulled back, dragging the wire out of the way. "You okay?"

"Fine." Tate bent once more and gripped the thick width of fence, hauling it up with both hands. "I'm fine."

"Could have fooled me."

Again, Tate ignored his brother as they walked toward the open fence line. As if by unspoken agreement, they both avoided the yellow tape that still fluttered in the afternoon breeze, even though they were free to remove the offending sign of intrusion on Reynolds land. The cops had taken their photos and their soil samples, clearing them to continue their use of the property.

Although he was glad to get the chore done, that subtle sense of menace that had ridden him all day still dogged his steps like an invisible weight around his neck. What should have been a ready distraction—kissing Belle until they were both oblivious of the world around them—hadn't done the trick.

Nor would ignoring the situation.

Someone had been murdered on their land. He'd seen the body himself—seen the ravages of what one human could do to another—and wondered if he'd somehow been implicit.

The steady increase in crime in the Pass was unsettling, but Tate had managed to keep his distance from it as he and his family worked to return Reynolds Station to its former glory. Their father's betrayal of all of them—using the illegal ranching practice of rendering to feed the cows—had nearly put them under. It was not permitted to feed livestock with the ground up by-products of already-slaughtered animals, yet their father had taken the shortcut that had brought down the ire of the press, their buyers and the FDA, as well as the never-ending headlines proclaiming how mad cow disease could come to Texas.

The discovery of Andrew Reynolds's crimes and his quick decline and death from a heart attack had only added to the nightmare of the situation.

But they'd found their way past it.

Ranching was good business and the land held enough life in her that their father's illegal practices hadn't put them fully under. Bit by bit, year by year, he, Ace and Hoyt had brought things back. For all his ribbing of her yoga and her meditation and her incense burning, Arden did more than her fair share and he commended her for it. She kept their books like a champ, managed payroll and saw to it that they even had an annual Christmas party for their staff. She'd also been instrumental in pushing him and his brothers toward PR opportunities that would highlight their focus on sustainability and off what had nearly ended their business.

While all that effort had gotten them back on track, their inward focus on rebuilding an honest, thriving business meant they hadn't done their part for their community. Beyond supporting the basic request of the police to put some outlying patrols on their land, they'd sat back and ignored what was happening around them.

On a hard sigh, Tate lowered his end of the fence to the ground, his motions matched with those of Ace. The two of them worked in silence, Ace's questions seeming at an end as they both worked to attach their ends of the fence to the thick posts that speared up out of the earth. It was boring work and he'd spent endless, tedious hours doing it as a kid, but in that moment, Tate would've done a mile of fence line if he could avoid the drive back to the main house with Ace.

Hell, he'd do the entire perimeter of the ranch five times over if it meant they didn't have to suddenly look inward—inside that fence line—hunting for a killer.

Sweat pooled at the base of his spine as a mental roster of their staff reeled through his mind. Ranger and Tris continued to nag at him, but as Tate considered their staff, he knew there was a huge difference between thinking a man was capable of drugs and making the far larger leap to murder. He and his brothers expected an honest day's labor from their team, but that didn't mean they knew all there was to know about the men who they hired to work their land. And no matter how well paid, for some there was no amount that satisfied a desperate craving for more.

Drugs were an easier leap than suspecting one of his employees had blood on his hands.

Ace broke the silence. "Belle settled in well."

"We should have put her in the mess hall."

"Kitchen's more comfortable."

The kitchen was considerably more comfortable— and intimate—if that blazing kiss with Belle was any indication. And damn it, he didn't want comfortable. Nor did he want the memory of her pressed against his body or the way her soft lips opened beneath his own haunting his thoughts.

But it was too late to rethink the impulse to drag her close.

Tate got to his feet from where he finished attaching a section of fence to the post. "Putting her in the kitchen means we look like turncoats. Like we're colluding with the cops."

"It sends a message."

"That we don't trust our men."

Tate wasn't quite sure why that bothered him so badly, but it did.

"There's no reason for anyone to think we're nothing more than interested, cooperative ranch owners aiding the police in a necessary investigation."

The argument fit snug as a coffin and was equally confining. "Like the police have done much to manage the troubles so far. They've done so well, in fact, that now they're sitting on a murder."

Ace stopped his work and got to his feet. His stare was direct, his words even more so. "You don't have a very high opinion of Midnight Pass's finest."

"And you do?" Tate shot back, ignoring the discomfort that lit up the nerves at the base of his spine.

"As a matter of fact, I do. They've been keeping up with a problem that's as big if not bigger than all the other border towns up and down the state. You know the Pass has always been vulnerable."

Which only reinforced the question that had dogged him for over a decade.

Why the hell did Belle want to mix herself up with any of that? Although the drug problem had grown worse of late, Ace was right. It's not like there hadn't always been whispers of trouble, going back as far as he could remember and likely well beyond.

"The Pass might have been vulnerable but we've stayed blessedly free of the seamier side of things. Even the breaches we've had up to now haven't felt personal. Not like this one."

"Then maybe we're due." Ace picked up the small length of wire he'd clipped off the edge of his post and headed for the truck.

He'd already poured two cups of water out of the large cooler they kept perpetually full on all ranch vehicles and extended a large plastic cup as Tate came up behind him. The water slid down easy and he was already reaching for the cooler to pour a second drink when Ace's words registered.

"Do you really think we're due?" Tate asked.

"I think we're fools if we put our heads in the sand and delude ourselves into thinking we're not at risk."

"We pay well. We screen our employees."

Ace crumpled his plastic cup and nestled it in a small covered bin in the back of the truck. "Which means jack if the wrong person starts whispering in the right ear. Means even less if that person gets in over their head and gets desperate."

"Do you think we're at fault here?" His earlier thoughts still chaffed, but Tate gave them a voice, trying them out. "If for no other reason than we've not done enough to stop it."

"I'm not quite ready to cop to fault. But I don't think we can remain impassive any longer. You and I may not see eye to eye on the capabilities of the Midnight Pass police force, but I do think they need all the help they can get. Those in a position to provide extra eyes need to do their fair share."

There was little he and his brothers didn't discuss, so it was startling to realize Ace's opinion was as well thought out as it was.

"You been thinking about this for a while?"

"A bit." Ace shrugged as he went around to get in the truck. "More since Dr. Torres's practice got hit a few months ago, by someone looking for drugs."

Ace's comment shot off warning bells, for both the crime that Tate had forgotten about and the fact that Ace had harbored such a concern. His brother and their large-animal vet had always had a tension simmering between them, but Ace's protective streak had clearly been notched up at Veronica's recent hardship.

Of course, if his brother was stubborn enough to ignore the attraction that still simmered between him and his old flame—an old flame that had dumped the idiot she'd married after her long-ago breakup with Ace, was now single again and had recently resettled in the Pass—that was his brother's problem. Ace was a grown man who normally exhibited better sense.

Or stubborn just runs in the family, Tate's conscience taunted him.

Since that line of thought was just uncomfortable—

especially with the coffee-flavored taste of Belle still on his lips—he focused on the discussion at hand. "You'd think maybe we could have done some advance planning on how we'd handle something like this?"

"Dad had a zero tolerance policy for drugs and drinking on the job. It was the one thing he did right. Grandpa had the same. It's in every contract. And no employer's required to keep on someone engaged in illegal activity."

An image of their wiry, wily grandfather seemed to shimmer in the air before them and Tate couldn't hold back the smile. "I thought Grandpa's only rule was to shoot first and ask questions later."

"He lawyered himself up a bit better than that. Protected Reynolds Station while he was at it. None of it changes the fact that a determined individual can do a lot of damage before we figure it out."

"Zero tolerance for an individual's behavior isn't sussing out a drug runner." Tate hesitated before adding, "Or a murderer."

"No," Ace sighed. "It sure as hell's not."

Their water break at an end, Tate climbed into the truck, the two of them moving in moments. He stifled a yawn, his early ride and the busy morning catching up with him.

"She really is a looker. Even prettier than she was in high school, if that's possible."

The urge to ignore the remark or shoot a silent finger gesture was strong but Tate did neither. He also refused to give free reign to the stubborn streak of jealousy that fired up at the fact his brother even noticed Belle was an attractive woman. Instead, he tamped down on all of it and forced a note of boredom into his tone. "Then you ask her out."

"You'd be okay with that? I figured since your lips were so busy with hers, you'd want a man to keep his distance."

"My lips weren't—" He snapped the offending appendages closed. "She's single. Last I heard, you were a single man. Although it sounds like Doc Torres might need a bit of protecting if you had a mind for it."

Ace's wide smile faded. "I am a single man. I'll clean up after we get back and see if I can't sweet-talk Belle once she's done interviewing the men."

"You do that."

Ace turned onto one of the dirt roads that cut through the property, the ride smoothing out as they no longer bumped over the ground. Tate stared out the front window, acre after acre spread out before him. This was his home. His life. And his livelihood.

And even with all that wide open space, something tight and hard and shockingly well barbed settled in his chest. Someone came onto his land—or was already here—and used his property to do unspeakable evil. All the work they'd done for the past decade to rebuild Reynolds Station was put at risk. His brother was going to ask Belle out...

Tate sat up, the sleep dogging his eyes vanishing as he stared at his brother. "Keep your thoughts and your sweet talk and your freshly showered ass off Belle."

"Why? So you can continue your specialized brand of Tate Reynolds charm that seems to come out only around her?"

"My charm's just fine. I haven't heard any women complaining."

"None of the women you've dated have been Belle either."

The neat snap of proverbial steel closed around his ankle, his crafty brother working it like the finest trapper. Damn, but he was getting slow if he couldn't see Ace's maneuvering from a mile away.

"It's called moving on. Belle and I had our time once and it passed." He risked another glance at Ace, surprised to see something quiet and wistful pass across his brother's face before it vanished. "Besides, you're not her type," Tate finished up lamely.

"No, little brother, I'm not. Not by a long shot."

Chapter 6

Belle fought the urge to rub her eyes and rest her head on that pretty Texas pine. The interviews had been endless and by the tenth, she could have scripted the conversation. Each ranch hand began the discussion wary and concerned. They moved quickly into a ready defense of their employers. And by the end, they swore up and down they knew of nothing horrible happening on Reynolds land.

Loyalty, she admired.

When it was pitch-black blind, not so much.

Even with assurance that she was asking questions to ensure everyone's safety, she was blocked at every turn.

Not that she'd walked in expecting much in the way of cooperation. But it was the endless repetition that made her twitchy.

Was the Reynolds family brainwashing their employees? Even as she flirted with the question, Belle dismissed the thought.

How did you fault a family for creating a place for good men to do good work for a good day's wage? While Midnight Pass wasn't painfully poor or depressed, it wasn't a thriving metropolis by a long shot. People valued good jobs for an honest day's wage.

It was obvious Reynolds Station provided that.

"You look like you need something considerably harder than another pot of coffee." Arden floated into the kitchen, a yoga mat over her shoulder and a gym bag in a matching color on the other. "Want to come with me to the studio?"

The offer was tempting—more so when Belle shifted and felt a line of fire shoot down her back and settle in a cramp at the base—but she had four more interviews to go and another report to wrap up. "Duty calls."

Arden frowned and settled her stuff on the floor. "You have a duty to your health, too."

"I'm good."

"Right." Arden marched over to the coffeepot and dumped the dregs into the sink.

"Hey—"

"If you don't stretch and breathe deep, you don't get to riddle your veins with stale caffeine. House rules."

"I'm made of sterner stuff."

"So am I." Arden moved on to the fridge and dragged out a water bottle. "Drink this and maybe I'll believe you."

"I see Tate's surly attitude and know-it-all personality have rubbed off on you." Belle made no effort to hide her own tone, but she did twist the cap off the water bottle and drink deeply. So she was in no position to argue when Arden shot her a finger gesture she'd clearly learned at the hands of her older brothers.

At least she did it with a smile.

"Come on. You deserve a break. You were called out here at six this morning. You've been at it ever since. Last time I checked, Chief Corden was running a police precinct, not managing a team of indentured servants."

"We have a limited window of time to get this wrapped up. Leads go cold way too quickly and I can't let that happen here."

"Have the men been helpful?"

Belle sighed. "Not at all."

"Then there are no leads to follow, cold or otherwise. Come with me. Clear your head. Maybe we'll go grab dinner after."

The offer to clear her head was tempting—especially with Tate's kisses still clouding it—and Belle admitted defeat. "Okay. Let me just text your foreman and tell him I'll pick up the remaining interviews in the morning."

"That's more like it."

They settled into a companionable silence as Arden rinsed the coffeepot and the mugs some of the ranch hands had used while Belle wrapped up. In moments, her phone dinged with confirmation from their foreman, Jarrett Brooks, that he'd send the rest of his men over by nine the next morning. She emailed the chief with the latest version of her report and knew she had run out of excuses to avoid leaving.

Despite his promise—or threat?—to come back, Tate hadn't shown up.

Which was just as well, but it still left her with a small kernel of embarrassment that she'd wanted him to. Or that maybe, somewhere deep inside, her desire to see him again had ensured she'd dragged out the afternoon.

She'd worked hard over the past decade to purge the man from her system. She'd dated off and on, enjoying her time getting to know some really great guys. Quite a few good men, actually, who'd somehow never quite measured up. A small part of her questioned just how well she was actually doing on that whole moving on thing, but there wasn't much to do about it right now.

Even if her heart had leaped every time the door opened or heavy boots stomped over the front porch.

"You ready to go?" Belle shoved the laptop into her workbag and added the pages of notes she'd taken by hand.

"Want me to loan you some workout clothes?"

"You *are* a good friend." Belle laughed at the offer. "But you could fit your entire body into one leg of my yoga pants."

"You're not that much bigger than me. In fact, while I never thought you were heavy, you're even more toned and fit than I remember."

"I keep a bag in the car and I've been working out before heading home. The Feds are all pretty fit and they've inspired me to work out a bit more. Stay on top of my game."

Arden's blue gaze lit up. "Anyone in particular offering extra inspiration?"

Her friend's interpretation of the situation—and the sad fact that the workouts had been a way to stave off boredom instead of actually putting herself in proximity to an attractive member of the opposite sex—had Belle shaking her head. She kept her tone light and casual, but the knowledge knocked another hole in her spirits. "Nope. Just for me."

"Well, you look fierce."

"Thank you."

Arden grabbed her things and Belle followed her out the door. A sharp dart of awareness skittered down her spine, but when she turned to look out past the stables and then on to the wide grazing land that stretched for the fifty thousand acres that made up Reynolds Station, she didn't see Tate.

And damn his gorgeous hide for making her look anyway.

She waited on the porch while Arden locked up, then walked toward their cars. Arden's gaze looked her over from head to toe once more. "Yep. You really are looking fierce. Maybe that's the reason my brother was kissing your brains out earlier today."

"Arden!"

"It's a simple fact."

Whether it was the raw emotions that always hovered near the surface where Tate Reynolds was concerned or the stress of the day, she wasn't sure. But the buoyed spirits that had carried her out the door and into the driveway faded. "There's nothing simple about it."

The humor faded from Arden's eyes, but the sharp, knowing gaze remained. "No, there isn't. Most things worth a spit are complicated and complex and hard."

"Tate and I are ancient history. A momentary lapse in judgment can't change that."

"Well, that's a shame."

Belle paused at the door to her SUV, her fingers brushing the handle. "Why?"

"Because I've always thought you and my brother's mutual lapses in judgment were the best things that had ever happened to either one of you. I've been hoping for about forever you two would have a few more."

Arden ducked into her car before Belle could say anything and she was grateful for the respite. Although they hadn't known each other well when they were younger because of their five-year age difference, over the past few years, Arden had become a good friend. Both had been diligent about keeping Tate out of their conversations and Belle was grateful for it.

So why was Arden pushing now?

It was only when she reached the edge of the Reynolds property and turned onto the main road that led into Midnight Pass proper that Belle realized she hadn't even asked the most important question.

Had Ace told Arden about the kiss? Because she knew with absolute certainty, Tate would never have admitted to a moment of weakness like that.

Nor was he likely to repeat it.

Tabasco Burns had owned the Border Line pool hall since he settled in Midnight Pass after serving in the Vietnam War. He lost two fingers and a foot in a skirmish that cost him half his platoon, received an honorable discharge and decided he'd head south to disappear.

It still seemed to tickle his old, grizzled features when someone pointed out that not only was he one of the most well-known denizens of Midnight Pass, but his pool hall saw roughly the entire population over twenty-one stroll through its doors on an annual basis. Even for those who didn't make themselves regulars, Tabasco's annual Thanksgiving Eve potluck and his Memorial Day barbecue ensured even the least social among Midnight Pass's citizens hit the Border Line.

The Reynolds boys, on the other hand—well, most would consider them regulars.

It wasn't the beer, Tate thought as he ordered his usual—the first of his two foamy lagers for the evening and a tequila chaser. Nor was it the company, as Ace or Hoyt were typically ribbing him about something.

But there was an incredible comfort and ease about walking into a room where the conversation was lively, the faces familiar and the work of a long day was over.

"Heard you had some trouble this morning?" Tabasco pulled the beer himself before grabbing a shot glass for the tequila.

"Bad news travels fast," Tate said.

"You have no idea, my friend." Tabasco handed over the beer and the chaser. "Especially when it's news like this."

While it stung to ask, Tate figured it was as good a time as any to see how much the cops were sharing and if they were committed to keeping the Reynolds family up to date as initially promised. "They identify him yet?"

"Not yet." Tabasco nodded to one of his waitresses, who hollered an order down the bar and began pouring the two glasses of wine she requested. "Word is it took them until almost five o'clock to move the body. Forensics, cops and Feds all needed their turn."

Tate took it in, the casual conversation like any other

he might have had at this very bar. Only this one was different.

This discussion was about what happened on his land.

Had it really only occurred that morning?

It had nagged and gnawed on him all day. What made him go out this morning? Although they checked the fences regularly, it could have been hours or even a few days before they'd have discovered the cut. And out of the thousands of acres of land, what had him riding Tot to that very section? He wasn't a fanciful man, nor did he believe in extrasensory talents. Yet something had pulled him to that section of the property this morning.

Tabasco handed over the wine, then returned his full focus to Tate. "Heard Belle caught your case."

Since it was a useless endeavor to ask Tabasco exactly how he knew anything, Tate just nodded. "Yep. Showed up at the ranch along with the sun this morning."

"She's been doing a fine job. Caught that smuggling case late last year and put away four slimeballs for life. Good riddance. She's also been active with the teens. Maeve Simpson's granddaughter thinks Belle hangs the moon. Has already started talking about heading to the academy after she graduates."

"Does Maeve want that for her granddaughter?"

"Since there was a time Maeve didn't think the girl would even graduate high school, I'd say she's thrilled."

As alternatives went, Tate figured Maeve Simpson's granddaughter was headed for a far better future. So why was it all he could imagine were the horrible things that could happen to the girl? The images in his head matched the same ones he'd always worried about for Belle.

"I saw a table opened up. I'm going to go grab it. Ace and Hoyt'll be here soon."

Tabasco nodded as he pulled out a glass for another order. "I'll send over fresh drinks for them when they get here."

His socializing at an end, Tate headed for a pool table that occupied the eastern corner, along the same wall as the front door. The table had been empty since he walked in, but it made for an easy excuse to quit talking about the glorious, sublime, independent Annabelle Granger.

And if given the chance, he'd make the polite lie again.

Which likely only added to the cosmic karma that had Belle and his sister walking in and intercepting him just as he passed the front door.

"We need to brace ourselves for the possibility this isn't the last."

Hayes Corden stood over the body of the victim they'd discovered earlier that day, laid out on the coroner's table, opposite Federal Agent Noah Ross. The Feds had set up shop in his town a few years earlier and the chief had come to accept their presence, first grudgingly, and recently, with more appreciation than he'd ever thought possible.

A big part of that was Ross, the team lead assigned to Midnight Pass.

"You didn't say first?"

"Observant as always," Ross said. "No, I didn't."

"You think we have a serial killer on our hands?"

"My agents have been running like crimes and two have popped so far. One over in El Paso in February and one down in Juarez last November that they nearly overlooked."

"What makes you think they're related?"

Ross pointed to the victim's throat. "Wounds match. So do the job histories of the dead."

Hayes took his job as the chief of police for Midnight Pass seriously. It wasn't running vice ops in Houston or tracking murderers in Dallas—both prior jobs—but it had its own challenges.

Some of those Hayes had expected, even anticipated. Small-town disputes between neighbors, rowdy teens after the prom and even the occasional run of petty crime like burglaries and light drugs.

Those things, he could handle.

Based on the years he'd spent in Texas's largest cities, he could also handle the serious stuff like drugs and all their associated crimes.

But he'd never expected a serial killer.

"You matched this guy?"

"About fifteen minutes ago. Prints finally hit in the database. Guy's been a known associate of *El Asesino* for the past five years."

Even though the news confirmed what he'd already suspected, Hayes couldn't quite make the leap to serial killer. "*El Asesino's* known to take care of his own. Did the guy go rogue?"

"This isn't an internal problem. We've got someone embedded in his organization. *El Asesino* doesn't know yet."

One of the border's largest drug lords, *El Asesino*—The Assassin—was known for his ruthlessness and his unwillingness to listen to excuses. Which made the news the FBI had gained entrance to his organization that much more dangerous. "You've got someone embedded?"

Ross never lost a moment of his calm demeanor. *Bastard.* "Classified information."

"Yeah, yeah. The standard Bureau line." Hayes pointed toward the body. "Was this the work of one of his enemies?"

"Those guys usually take credit a lot quicker than that."

Hayes had worked the Pass long enough to know Ross's words for truth. "Lay it out for me, then."

Step by step, the agent filled him in.

The similar crimes, all perpetrated against known drug runners. The matched style of cuts on the neck. And a small, deep nick made postmortem in the heart.

It was that nick that had Ross's full focus as he pointed out the same abuse on the body that lay before them. "That's a mark. A code, if you will, that says, 'I'm in control.'"

"You think drugs are a front?" Hayes asked, leaning closer to inspect the wound.

"Maybe yes, maybe no."

While Hayes respected the man's ability to consider a problem from all angles, if a killer was on the loose, they didn't have time for considerations. They needed to act. "Well, which is it?"

"Drugs may be at the center. I'd wager it's no coincidence the three victims we've identified are all involved in the drug trade."

"But?" Hayes probed.

"But this doesn't seem like gang warfare or the outcome of a turf battle."

"Guns are easier. Quicker." Hayes brushed a plastic-covered finger over the heart wound. "A knife's personal. Intimate."

"That's what bothers me."

Hayes gave himself a moment to inspect the wounds in the new light of Ross's findings. The position of the body in the ravine and the subsequent review by the forensics team had confirmed the victim wasn't killed there. The team was still reviewing the soil samples from the Reynolds ranch along with canvasing the neighboring ranches but preliminary thinking put the murder on Reynolds' property before transport to the ravine.

The question was, why go to the trouble? If the killer had completed the task while still on the ranch, why move the body? Why not leave it where it fell?

He was good at the questions—he'd been trained to ask them and he'd taught his team to do the same.

But Hayes Corden was used to having answers.

And at the moment, he had none.

Annabelle felt the muscles in her back tighten right back to where they'd been at four o'clock that afternoon and wondered why she'd bothered with the yoga. Especially when Arden charged fifteen bucks a session.

"A latte would have been cheaper and easier," she muttered to herself.

"What's that?" Arden's gaze narrowed as she passed over the cosmo Belle had ordered from their waitress.

"Oh, nothing. Just thinking about the large latte I'm ordering in the morning."

"Feeding the addiction?" Tate glanced up as he lined up his shot, preparing to make the first break.

She ignored him in favor of a sip of her drink. And watched as he neatly broke the fifteen balls, sending them caroming over the table. Smooth and easy.

Vintage Tate Reynolds.

Arden had worked them hard in yoga, focusing on their legs and their core for the majority of their hour-long workout. It had to be the only reason Belle's legs were shaking.

She refused to believe the large shoulders, bent over the pool table lining up the next shot, could be at all responsible.

Even if Tate's focus on the game did give her a moment to unobtrusively look her fill.

His blondish-brown hair was cut short and she knew a few more months of work outdoors would have a series of blond streaks coming to the fore. He'd put on a black T-shirt for the evening out, a superhero in fighting stance covering the front, and it nearly made her laugh out loud.

Who knew his childhood obsession with superheroes would pay dividends as an adult? As a child, he'd worn his heroes whenever possible, plastered on his clothes, his lunch box and even his underwear. A fact she knew from an unfortunate incident at recess during the third grade.

What had branded him as a goof at Midnight Pass Elementary had grown into the self-possessed cool of a confident adult male. A solid chest and thick biceps peeping out of tight T-shirt sleeves didn't hurt.

Not one bit, Belle thought to herself.

Arden's catcall when Tate missed his next attempt

to keep up his run of the table pulled Belle from her musings and she stepped up to the rack and selected her cue. She'd reluctantly followed Arden to the Border Line, agreeing to one drink after their workout, but knew to back out now or turn tail and run home would brand her the loser of this round of wills.

And there was no way pool with Tate was anything but a battle of wills.

"Table's all yours, Belly." Tate reached over and took a sip of his beer.

She ignored the name and wished it didn't have such power over her. It was silly and stupid. A taunt from around the same time she caught sight of an eight-year-old's superhero underwear.

Yet it had stuck.

Just like this stubborn attraction.

The kiss from earlier that still lingered on her lips only confirmed the fact that she'd found herself in this situation steadily throughout her life. From the playground to the chemistry lab to those tension-filled months they'd danced around each other after graduation.

Until that one glorious night when it had all swung wildly, perfectly together, just like those caroming pool balls.

Lust. Need. Desire. Attraction.

And love.

Whatever else she'd experienced with Tate Reynolds, love had been a part of it all. It had intensified every moment together and had made the time after agonizing. But she'd survived. More, she'd thrived. Most of the time.

Which only made the moping and the raw feelings

and the stubborn ache since meeting up with him this morning such an indignity.

She'd moved past it all. Moved past him and created a life for herself.

So how mortifying to realize that all it took was one kiss to prove she hadn't moved that far forward at all.

Chapter 7

Tate lined up his shot and took some small measure of satisfaction when the balls went flying just as he'd planned, dropping the six neatly into the corner pocket. At least something bent to his will. The crime on the ranch certainly hadn't.

Nor had Belle.

He'd spent as little time as possible in the house—especially after that explosive kiss—yet her presence around his home had haunted him all day. Each ranch hand who spoke to her talked up a storm about the attractive cop once they'd come back to their duties. His hands had balled into fists at every mention—which had basically been all damn day—and it was a wonder he'd gotten anything done.

And now here she was. She and Arden looked as thick as thieves, sitting there sipping their pink drinks and watching the game.

She'd taken the cue when he'd teased her, doing a fine job of knocking in the eleven. But she was out of a turn on the next shot, pocketing the cue ball by mistake.

If he didn't know her better, he'd have said it was on purpose. But Belle Granger never lost at anything on purpose. Ever. The woman had a competitive streak to rival his and it was one of the things he'd always liked about her.

There was no artifice or attempts at being something she wasn't. What you saw was what you got.

He'd spent the past decade fighting against that knowledge but knew the same personality trait that drove her to win made her work extra hard at her job.

Made her a good cop.

"Come on, cowboy. Run the table."

The not-so-subtle purr rippled over the green baize, accompanied by a broad, sexy grin when he glanced up. It took him a few moments to shift from his thoughts of Belle to the over-the-top image that stood in front of him.

Dove Anthony.

The woman was a piece of work. Long, lean and in possession of a sizeable pair of breasts, he'd been the object of her attention and misguided affection since the seventh grade. Despite the whispers around town, he'd never sampled the lovely Dove, but it wasn't for her lack of trying.

Or for her seeming sheer enjoyment of flirting with him whenever Belle was nearby.

Focusing on his shot, he re-lined up the balls, slamming the cue ball into the three he'd aimed for, pleased when it hit the side pocket as he'd intended. Ignoring the clapping, he stood to his full height and mimed tipping his hat. "Hey, Dove."

"That was a lucky shot." She worked her way around the table, lush hips grazing the edges as she moved determinedly toward him. "Must be because I'm here."

She ran a long finger down his biceps and Tate shifted out of range, softening the rejection with a broad smile. "Luck and pool go hand in hand. Let me buy you a glass of what you're drinking as my thanks."

Their waitress had been watching with interest from the wings and rushed over at his offer, taking Dove's order of a light beer. The waitress had nearly rushed off when she remembered the rest of the crowd and took refills from everyone else. Tate didn't miss Belle's sharp stare—or her order of club soda—and fought the urge to ask Dove to leave.

He wasn't beholden to Belle Granger and hadn't been for a long time. He could talk to Dove or any other woman in the bar if he wanted to.

So why did it feel so crass and low to allow another woman to stand between them?

Belle stood it as long as she could. Since "standing it" included four more games of stripes and solids and a lone game of nine-ball as well as endless refills of club soda, she figured she'd given a good, solid air of enjoying the evening out with friends.

Even if she was dying inside.

Dove Anthony had finally gotten the hint and gone back to her friends at the table next to them, but it hadn't stopped her from shamelessly flirting with Tate. The story had remained unchanged since middle school, with the Dove showing up at the worst moments.

Annabelle wanted to be mad. Worse, she wanted to sit and wallow in a bottle of wine and feel sorry for herself about how easy it was for Dove to flirt and tease Tate, running her hands all over him, while she sat back and was forced to watch, a polite smile pasted over her face.

But she had no right. Nor had she had that right in a very long time.

Mentally slut-shaming Dove for it was not only small and petty, but it flew in the face of how Annabelle chose to see the world and her fellow females. The woman had every right to flirt with Tate. To be attracted to all that male virility and sweet charm.

And to let him know it if she chose.

"Do you always think so hard on an evening out?" Arden's voice was a low whisper but it was enough to pull Belle from her morose thoughts.

"Sorry?"

"I can practically see the ax sharpening in a thought bubble above your head."

Belle smiled at the image, well aware it wasn't too far from the truth. "I prefer to think of it as a bit of an internal talking-to, but an ax makes me sound fiercer, so I'll take your version. What I also am is tired, since my day started when it was still dark outside this morning."

Arden nodded. "Fair enough. I'm still glad you came out."

"I'm glad, too."

Oddly, for all the emotional turmoil, she was glad. The evening hadn't been terrible and it was nice to be out with people her own age. She'd been so focused on her job of late and the additional layer of work they'd all taken on helping the Feds that she hadn't been out in a while.

If she could take away the pining for Tate Reynolds, she might even have chalked it up to a truly successful evening. As it was, she was going to make her exit and head home to a bubble bath and bed.

She said a few quick goodbyes and made a point to give Tate the same courtesy. So it was a bit of a shock when he strolled up behind her, his long legs catching up just before she reached the front door. "Leaving so soon?"

As she pushed through the door, Tate followed in her wake. "It's been a long day."

Tate walked beside her toward the parked cars. "You can say that again."

Belle visualized the techniques she'd learned in training—staying calm, cool and in control in the face of a threatening situation—and forced a quiet friendliness into her tone.

"I appreciate it but you don't need to walk me to my car. I'm interrupting your game."

"Sure I do. No game is more important than a woman's safety."

The quiet agreement, and lack of fight in his tone, had Belle taking a good hard look at him in the glare of the overhead parking lot lights.

He looked tired.

The thought caught her so quickly she nearly said something before holding back the observation. If she said something, the quiet moment would inevitably be broken and she would miss her opportunity to really study him. To get a sense of what was going on.

And in the quiet, she saw that Tate was more than tired. He looked sad.

"You okay?"

"I just won five games in a row. Of course I'm okay."

The response was vintage Tate—evasive and overlaid with that casual charm that made people rarely look deeper.

"That's not what I meant."

"Of course it's not."

When the usual thread of teasing or light mocking failed to materialize, Belle went for broke. "Are we okay?"

"You and me are always okay."

They'd come to a stop against her car, the cool night air swirling around them. Rain scented the air but that bite of cold that had nipped at them that morning was gone, replaced by the heavy, muggy air. The vagaries of spring weather in Texas at its finest.

"I'm going to need to spend a few more days at the ranch."

"The kitchen's yours."

"Thanks for that."

"No problem."

Annabelle mentally shook her head. Was it even possible she was having such a pedestrian conversation with Tate? Hoyt or Ace, she could see. But Tate? He usually shot first and considered asking questions later. "I'll do my best to be as unobtrusive as possible. I appreciate your willingness to give your ranch hands the time to talk to me."

She turned away from him and reached for her keys,

her hand nearly closing over them in the front pocket of her purse before her movements were upended. Tate had her whirled around, his arms wrapping around her and his mouth slamming down on hers.

The move was overbearing and unexpected and…

Wonderful.

The man had the speed and the graceful finesse of a rattler and that should irritate her. But when all that seductive male strength gathered her close, his tongue finding its way into her mouth with artful purpose, Belle forgot to be mad.

She also nearly forgot to breathe, the urge to devour him coming on as strong and as fast as the kiss. Willing her mind to still, Belle chose to focus on the moment.

And the way *this* man made her feel.

Nothing pedestrian about that.

It had been like this forever. Even before she'd understood the depths of her feelings and the sexual desire that paired with it, she wanted Tate. Wanted to be around him, despite the taunting and the teasing on the playground. Wanted to be his partner in science lab and his study buddy at the library. She'd even enjoyed going head-to-head when they played sports in gym class, the battle of athletic talent exhilarating and fun.

If given a choice, she wanted to be in his orbit. Close to him and reveling in the way everything inside of her heightened and sharpened when they were together.

In so many ways, that was what she'd missed most in their years apart. That sharp, sweet need and awareness that marked their time together.

Everything else felt like going through the motions.

Tate shifted closer, his body pressed fully against hers and her back to the car door. She let her hands drift down to grip the edges of his shirt, fisting the soft material in a restless attempt to assuage the fire that burned inside.

She wanted him. Had never stopped wanting him, really. But this renewed awareness was dangerous. She wouldn't be able to do her usual avoidance dance, skipping out on events she knew he'd be at or keeping her distance from the end of town that housed Reynolds Station.

For the next several days and weeks, she'd be back inside the orbit that drew her in so close.

And she was going to have to do the job of her life to keep herself from getting lost there.

Tate felt the ground shifting beneath his feet. There really wasn't any other word for it. The tension that had ridden him all day—from the moment Belle had showed up on the ranch, her police-issued vehicle bumping over the uneven ground—finally abated as he gave in to the needs that always hovered so close to the surface.

Oh, how he wanted this woman.

The need that burned inside like an out of control fire continued to flicker and flame, drew him toward her. His body was tight, his muscles taut as he held her close and learned once more the achingly familiar shape of her mouth and the lush curves that pressed against him.

They'd kissed earlier in the kitchen but it was nothing like this. The exhaustion that dragged at them both, the dark that surrounded them and the quiet of the parking lot all combined to loosen the ironclad guard each kept up around the other.

He felt his weaken and recognized the same in Belle.

"Tate." His name was a husky whisper on her lips, but when her hands went to his shoulders to slow him down, he renewed the kiss. There would be time enough tomorrow for recrimination and frustration things had gone this far. Even more time to restore the battle armor they both clung to like lifelines. For now, he just wanted a few more moments with her.

The pressure on his shoulders shifted, became more of a pull toward her than a push away, and Tate groaned against her lips when she matched the movement with the press of her body against his groin.

Sparks shot through him and he briefly wondered if she'd manage to unman him still fully clad in his jeans.

Without warning, all of it stopped. The intimate press against his body. The warm welcome of her lips. Instead, the woman in his arms stiffened, her body shifting from liquid and languid to sharp and alert in the span of a heartbeat.

"Tate!" Urgency whispered through her quiet tone.

"Hmmm?"

He knew he needed to keep up with the change in mood but couldn't quite understand why. Her lips felt so good and her body was so warm. So welcoming.

It was only the shift of her hand to cover his ass and the firm squeeze that wasn't designed to tempt and tease that finally had him opening his eyes. "Stay with me, cowboy, and don't move."

That husky whisper was still in place but the iron beneath her words was all cop. "Tate. Someone's out there."

Her words finally caught up with the shift in mood and Tate focused on her. "What?"

"Someone's out there. Watching." With her free hand, she kept a firm grip on the back of his head, holding him still before he could shift to look around. "Kiss my neck so I can get a look behind you."

Tate complied, the light taste of salt from her skin coating his lips. The joy he'd have taken from that move only a few moments before had vanished, replaced by the overwhelming urge to cover her with his body while he wrestled her into the safety of the car.

"Do you see anything?"

"No. The lot's clear and I don't see anybody walking around." She arched her neck, the move appearing to anyone watching that she was in the moment, enjoying the pleasures of the man she was with. The bulleted description he received, matched in the rumble of her vocal chords beneath his lips, told another story.

She was back on the job and his presence had become unnecessary.

Tate pulled away, that reality as effective as a cold shower. He wasn't going to apologize for the past few minutes but he was damned if he was going to stand there and play undercover stud either.

"Where are you going?"

"You seem to have a handle on things. I don't think my lips are necessary any longer."

"You're picking a fight with me?"

"Geez, Belle, I don't know. One moment we're kissing each other's brains out and the next you're ready to race off into the night. I'm not gonna lie, it messes with a man's head."

"I'm not going to apologize for thinking we were in danger. You of all people should understand that.

We found a dead man practically on your property this morning."

"I'm well aware of that."

"Then why the sudden pout?"

She always knew the right turn of phrase to reduce their exchange to a heated debate and had succeeded once again. Tate turned in a wide arc, his arms held high and his voice rising several decibels. "Anyone out there? Anyone watching?"

"Tate!"

She tugged at him but he stepped out of range, his gaze roaming over the parking lot as he kept up the steady shouting. "Who's out there? Getting your rocks off on a couple making out in the bar parking lot? Where are you hiding, you bastard?"

"That's enough!"

Belle got a better grip on him this time, dragging on his arm and pulling him toward her. The move was enough to catch him off balance and his other arm windmilled as he stumbled a few feet over the gravel parking lot. He caught himself and added his own personal layer of armor, pushing every ounce of smart ass he had into his tone. "If this is how you get a man on his back, I'd say you're not very good at this game, Belly."

"I'm trying to keep you from being a target."

"Of what? Some perv's attention?"

"Or a killer."

Her heavy hiss struck a chord but he'd be damned if he was going to show it. She'd hurt his feelings— worse, she'd dismissed him and what they'd shared— and he wasn't ready to think rationally.

Nor was he willing to be reasonable.

"Won't that be nice? One more feather in your cap when you bring down a killer."

"I'm looking for justice."

"You have fun with that." He gestured toward the car. "I'm not leaving until your fine ass is in that car, driving away."

"I'm a cop. I can handle myself."

"And I'm still the gentleman Betsy Reynolds raised." He crossed his arms, anger and confusion and the sheer agony of having their sweet moments ripped away all churning inside. "The sooner you drive away the sooner I'll go back into the bar."

"Back to Dove?"

It would be easy—too easy—to use the jab to his favor. Which was the exact reason he didn't. That and his basic respect for Dove Anthony and the reality that she had nothing to do with what went on between him and Belle. "I said back inside."

The light of battle and innate competitiveness flared once more in her gaze before she seemed to come to some sort of internal decision. Belle dug in her purse for her keys, unlocking the car. She climbed into the driver's seat, the engine rumbling to life beneath her calm, efficient movements. In moments, she was driving away, leaving Tate with nothing but images of their exchange.

And the memory of how her hand shook when she'd unlocked the car.

Chapter 8

Ten days.

Ten whole days with nothing to show for her efforts, other than a heap of notes and the endless reports those notes generated. The dead body discovered on Reynolds property had long since been released from the coroner's office, horrified next of kin eventually found and notified. The funeral was scheduled for the weekend to bury one Jesse Abrogato, son of a grieving mother and three heartbroken sisters, and former runner for one of Mexico's biggest drug lords.

Belle fought the urge to drop her head to her desk as she flipped to the calendar in her email program. She hadn't had a day off in three weeks and it didn't look like she was getting much of one this weekend either.

She would attend the funeral. She was initially surprised it had been planned in a town an hour away from Midnight Pass instead of in the victim's native Mexico, but then Abrogato's chatty youngest sister had informed her the family had moved to Texas to escape some of the unsavory influences of their hometown. She'd then sobbed at how poorly they'd failed.

Belle shook off the sad conversation and the bone-deep grief that had punctuated the woman's need to talk. She had a job to do and she needed to focus on finding who murdered Jesse. He may have made poor choices in life, but it was her duty to see he got justice in death. And since there was always a chance the killer would attend the funeral, Belle refused to miss the opportunity to assess the scene and watch carefully in the role of mourner.

Five o'clock had long since come and gone, and she finally gave in, shutting down her computer and vowing to clear her mind for a few hours. She'd shot off her latest reports to Chief Corden and was nearly out the door when she heard a soft goodbye from the office next to Corden's.

"Captain Grantham." Belle stopped, always happy to spend some time with her captain and all-too-often mentor. His brown eyes and fatherly smile never failed to bring her smile out in return. "You're working late."

"I could say the same about you."

"It's been a busy few weeks."

Grantham nodded, that warm gaze going serious. "Murder's terrible business. How is the Reynolds family holding up?"

The heated image of her late-night kisses with Tate in the Border Line parking lot filled her thoughts before Belle resolutely pushed them down. Despite her best intentions, they'd hovered way too close to the surface for the past week and a half. Even as the infuriating man had kept his distance, leaving her to sit in his kitchen day after day with a full pot of coffee, an equally full refrigerator and absolutely no contact whatsoever.

Jerk.

She mentally stuck her tongue out before returning her focus to the captain.

"They're doing okay. Wary, but moving past it all."

"Glad to hear it. Reese said she spoke to Arden. Had the same impression that they're handling it."

Belle thought of the chief's daughter, Reese, a few years younger than her and one of the town's favorite teachers. She was a kind woman and had borne up under an unbearable tragedy of her own when her brother had succumbed to a drug overdose in high school. She'd become one of Midnight Pass's biggest anti-drug champions and led several programs in the schools to battle the insidiousness of the trade against their town and along the border.

Amazingly, her students loved her enough to pay attention and she'd begun to make a real difference at the high school. Drug-related crimes among the students had dropped off significantly since Reese had started her initiative three years before.

"Please tell her I said hi."

The captain smiled. "I'll be sure to. And if you're looking for something to do to take your mind off things, Reese is neck-deep in building the decorations with the prom committee. I have no doubt she'd love another adult opinion that doesn't involve high school drama, a push for emoji-based decorations or anything involving teenage rebellion."

Belle fought the shudder. "There's a reason I chose killers over teenagers."

Captain Grantham's grin was broad. "You and me both."

She headed off with a smile, feeling considerably better than when she'd shut off her computer. The smile carried her out of the precinct and straight to her car, fading only when she caught sight of Tate leaning against it.

Something hard and needy clawed at her stomach. The man really was lethal, those long legs clad in faded jeans, pointed cowboy boots on his feet. An afternoon rainstorm had cooled the air but he looked as stormy as the still-cloudy skies, a gray T-shirt spread across his firm, wide chest.

Boy howdy, but the man looked good.

"Belle." He spoke first, his greeting as gruff as the dark look that rode his face.

"Tate." She'd been at his house for over a week and then he'd ghosted her. Yet here he was, front and center on a Friday night? "What's going on?"

"I need to talk to you."

"Okay."

"Not here."

Warning bells began clanging in the back of her mind, overshadowing the shot of lust that still stirred in her belly. "Where?"

"Follow me up to Mesa Creek."

Mesa Creek was a small, quiet town about a half hour from the Pass. They'd likely meet no one, which was what made it so perfect. "Manuel's Kitchen?"

"Yep." He nodded as something briefly flickered

in his eyes before he shut it down. "We'll snag the back booth."

Belle wasn't so sure the back booth would be available on a Friday night but she said nothing. "Want me to drive?"

"Let's go separate. No one needs to see us together."

She fought the stab of pain conjured by his words and only nodded instead. Whatever mood he was in, she wasn't going to get him out of it by arguing.

And at the moment, the exhaustion that had ridden her as she wrapped up her reports returned in full force. She was tired and lonely and hadn't quite gotten past the anger at their fight in the Border Line parking lot. Maybe some distance from Midnight Pass would do them some good.

Or maybe it would only add even more between them.

Tate knew he'd hurt Belle's feelings and he was sorry for it, but he had to talk to her and he didn't need anyone wondering *why* he was talking to her. He'd briefly toyed with the idea of trying some sort of pretend date scenario but knew that was as dangerous for himself as it was for her. Letting the entire damn town think they were an item again had a set of risks he wasn't quite ready to explore yet. Didn't mean he wouldn't go there if Tris Bradshaw's suspicions panned out, but he wasn't ready for that quite yet.

So he'd settled on an alternative approach. Years back, they'd spent more than a few evenings shut up in a cozy booth at Manuel's, away from the prying eyes of the Pass, caught up in each other. They could do it again, keeping their distance from anyone who might take an interest in noticing the two of them together.

Her headlights trailed behind him as he wound his way out of town, following when he turned onto the highway that led up to Mesa Creek. The drive was quiet, their corner of Texas still not infiltrated by rush hour traffic, crazed commuters or endless waits to get to and from office meccas.

Even the thought of a life like that gave him the willies. He liked wide open spaces, time spent out and about on Tot and working the land. Being shut up at a desk all day was, to him, the epitome of hell on earth and he'd often wondered what that sort of focus did to a man's soul.

He usually shrugged the question off, assuming people were well able to make their own decisions, but had never been able to fully shrug off the idea that a life like that would feel like he lived his days in a coffin.

The bright neon lights of Manuel's Kitchen came up on his right and he turned off, images of riding a desk and staring at a computer all day fading as fresh tortillas and warm tacos filled his mind instead. He swung into a parking space and saw Belle find one a few cars down. He strolled down to meet her, curious to see she'd added lipstick and had done something to her eyes.

"Makeup for Manuel's?"

"It's a Friday night out. Even if it's only with you, it's nice to remember I do have lady parts every now and again. I fixed up because it might be nice if someone took an interest in looking at them."

The dig was direct and intentional and he knew damn well not to rise to the bait. Which made it that much more fun to do so. He leaned in, effectively caging her between her seat and open door. "Darlin'. I always notice your lady parts."

"Oh, Tate. Such sweet words." She fluttered her eyes in exaggerated movements. "It wasn't your notice that was the problem. It's how you struggled with the fact I have a brain that caused our problems."

Belle ducked out beneath his arm, effectively escaping the small area and neatly turning the moment on him. He had to give her credit for execution *and* a direct hit and slammed the door in her wake.

Point one, Granger.

He followed behind like a puppy, the sexy sway of her hips adding a second point to her side of the tally column. Tate cursed himself for the foolish decision to head here instead of cornering her in the kitchen that morning and telling her what he knew. What had seemed like a good idea at the time was fast shaping up to be one of his dumber moves and he sped up to grab the front door of Manuel's, determined to maintain that small measure of gentlemanly behavior.

He knew damn well the woman had a brain. And contrary to what she thought, his issue wasn't with what went on in her head. It was the stubborn persistence in her heart that caused their problems.

Manuel's was busy but they'd managed to hit a rare lull and were given the back booth as requested. The hostess didn't recognize them and for that Tate was grateful. He wanted quiet time with Belle and nobody paying attention. Nor was he interested in having gossip travel its way back up to the Pass.

"I haven't been here in forever," said Belle. "It's nice to see it hasn't really changed."

"I haven't been here in a dog's age myself."

The disbelief on Belle's face registered momentarily before she seemed to pull back, the surprise in those slightly widened eyes vanishing. "I guess I figured you would've come here more often."

"Just never seemed like the place to come back to."

And it hadn't. Although it hadn't struck him before they began dating, it soon became evident that everybody in Midnight Pass was interested in watching the evolving romance between Belle Granger and Tate Reynolds. The romance had been new enough for the two of them and they'd both quickly realized they needed a few places to call their own.

So they'd gone exploring. And in their explorations had found places like Manuel's, as well as a quiet holler near Reynolds land and the back study cubby at the seldom-visited Midnight Pass library. They'd also found a park near El Paso and more fun than either would have expected watching the elephants at the El Paso Zoo. Those quiet places had been theirs. Spots they ran to where they could be alone with each other.

A few special places to shut out the world.

Their waitress came to take their order. She had the look of the harried and slightly hapless, and Tate gave her his broadest smile. "Hey there." The smile did its job, putting their waitress at ease, and in a matter of moments she had their drink orders and was reading off the specials.

Tate ordered an old favorite—beef enchiladas—and knew from experience they'd be perfect. Belle seconded the order and their waitress toddled off, promising a quick delivery on the drinks and a basket of hot tortilla chips coming right out.

"How do you do that?" Belle asked.

"Do what?"

"It's so effortless. You smile and people just seem to fall in line. Women," Belle added, "especially."

"For the record, I did nothing but be nice. And for the second record, you're the only one who doesn't fall in line effortlessly." He had no idea why he went there, but the fact they seemed unable to spend ten civil minutes with each other likely had something to do with it.

How did she do this to him? It was oddly effortless, yet always present.

More to the point, why couldn't he resist?

Despite being a youth who had committed more than his fair share of high jinks, he *had* grown up. He was an adult who had responsibilities to his family, to their ranch and to the business of Reynolds Station.

Even more important than having responsibilities, he actually liked having them. Living a life with purpose, rising each day to conquer their corner of the world—it mattered.

And so, he acknowledged, did Belle.

And wasn't that the problem?

"What did you want to talk about?" Belle asked. The subject change was obvious, but at least it got them past their earlier, tense words.

"You met one of my ranch hands, Tris Bradshaw, last week during the interviews?"

"Yes."

"Tris is pretty new to the ranch and I haven't known him very long, but I think this is worth sharing."

"Do you suspect him of something?"

"I considered it at first. But now I'm not so sure."

Belle's eyes sharpened as she leaned forward. "Do you know something, Tate?"

"Tris mentioned to me he's seen things out at the far end of the ranch. We put him on fence line detail his first few months. It's a good way to grow familiar with the land and the property, understanding what's ours and the vast area that Reynolds Station covers. Anyway, he mentioned seeing some depressions in the grass and evidence of some strange pressure against the fence line."

"Pressure?"

"Not the sort an animal would make, but what looked like a human testing the fence line. Like a piece or two of fence that had bent and come loose from the post."

"Was it in the same area we found the body?"

"No, and that's what was so interesting about Tris's remarks. He said he's found these pressure points at different places and at different ends of the property. Said it seemed weird at the time but not weird enough to give it much notice. He fixed the gaps and moved on. Until now."

Belle Granger might have a poker face, but Tate still saw the telltale signs of her interest. She was mad, and if he wasn't mistaken—and he didn't think he was—disappointed, as well.

"I interviewed him. He never mentioned a word about this." Belle's eyes flashed with irritation, those pretty blue depths going full cop on him.

"Before you get your back up, why don't you hear me out?"

"I'm not getting my back up. I'm trying to understand why an interview subject didn't tell me pertinent information. Information I probed for repeatedly."

Tate got why she was mad. If the situation had been reversed, he couldn't honestly deny that he wouldn't be pissed off, too. But he also couldn't stand by and let one of his men be dismissed. Or let their worry over losing their job cloud his judgment.

"You don't think they're scared of you? Scared of what happened on the ranch?" Tate fought to keep his voice level, but all of a sudden, the fear he'd been hiding inside himself needed to find a way out. "You don't think this is disruptive and upsetting? To all of us."

"Believe me, I understand the disruption. I'm investigating a murder in my own town. On the land of people I care about. Deeply."

The confession caught him off guard momentarily, but he rallied quickly. "You don't think these men aren't questioning that you think they did it?"

"I'm not suggesting Tris or anyone else committed a crime. I'm suggesting I need to know what happened. Asking questions is the way to find that out. To find leads. Tris's instincts are real, a product of working the land like he does. What he found is something we need to look into so we can capture the person who did do this. His unwillingness to talk to me has now let this go for almost ten days."

Ten days.

Belle's words leaped up and slapped him in the face. Ten days when the police could have been investigating, looking for information or perhaps finding a lead to catch a killer.

"I'm doing my job, Tate. What don't you understand that?"

"I understand it fine. Just fine."

He more than understood it. In this case, his own

stubborn behavior had contributed to making the situation worse.

"But you don't like it. Which brings us right back to the same place we always land."

"What place is that?" The question was a lie because he knew exactly what place Belle spoke of. How could he not? The repetition of their fights was something he could set his watch by.

And by keeping this to himself for a few days—by not encouraging his men to speak to her when they had a chance—he allowed his pride to contribute to a killer roaming free.

Belle took the last bite of her enchiladas and fought the groan working its way up her throat. She'd eaten too much. Of course, it had been inevitable. The mix of fresh tortillas wrapped around beef so tender it practically melted would cause anyone to overeat.

That and the fact that shoving food into her mouth had kept it occupied and off a conversation with Tate.

She'd try to remember that tidbit in the morning when her pants didn't button.

God, would they ever find a way past their endlessly circular arguments? Even if her comments had put Tate in his place.

She understood his ranch hand's fear. People didn't like talking to cops. Whether it was the over-dramatization of far too many TV shows or the simple reality of standing next to somebody who had the power to change their life.

But dammit, Tris's fence line information was something she could've used.

The past week had provided surprisingly few leads, despite the fact that the entire department was working the case, either directly or during free time. They'd tugged hard on the drug angle, but so far, those loyal to the region's runners had been unwilling to give up information. The entire department, as well as the Feds, had all tried various tactics on each of their informants but to no avail.

When sources like that dried out, Belle knew, things were in a bad place.

Even *El Asesino* had gone to ground.

The fact that all the normal chatter they recorded on his business had gone quiet for the past week and a half was a significant indicator that something was going on.

What the time had given them, was an opportunity to investigate similar crimes. Just the day before, she'd been pulled into a small, top secret task force and briefed on the details discovered on Jesse Abrogato's body. The findings had been concerning, but it was even more troubling to realize this MO appeared to be a match for two other open investigations.

The initial irritation that had flowed freely at being kept in the dark on the details had morphed and changed quickly. Upon closer reflection and a deeper dive into the first two murders, Belle better understood the hesitation of the department brass.

It appeared as if they had a serial killer on their hands.

And the department's complete inability to capture— or even garner a working lead on—a very elusive killer had the brass worried. The Feds, too.

She'd been brought into a small circle of trust because it was her case—a circle that didn't extend too far past the chief, the Feds assigned to the Pass and the captain. And since the crimes had all been perpetrated against criminals, word had been contained up to now. The public's general safety realistically wasn't at risk.

But Belle also knew that if something like this got out—especially the holding back of it—the news had the potential to cause significant damage to people's confidence. Confidence that was already stretched because of all the problems that flowed back and forth over the border.

"Why so serious, Belly? Didn't you like your enchiladas?"

She fought the grimace at his use of that stupid nickname and ignored the shot of warmth it sent to the very place he mentioned. "I liked my enchiladas just fine. What about you?"

Tate patted his stomach and sat back. "I've missed these. And somehow managed to forget just how good and perfect they are."

Sort of like you, Belle thought to herself. "You really haven't come back here?"

"No."

She wondered at the quick response. More to the point, wondered that he didn't elaborate. "I haven't been here either. Not since—" she hesitated, then continued. "Not since we used to come here. It's nice to know it's still just as good as before."

"Some things just have staying power, I guess."

She didn't miss the innuendo, or the reality that the two of them hadn't had staying power, but something in his words stung all the same. It was silly to wish for things that couldn't be.

It was even worse to long for the things that you couldn't have.

* * *

Jesse Abrogato's funeral was a joke. An atrocity. How could anyone, including a priest, stand over the casket and intone words of praise and love and forgiveness on a killer? How could a man of the cloth speak of things like perpetual light and eternal rest? In hell, he hoped.

No, he corrected the line of his thoughts. He prayed. Prayed his deeds would be rewarded and his willingness to do the work others refused would someday be recognized for the gift to humanity it really was.

From his view at the back, he could see how the weeping women had assembled themselves beside the casket. A line of solidarity.

A mother's love. A sister's devotion.

What a laugh.

The woman had raised a killer and the sisters had turned a blind eye, and he was expected to feel sympathy? They all were?

Yet somehow they did. Everyone assembled had their tissues and their tears, their kind words of sympathy and their memories of the dead as they spoke to the grieving mother, the crying sisters.

Where was the censure? The questions? When had the woman lost her focus on being a good mother, raising a fine and honorable son? Why hadn't she forced the boy to change his life?

Even now, she wore clothing that was likely paid for by drug money. Wore jewelry that came from the same. And she stood in the midst of a rich funeral and cried for the dead.

Yet he was supposed to feel bad or guilty or bereft

at her loss? Supposed to feel bad or guilty for his own decision to act? To do something?

Never, he thought to himself as he settled into the back row and watched the assembled crowd. He'd burn in hell first.

Chapter 9

Belle reread the small funeral card before slipping it into her purse. She'd purposely arrived early, hoping to recognize anyone who appeared out of place or unusual, but saw nothing. Even now, well after the body had been laid to rest, she hadn't seen anything out of place.

Instead, she watched the steady tears and endless grief of a family torn apart.

Another soul lost to the drug trade. Was that part of the grief? Part of the sadness? His family's realization that they not only lost a loved one, but one who'd hurt others?

She'd been a cop long enough to have developed a thick skin. She understood you couldn't save everyone, nor were you meant to. But dammit, some days it hurt more than others. And in the worst way, today was about loss.

The loss of a life. The loss of a loved one. And the loss of ever having an opportunity to make different choices.

Belle glanced around the funeral home, her gaze skittering from family members to friends to what were likely acquaintances. Friends of the mother and sisters, all there to show their support. She saw the plainclothes they'd put in the back, there to keep additional eyes on the proceedings and make sure that nothing inappropriate went on. Jesse Abrogato had lived a tough life and while they been unable to pin his murder on another rival gang, no one was taking any chances.

And didn't that sting?

It had been eleven days since the body was found and they were no closer to having any leads than when it started. She'd been over and over Reynolds land with the chief and had scheduled a follow-up on the lead from Tate. She planned to ride the fence line on Monday with his ranch hand Tris Bradshaw. Since the line had been repaired, she had little hope it would make a difference, but she'd do it.

She had to do it. Had to do something.

Because so far they'd found nothing.

Belle originally wanted to believe it was all a random act of violence—something that was once and done, a tragic end to a life full of poor decisions—but the recent news from the chief made that impossible.

Abrogato's death wasn't a one-time occurrence. Nor were the implications of a killer on the loose something they could ignore. It didn't matter who the killer had targeted; it was their job to find him or her and take them down. Hard.

* * *

Belle drove through the downtown streets of Midnight Pass, the sorrow and melancholy that had ridden her throughout the funeral not quite done with her. That weird mix of sadness and vengeance didn't sit well with her, and all she wanted was to clear her head.

It was Saturday, which meant she didn't need to go back to work. And she was smart enough to know that eleven days straight without a break wasn't smart either. So the rest of the afternoon would be for her. Taking a right at the edge of town, she headed for the small park that had been updated and refined over the past few years.

They had a park when her grandparents were young, but it had fallen into disrepair. Those days of Buddy Holly's West Texas had faded for quite a while and it was only in the past few years that the town council had seen fit to bring a bit of it back. A nostalgic yearning? Belle asked herself as she pulled into a parking space. Or just the realization that it was time to face the future?

Whatever it was, the sounds of children playing filled the air as she stepped out of the car and she knew it was the right choice to come here. Midnight Pass had a future. A good one, if the people she'd come to know over the past decade were any indication.

That reality made Tate's attitude all the harder to bear. He was so focused on the dangers of her job, he'd taken no time to recognize the good parts. The people she met. The lives she'd affected. And the lives that had affected her.

Since joining the force, she'd met any number of people from the Pass. Good people who wanted to make a difference. There was Sandy Ramirez, the young mother who ran the coffee shop downtown. Random vandalism just before she opened her shop could have shut her down for good, but Belle had helped find the men responsible, and then had organized a group more than willing to help Sandy set the shop to rights.

Then there was the Vasquez family, longtime rivals to the Reynolds. They had faced a series of poachers on their lands, but through diligent police work, Belle's colleague had caught the man responsible—a cousin who'd tried to make trouble for the family. Vasquez beef was back in high demand, just as it had always been, because committed cops had seen to it that the family received justice and their commitment to uncovering a crime.

"It's a fine day for the park."

Belle turned to see Tate standing behind her, the sun highlighting the back of his head like a halo. A traitorous snap of heat skittered down her spine, even as she wondered how he'd found her.

Or why he was even there.

"Hey." She grasped at something to say, but realized there wasn't anything but small talk. Especially not after their bickering the night before. "Just enjoying the day."

"Me, too. I was sick of my own company and just wanted out of the ranch."

Belle was surprised at how closely his thoughts mirrored hers, and he gave her the opening that she wanted. "I attended Jesse Abrogato's funeral this morning. It left me sad and out of sorts, and I figured some fresh air and sunshine might do me good."

"I didn't know you had to go to those."

"Technically I don't. But I thought it might give me a chance to check out the situation. See if the killer was somewhere in the room, watching like an audience member."

His eyes grew dark at her admission, and she braced for another round of "what you do is dangerous," but he refrained from saying anything contentious. "Find anyone?"

"No. And I wasn't there by myself. Although I attended as the department representative, there were plainclothes in the back. And more officers nearby on call."

"Sounds like quite an operation."

"One that's all too necessary."

"You see anything out of place?"

"Nope. Not a thing."

Tate's attention drifted to a group of children playing on a swing set. Their shrieks and screams as they pumped their legs, forcing them higher and higher into the air, grew louder. They both watched them through the cycle, going high, then low, then high again, before their momentum finally slowed and they all came to a stop in a heap of giggles and kid-level trash talk.

"I remember being that little," he said. "That carefree."

"Me, too." With the admission came a memory of the two of them on the swing sets at school recess, along with a few of their classmates. She and Tate had egged each other on, higher and higher, sneakers pointed toward the sun.

It had been so easy then. Of course, it was supposed to be. They were children. And they had the worries of children.

It was only when those worries had grown far too serious in much too short a time that they'd all been forced to grow up. Her mother's worsening addiction. His father's poor choices in raising beef outside of normal practices.

"You ever think about how easy it used to be?" She turned to him as she asked the question, intrigued to see the flash of memory wash over him. His stubble-filled jaw firmed and when he turned to her, the normal teasing in his gaze was nowhere in evidence.

"I do think about it sometimes. Those days before I knew what my father really was. The days before my brothers and sister and I had so much responsibility. Those days when we believed the Reynolds name mattered."

"It still matters. You and Ace and Hoyt and Arden have seen to that. You've made it count for something."

"Some days I think you're right. Others I realize we still have a lot of work to do."

"Has something happened?"

"You mean besides a murder happening on my property?"

"But, Tate, that's not about you. Or your family. That's about a bad person who made a violent choice and dragged you all into it."

"Maybe so." He shrugged. "But it certainly feels personal."

It wasn't personal. Belle knew that. Empirically, she did and somewhere deep inside believed he did, too.

But it sure as hell felt personal.

Tate watched the way the spring breeze blew Belle's hair around her face. He wanted to reach out and touch one of those smooth tendrils, but he kept his hands firmly at his sides. He had no right to touch her. More, he had no right to think about touching her. They had an attraction, yes, but it simply had no room to breathe between them.

They'd both seen to that. It wasn't just the bickering or verbal swatting at each other. It was that firm, implacable line that neither of them would budge on.

But oh, how he wanted her.

And in the moments of madness when he forgot that he even had a line to stand on, he realized just how good things truly were between them.

Pushing aside those feelings of want and what couldn't be, he let his mind drift to the simple days she'd reminded him of. Laughter and teasing on the schoolyard. Working through math problems during study hall. Even those endless hours they spent in physics class when he understood the meaning behind physical principles, but had no idea how to write out the definitions for their tests.

She'd worked with him then. So patient and so determined to help him succeed. While she wasn't the only person in his life who supported him, she was the first one outside of his family to champion him.

His mother had certainly loved her. Betsy Reynolds had always made a point to ask about Belle. Whether it was a casual request while eating cookies and drinking milk after school, or more probing questions about who he was going to take to the school dance, his mother had seemed to understand the connection between her son and Belle Granger.

More than that, she'd sensed his feelings even before he could put them into words.

He missed his mother every day, but at that moment, it was a sharp, acute need that settled beneath his breastbone and stole his breath. And it only added to that feeling of being at odds that he'd woken up with.

"My mother loved you, you know."

He saw that he'd caught her off guard, and was pleased for it.

"Your mother?" Belle pushed at those tendrils, sweeping them behind her ear.

"Yes. She thought the world of you. And she always made a point to ask about you."

"Well, that's a funny coincidence." Belle smiled, her dark eyes all soft and misty. "I thought the world of her, too. She was one of the most beautiful, gentle women I have ever known."

That pain beneath his breastbone subsided slightly, easing as her words sunk in. Those moments when it hurt so bad—when he missed his mother so clearly— he would've thought it would be hard to talk about her. But instead, he found that talking about her actually eased the pain.

It was talk about his father, on the other hand, that hurt. That left him feeling bereft and edgy and empty.

"I remember that time she brought cupcakes for your birthday."

Belle's words crashed right through the memories of his father, effectively knocking them over like bowling pins.

"Which birthday?" he asked.

"We were in second or third grade, I think." The

corners of Belle's mouth twitched up as she got into her story. "She brought chocolate and vanilla, and what I think was carrot."

"You know carrot with cream cheese frosting is my favorite."

Belle shook her head. "A weird choice for a kid, but yes, I do remember." She gave an exaggerated shiver. "Carrot. Yick."

"They're delicious."

"They're gross. But I realize that's a useless argument with you. Anyway, she'd only put a few carrot ones into the box, but Johnny Tambor and Amber Michaels ended up getting them."

Tate got into the story, the memories flooding back. "And both had already taken large bites before basically spitting them out."

"Because—" Belle poked him in the shoulder "—no one likes carrot cake."

"Certainly not eight-year-olds."

"And by the time your mother realized they'd been mis-distributed, it was too late."

Tate shook his head, projecting his best impression of puppy dog eyes. "I was a puddle of tears in the birthday boy seat, stuck with my vanilla cupcake."

"Poor, poor little Tate."

"Eight-year-old trauma at its finest."

The memory went a long way toward easing the grief over his mother. Even more than that, it had given him a small reprieve from the adult tensions that seemed to pervade his life. The murder on the ranch. The lingering embarrassment over his father's dealings that had been like a shroud over the entire enterprise of Reynolds Station. And the impasse with Belle.

For a few precious moments, he was eight again. No responsibilities or hurts beyond a vanilla cupcake in place of a carrot one. The memory of that long-ago birthday had reminded him of one other thing. A funny little incident that had been long forgotten, yet now filled his mind's eyes as if it had happened yesterday.

When he'd walked through the door at the end of that school day, there had been a plate full of carrot cupcakes greeting him on the kitchen table.

Tate walked into the kitchen later that afternoon and could've sworn he smelled the lingering scent of carrot cake. It was silly, and not remotely possible, yet it left him with a small smile he couldn't fully shake. When he left earlier, he'd been tired and out of sorts. Now, although he was little melancholy, he'd gained his equilibrium again.

"You look way more human and quite a bit less like a bear," Arden said.

"I never look like a bear."

Arden just snorted, before adding, "Look in the mirror much?"

Since he knew she hated it, he ruffled her hair as he walked toward the fridge to snag a beer. "I may get the jackass award, but I'm very rarely a bear. Ace and Hoyt battle rather well for that title."

"Fair point." Arden smoothed her hair. "Where have you been?"

"The park." Tate opened his beer and took a deep swig before taking a seat next to her.

"Well, the fresh air did you good. Our grizzled

brothers should take a lesson and head over there, too. Especially if it has such transformative effects."

"The fresh air and a really nice conversation about mom did the trick."

He saw how the mention of their mother stilled Arden's motions, her blue eyes clouding for the briefest of moments. "Mom?"

"I went to the park to clear my head for a bit, and found Belle sitting on a park bench."

"Oh?" Those clouds moved on quickly as a strange eagerness filled their place. "What was she doing there?"

"Clearing her head, too. Must be the day for it."

"She's had a lot on her mind. We all have."

"She went to the funeral."

"Of the guy?" Arden took a deep breath. "The one that was killed?"

"That's the one."

"I didn't realize she was required to go to those."

Tate ignored the fear, keeping it firmly bottled inside. "She went looking for anyone suspicious."

"Did she find anyone?"

"I don't think so. Or at least she didn't say she did."

Come to think of it, Belle had changed the subject rather quickly. Had she seen something at the funeral? Or did she just know it was dangerous ground to keep that conversation going between the two of them?

Since he'd found her in the park instead of running down bad guys, Tate chalked it up to their own problems.

"So you talked about Mom instead?"

"Belle reminded me of a particularly funny story from the year I turned eight."

"She remembers that long ago?"

"I guess she does. I'd forgotten myself, but it came back pretty quickly when I was forced to remember how I missed out on one of Mom's carrot cake cupcakes."

"I don't think I know the story. Was there a tantrum? Tears?"

"Definitely tears. And a lot of sulking."

"You do love your carrot cake."

"Always have."

Again, it struck him that conversations about carrot cake and swinging on swing sets and memories of school were so easy. So simple. He wasn't afraid of being an adult, nor did he really want to go backward, but there were moments when it surprised him just how hard it all was. How no one prepared you for that reality.

"And there you go, looking so thoughtful again." Arden laid a hand on his forearm. "Are you okay?"

"Just acknowledging that horrible realization that being an adult isn't often very fun."

"Except for the sex. It's sort of like a reward for being a grown-up."

Tate laughed in spite of himself *and* in spite of the fact it was his baby sister mentioning the subject. "There is that."

"I bet sex with Belle is a lot of fun."

He pointed his beer at her. "Don't go there."

"You certainly won't go there." Arden shook her head. "And for the life of me I have no idea why. Literal sparks fly off the two of you when you stand next to each other."

"I think you need to look up the definition of literal."

"And I think you need to get your head out of your ass."

Despite his best efforts, the pleasant mood he walked in with was moving determinedly in a sour direction. "Are you truly trying to spoil my good mood?"

"What are little sisters for?"

"Support? Hero worship?"

"Oh, you stubborn man. Can't you see that's exactly what I'm doing?"

Figuring a hasty retreat was better than sitting there delving into things he did not want to discuss, Tate stood up. "I'm taking my beer into the other room and catching an early-season ball game."

"Good. I can have the kitchen to myself again."

"Why would you want that?"

"I was already planning what I was going to cook for dinner. Now I can have some peace to do just that."

"You're cooking?" Tate asked. "Seriously?"

"I do that from time to time, you know."

"Yeah, but I thought after the last round you had no interest in cooking for us heathens again." Tate remembered the wicked battle that had ensued when Ace had dared to mention the mashed potatoes were a little thick.

"I've gotten over my anger over potatoes and boorish brothers who remark on them. And besides, I'm in the mood to cook something."

"Far be it for me to argue over a home-cooked meal. I was planning on a sandwich for dinner, so Chef Boyardee would be an improvement."

"Sandwiches are for lunch, not for dinner. And

Chef B should be for never. We're going to have something good. I may even serve wine with it."

Arden's stubborn interest in cooking a meal finally penetrated his thick skull. It was so obvious, yet he'd missed it at first. Like the rest of them, she was as out of her element as they were. Their lives had been upended and maybe a few hours together, over some home-cooked food, would let them forget for a while.

On impulse, he gave her a quick kiss on the cheek, surprised as always by just how soft her skin was. She was his baby sister, but she was also a grown woman. And in the same way he had concerns, so did she. Adult concerns.

Grown-up concerns.

The sorts of things that kept one up at night.

"A home-cooked meal with wine sounds perfect."

"Go enjoy your ball game, even if it's too early in the season to count. I'm gonna finish making my plans and then run out to the market, so I'll see you later."

"I can run for you."

"It'd be a shame to waste that beer. I can go, no problem."

Tate walked into the living room, snagging the remote control as he went. He settled into the couch and took another swig of his beer. Being an adult wasn't so easy, but it was a lot easier when you shared the load with others.

And, as his sister had so wisely pointed out, there was sex.

He might be short of that of late, but there was also liquor and comfy couches. As he stretched out with his beer, he fought the image of sex with Belle that Arden had managed to plant in his head.

And took what comfort he could in his welcoming couch and an impending home-cooked meal.

Chapter 10

Belle knocked on the front door of the Reynolds ranch house and wondered if she should have gone to the kitchen door. Why was she so nervous? The thin tissue paper that wrapped around the base of the flowers she held was growing warm from her hands and she had nearly reconsidered coming about six times on the drive over.

And that drive only took ten minutes.

Why was she here? Why had she said yes to Arden's kind invitation? Why was she so panicked over dinner with old friends?

Why, why, why? Nothing but whys.

Only she did have a reason. A big one that had started with the afternoon she spent sitting next to Tate in the park. The talk of his mother and the laughs over when they had been children had chased away the initial disquiet that had followed her into the park. Only chasing that unrest away had left an odd, empty melancholy in its place.

Arden's text had caught her in a vulnerable moment, and the call that followed quickly on its heels even more so.

So here she was. Flowers in hand, knocking on the front door of the Reynoldses' house. She'd almost laugh over it, and the weird role reversal, if she wasn't so nervous.

And dammit, why was she nervous?

These were her friends. People she'd known nearly her entire life. People who she should be comfortable having dinner with along with a few laughs. Of course, they *were* people she was comfortable having dinner with. It was only one person who made her uncomfortable.

Which was just stupid, because she'd been here thousands of times and there was nothing to be nervous about. Except she was.

Belle knocked and practiced the calming breaths she'd learned at the Academy.

And hoped like hell Arden answered instead of Tate, because then he'd see her acting like an expectant mother doing Lamaze on his front porch.

At that image, she stopped breathing all-together.

Ugh! Why wasn't she making any sense?

"You look lovely." Arden stood framed in the screen door, her hair falling over her shoulders in glossy waves. "I'm so glad you could make it."

"Thank you for the invitation. It was—" Belle broke off. Did she say what she was thinking? Or would she put on the polite platitudes like she did for everyone else? "It was nice to receive the invitation. I needed this more than I realized."

"Then I'm glad you're here." Arden gestured her inside, following behind after she closed the door.

Warm, rich scents bathed the air, a mix of tomato sauce and baking bread. Her stomach answered immediately, nearly roaring in the sensual wave of such deliciousness.

When was the last time she had a meal like this? She very rarely cooked for herself, a mix of seeking quick options and general lack of interest in cooking that kept her away from the stove. Sandwiches, a quick batch of scrambled eggs or frozen dinners were way easier than building a full meal.

And when had that become her reality?

"What can I do to help?" Belle asked the question, anxious to get out of her own head and *do* something. Something useful and helpful and active. She'd spent way too much time in her own thoughts of late and she was getting rather sick of the poor company.

Arden had gone to all this trouble. It certainly wouldn't do to stand in the middle of the woman's kitchen with a sourpuss on.

"I'd love some last-minute help with the garlic bread." Arden pointed toward a row of items already set up on the counter. Belle took each one of the items in, from the fresh garlic to the large bottle of olive oil to the already chopped parsley.

"When you say you're cooking dinner, you don't mess around."

Arden turned from where she stirred sauce on the stove. "It really is nice to have a woman around. The last time I cooked like this, I had a wicked, epic fight with my brothers."

"What happened?"

"Let's just say not one of the Reynolds boys will ever again think up an offhand comment about too-thick mashed potatoes and feel they need to put the observation into words."

Belle laughed in spite of herself, picturing the incident. Whether it was having three brothers or just the way she was made, Arden Reynolds didn't take crap off of anybody. Belle suspected that would be even truer of the three men she shared blood with.

"Which brother was it?"

"I think it might've been Ace who actually said it, but the other two jumped in quickly enough it was hard to blame him directly."

Words she'd heard many times in her youth played through her mind. "My mother always said if something should be left unsaid, it should be."

"Amen," Arden said. "Wise advice indeed."

"Are we rehashing the potato incident again?" Ace Reynolds walked into the kitchen, his smile bright and warm as he walked directly to Belle. His big arms wrapped around her and she nestled into the hug, taking care not to rub her hands—full of minced garlic—all over his shirt.

More than one woman in Midnight Pass had swooned over Ace, though none had managed to capture the big cowboy's heart. The oldest of the Reynolds boys, Ace was known throughout the Pass and beyond as the stoic, stalwart head of the Reynolds family. Where Tate was known for his humor and Hoyt for his all-around surliness, Ace was the Steady Eddie. Solid, sure of himself and always quick to tip his hat to a lady, Ace Reynolds was the quintessential Texas cowboy.

She certainly found him attractive, but Belle had only ever seen him as an older brother. Since he'd only ever seen her as a little sister, it worked nicely.

"Glad you're joining us tonight, Belle."

"I appreciate the invitation. And it smells amazing in here." She hesitated a moment, before going for broke. "And not a potato in sight."

Ace guffawed at that, leaning in and pressing a kiss to her cheek. "I see Arden has pulled you into her more-than-righteous chef's anger. If the woman has her way, we'll never hear the end of the potato story."

"I should think you wouldn't." She was about to say something else when Ace was pulled away, a harsh curse lighting up the air.

"Get your damn hands off her!" Tate bellowed.

"Jealous, little brother?" Ace made a point to get up in Tate's face before stepping back to snatch a carrot off the counter. "Never did like seeing a man touching your woman, did you?"

Before she could protest the distinction of being Tate's *woman*, Tate beat her to the punch. "I just don't like seeing a woman, any woman, get pawed at by my stupid brother."

"Pawing? That's what we're calling it?" Ace just munched on his carrot, his grin cocky.

"Don't be crass," Tate shot back.

"And quit carrying on in my kitchen."

Both men looked momentarily contrite at Arden's warning, but Ace still managed to get in the last lick with a muttered, "Your problem is you haven't done enough pawing."

Hoyt interrupted any further tussle as he slammed through the swinging door into the kitchen. "Hey, Belle. Welcome to the zoo."

Belle wanted to laugh at the artful display of testosterone that seemed to overpower the kitchen, but opted for a shoulder shrug at Arden instead. She knew her friend loved her brothers, but the little display—reminiscent of a herd of male rhinos—made Belle realize that perhaps being an only child had a little more merit than she'd always suspected.

Arden waved a hand with a wooden spoon covered in spaghetti sauce. "Would you all just get out of my kitchen and give me a chance to have a little bit of girl talk?"

"We just came in to help," Hoyt said before snatching a half-cut roll on the counter. A roll Belle had just smothered in olive oil and garlic.

"Help?" Arden raised a lone eyebrow at Hoyt. "Help my ass. Now get out."

Amazingly, all three men did as she asked.

Belle watched each of them leave, filing back through the swinging door in the same order they came in. It was only once they were gone that she turned to her friend. "That is a rare and fine skill. Someday you're going to have to teach me how you did that."

"On one condition."

"What's that?" Belle asked.

"You teach me how you manage to possess a gun, yet seem to restrain yourself from shooting imbeciles with it."

Tate ignored the persistent image of his brother kissing Belle's cheek in their kitchen and focused on the doubleheader on the TV. He knew there wasn't any-thing between Belle and Ace. He knew it.

So why did it bother him so bad to see another man—even one he loved and respected as much as he did Ace—with his arms wrapped around Belle Granger?

"You cool off yet?" Ace asked him, as if reading his thoughts.

"Nothing to cool off about." Tate never removed his gaze from the screen. The Rangers were playing the Cardinals and he wanted to see the new pitcher the Rangers were debuting tonight.

"Right." Ace reached for his beer on the coffee table, picking it up and then replacing it with his feet.

"Would you get your feet off there?"

"Are you my mother?" Ace shot back.

"You could behave a little nicer when company's here."

Ace never removed his feet, but the subtle humor that had ridden his earlier response had vanished. "Belle is hardly a guest. Not only was she here for over a week talking to our staff, but she's been coming here since she was small. She knows what the house looks like, and she knows what my feet look like up on my own damn coffee table."

"I just think you could show little bit of respect." Tate heard the words spilling from his own lips and knew what a priggish schoolmarm he sounded like. Feet? Coffee table? Was he really going there?

"And I think you should mind your own business." Ace tossed back the remark and added a finger gesture to make his point. It was vintage Ace—and a move they'd all practiced to the point of excellence through the years—but it still stung.

Tate pushed to his feet, not sure where he was going with the action but determined to remove his brother's feet from the coffee table. "I said, we have company."

Hoyt let out a low groan before finally leaning forward, moving into the melee. He slapped his hands on Ace's feet, dislodging them from the coffee table, before turning his attention on Tate. "Are you both trying to screw up dinner? None of us have had a home-cooked meal that didn't come out of the bunkhouse in over a month, all because of Big Mouth over here and his damn potatoes. I think you could both find a way to behave."

Hoyt grabbed his beer before adding, "And this is coming from the brother generally thought of as the jerk of the family."

"You *are* the jerk of the family." Since his response was nearly identical to Ace's, Tate wasn't sure it was a real victory, but it did ease the tension a bit.

"You cooled off?" Ace shot him a sideways glance but kept his feet firmly on the ground, their childish argument about feet on the coffee table already fading away.

It *was* childish, and Tate knew it. But for reasons that continued to escape him, he'd somehow managed to fall down the rabbit hole of schoolyard memories, playground insults and sibling rivalry the likes of which he hadn't seen since he was ten.

"Why is everybody so convinced I need to cool down?"

"Um, maybe because you do," Hoyt said.

"I can't seriously be the only one upset about what's

going on around here. Or has it escaped your notice we had a murder on our property a week and a half ago?"

"It hasn't escaped anyone's notice, Tate." Ace was quick to push at him, his attention no longer on the TV. "But it also can't change the way we live our lives. Nor can you continue to let it get to you that Belle Granger is the one investigating this murder."

"It's dangerous."

"Yes, it is," Ace said. "And it's what she's chosen to do with her life. She's a good cop. Why is it the rest of us can see that and you can't?"

"I can see it."

"But you don't like it," said Hoyt. "That's the real rub, isn't it?"

His little brother came a bit too close to the underlying problem and it chafed to be quite that transparent. His family all knew he and Belle had parted ways years ago and in the throes of a few whiskey-fueled evenings, he'd told his brothers the truth of why they'd broken up. That didn't mean he needed to rehash it now.

Nor did he mean he wanted to rehash it ever.

He and Belle had stood on opposite sides of a very large fence. One that in the ensuing years had become a wall, built of emotional concrete and practically impenetrable from either side. After the embarrassment of his father's actions, he'd learned to push his way through just about anything. Bank loans, skeptical lawyers, even the town's questions about the quality of the Reynolds boys and the beef they brought to market.

He'd pushed through all of that and found a path. One that was good, honorable and decent. One that had garnered him and his family some success and had begun to put Reynolds Station back on the map. He wasn't afraid to power through challenges, nor was he afraid to push forward toward the answer he wanted.

Yet despite all he'd learned, he had no idea how to carve a path back to Belle.

Belle hadn't enjoyed an evening this much in a long time. Unlike her evening out at the Border Line with Arden a couple of weeks back, this was relaxed, without the prying eyes of half of the town. Or the roaming hands and suggestive glances of Dove Anthony.

The evening had also given her a chance to reacquaint herself with the Reynolds family. It was funny, she realized, how much her time with Tate had colored how she thought of them. Through Tate, she'd known that Ace was the well-respected older brother, Hoyt was the grumpy younger brother and Arden was the baby sister and family free spirit. Observing them on her own and especially watching them together had shown her that while those traits and qualities were true, they were also rather broad brushstrokes.

It had been fun to see how Ace worked really hard throughout dinner to compliment Arden's cooking. Not only had he seemed contrite about the overstep on the potatoes, but he'd realized that underneath the comment, he'd hurt her feelings and he wanted to make it right.

And then there was Hoyt. Yes, he might be grumpy, but underneath the old man facade was someone who was bright, artistic and funny. He'd gotten more than a few jokes in, about the family and, more expansively, around his observations of the people in town.

While she knew Arden better than most of the men,

it was interesting to see the way her friend interacted with her brothers. Some ribbing, some battling and a little bit of sweet-talking seemed to make up their collective family dynamic. Yet underneath it all, Belle saw an affection that was real and tangible. Her brothers made her crazy, that was obvious, but Arden also loved them all to distraction.

And then there was Tate.

In many ways, Belle saw what she wanted to see and always had. The sweet boy who'd captivated her had become the sexy man who enthralled her, in spite of her best efforts to feel otherwise. Even with the knowledge that she was biased, it was fascinating to see him with his family, as much a part of the dynamic as Arden, Ace and Hoyt.

When they'd dated, things had been so new between them—so fresh and more than a little overwhelming—they'd spent little time in the company of others. And then once they broke up, they'd avoided each other as diligently as possible.

This evening was the first in years she'd spent any amount of time with the Reynolds family collectively. It was nice to see some of her perceptions change, like a kaleidoscope that she shifted just enough to get a new image. A new picture. And maybe, she realized, a new understanding as additional colors fell into place.

As a family, they'd been through a lot. Although Tate's father's disgrace had happened shortly after they'd broken up, she knew the basic story. His father had taken the family business to the brink of bankruptcy and had ultimately soiled the Reynolds name throughout the beef industry with his illegal cattle-feeding practices. His death from a heart attack less than a year later had ended any real sense of responsibility or liability for his actions.

Yet his children had done right by the legacy. They'd worked the land, built a business plan to bring in new cattle and they ultimately restored the name of Reynolds in Texas and beyond.

It was impressive, she knew, and more than a little daunting to realize all they'd accomplished in so short a time. While she certainly hadn't felt that she'd wasted the past ten years of her life, it was humbling to see all that Tate and his family had built in the same decade.

She'd learned criminal theories and had put the occasional bad guy away.

He'd built a business.

They had different lives with different goals and it wasn't fair to compare. But they did compare themselves to each other and had throughout the time they were dating. He'd pressed for her to take a different path—had nearly pleaded it on several occasions—and she'd stubbornly refused to change her mind.

Why had that always stood between them instead of making them stronger together?

They both valued hard work. And underneath the constant swatting at each other, there was respect and always had been.

She did understand his concerns about her safety. There wasn't a single person in a relationship with a cop who didn't worry about that. Yet many people made relationships and marriages work. And yes, while some relationships still didn't make it under the pressure and the scrutiny, many did.

Look at Captain Grantham, for Pete's sake. He and his wife had raised two children and had spent a lifetime together. They'd even survived the pain of losing a child and were still together.

A life of public service and a marriage could work. But, she acknowledged to herself, both parties had to want to make it work.

"How about some strawberry shortcake?" Arden's offer of dessert broke into her thoughts and Belle was thankful for the reprieve.

Hoyt, Ace and Tate practically fell over themselves in order to pull the dishes off the table. One stacked plates in the sink, another put coffee on, while the third went to the counter to pull out forks and knives and then dessert plates from the cabinet.

"I think I need to get me some of these," Belle said in an exaggerated whisper to Arden as she pointed toward the fast-moving Reynolds men. "How did you get them to fall into line?"

"I simply employed a few tactics that my mother taught me."

"What are those?" Belle already imagined how she might get some of the men at work to clean up the break room and put their coffee mugs in the dishwasher.

"A well-fed man is far easier to manipulate than one with an empty stomach."

"Manipulation?"

"You bet." An unholy light lit Arden's eyes. "I'm a woman with a plan and I'm going to do what I need to in order to see it through."

"A plan for what?"

"A rather elaborate plan to get my brother's head out of his ass."

"Can you be more specific? You do have three of them."

Arden reached over and Belle felt the woman's fingers close tight over hers. Arden lowered her voice so she wasn't heard in the midst of the clanking plates and slamming cabinet doors behind them. "I think you know which brother I mean."

"Arden, come on, that's not why I'm here."

"I know that's not why you're here. Nor is it the only reason I invited you."

"Then why bring it up?"

"Because I'm a woman on a mission and I refuse to lose. You and my brother belong together."

"That ship sailed a long time ago."

"I don't see a shoreline anywhere around here." Arden's grip tightened slightly. "I don't see why you keep running."

"I'm not running anywhere. I just know what's not right for me. What hasn't been right for me for a long time."

"You don't think everything happens for a reason?"

"Some things do." And she did believe that. She'd lived long enough and had experienced enough to understand that sometimes things did happen for a reason. She'd also lived long enough to know that sometimes they didn't.

Tate's father's bad business choices. Her own mother's inability to really show love and affection. Even the random murder that had happened on Reynolds property. Not everything had a reason.

Sometimes it just sucked.

Chapter 11

A warm, soggy rain coated the air with thick humidity as Belle trudged into the precinct the following Wednesday. She felt wet to the bone and that, along with a layer of perspiration, had her feeling like a cat in a bathtub.

Irritated and more than ready to escape.

There was no question about it. Spring had fully sprung in southwest Texas.

"Don't you look pretty as a picture."

Belle wasn't sure if their head dispatcher was trying to be funny, or if he meant it, so she went with her first instinct. "Aren't you a funny guy, Willie?"

"Hey." Willie's hands went up in a don't shoot gesture. "I was just trying to be nice."

"As I look like a drowned rat, you can keep your platitudes to yourself."

Willie let out a low whistle. "Wow, someone's having a bad day."

She wanted to be mad. Knew she was probably entitled to be. But being mad at the clueless Willie would take far too much time and effort and she wasn't willing to give him either.

A lead had come in overnight. Someone who had come forward anonymously, claiming they knew a few of Jesse Abrogato's contacts and a possible place near the border that he used as a drop point. Not quite a snitch and not really a hard clue either. She'd still grasped at it like a drowning person gasped for air. Only to realize by midday that she had nothing to show for it except for a bunch of sweaty work digging and clawing at some mud in a ravine down near the border, just outside of Midnight Pass.

Two weeks. It had been over two weeks since Abrogato's body was found on Tate's land and they were no closer to finding a killer.

"Belle?" The chief poked his head out of his office the moment she came near his door. "You have a second?"

"Of course." She brushed her hair and hoped that it wasn't quite as wild looking as she imagined. "Be right there."

She dropped a few things off at her desk and shrugged out of her coat, curious why Chief Corden had flagged her so quickly. Although he was always willing to take downtime with his team—his approach was more hands on than desk jockey—he rarely summoned anyone into his office, acting as if he'd been waiting for them.

"What can I do for you, Chief?"

Chief Corden gestured toward his door. "Would you mind closing that first?"

"Of course." Belle did as he asked, growing even more curious at what might be going on.

"I'd like to talk you about the current case, Belle."

"Anything, sir. What can I tell you?"

"How did this morning's lead pan out?"

She avoided the grimace that threatened, as well as the sense of failure that the time she'd spent chasing the lead was unproductive, and focused on the facts. "Unfortunately, sir, it didn't pan out at all."

"Do you think it was bad information?"

"At this point I'm not sure. The lead seemed solid. Although—" she broke off, hesitating for a moment. "Although at this point I must be honest and say I've hit the stage where it feels as if I'm grasping at straws."

"It happens."

"It's not how I like to manage a case. When you start grasping, it feels like you run too much risk of potentially accusing the wrong person. But no one, least of all me, can seem to get a bead on this. Leads feel half-baked and no matter how hard we look for clues, no one can find a pattern."

"The fact you acknowledge that can't be taught at the academy. Don't lose that spirit or that vigilance, Granger."

"Thank you, Chief."

The news she and Corden had shared the week before—that they were potentially dealing with a serial killer—hadn't been far from her thoughts. She tried to keep an open mind, but if they *were* dealing with one, this entire situation had an added dimension layered on top of it that was nearly impossible to fully imagine.

Murder was never simple, but this had a complexity that she struggled to process. Something this cold and calculated was on a level the Midnight Pass Police Department had never experienced before. Of course she knew serial killers existed—she'd studied them in the course of her career and had often read up on them in her free time—but to actually be faced with one?

It just wasn't anything she'd ever expected would cross her path.

Like the rest of the department, she'd chafed when the Feds had first arrived in town. The underlying insinuation, whether true or not, was that Midnight Pass couldn't police its own and that the drug trade had flourished too far and too fast to keep under control.

Now, she'd never been more grateful they were here.

"What does Agent Ross think about it?"

"He's asked for reinforcements but has so far been unsuccessful."

"You can't be serious?"

The chief shrugged, but the motion was anything but casual. Something strong and steady burned in his gray gaze. "I wish I was making it up. Ross is pretty pissed about it and I can't say I blame him. He was sent down here to manage the drug trade and suddenly finds himself in the middle of an investigation over a serial killer. Now his home office won't even give him and his small staff a hand. They were underwater to begin with."

"And his bosses really don't see this as a crime?"

"I wouldn't go quite that far. But they certainly don't see it with the degree of urgency one would hope. Killing drug dealers is still a crime, but their chosen profession does color their deaths."

Belle did her best to digest the chief's words, but on a level she couldn't quite define, she struggled with what they truly meant. Regardless of what behavior had put someone in the crosshairs of the killer, the fact remained there were now three people that had been murdered. How could a group of qualified individuals who'd studied and who understood the workings of the minds of serial killers not feel compelled to take action?

For all her defense of the criminal justice system, it was moments like these where Belle had to admit that Tate and his ready cynicism had a point. When he managed to get his jabs in, he often pointed out that the police rarely did as little good as people thought they did. She'd argued the point over and over, that justice didn't work that way, but she'd known that he wasn't completely wrong. Yes, there were plenty of good men and women who worked for the greater good. A tremendous number, actually.

But there were also a few who didn't.

People who were either too lazy, too inept or too self-involved to make a difference. Or even worse than that, people who'd somehow convinced themselves that a badge and a weapon made them invincible.

She'd never had time for that morally superior attitude and when given a chance to set an example for incoming recruits or help in their training and development, she'd immediately squelch even the slightest whiff of that.

Being a cop was a responsibility. It was a responsibility to others and it was a responsibility to herself. Even more though, it was a responsibility to the public. She took that seriously, and she expected others to do the same.

"While we're not trying to hide anything, we do need to continue to keep the serial nature of this information contained." Thoughts of her decadelong impasse with Tate vanished at the chief's instruction.

"Of course, sir. I've not spoken to anyone about this as you instructed me."

"Thank you. I knew you could be trusted on this."

While it was nice to hear, and while she also knew the chief was under tremendous pressure, she struggled a bit with the secrecy. "Chief. May I ask you a question?"

Upon his silent nod she continued. "I appreciate the need to play this close to the vest, but wouldn't it be better if the staff knew? More eyes, and all that, focused on the problem?"

"We're not exactly a small department, but we are a small town. Do you honestly think people could keep this to themselves? And once one person knows, it will be through town faster than a fire."

She'd lived here her entire life and she knew how the gossip flew. Something like this would be irresistible. "No, I suppose not."

"I don't like the secrecy either. And if it were up to me, I would take a few more people into my confidence. But Agent Ross has suggested we play this close to the vest for now and I'm inclined to trust his experience and his expertise."

"I understand." She stood from her chair, aware the discussion was at an end. She'd nearly turned for the door when Belle stopped. "Sir? One more question, if I may."

"Yes?"

"Do you think he will strike again?"

"I do."

"Do you think we'll catch him before he does?"

"Truth?"

She nodded. "Of course."

"With the limited information we have? No. I don't think we will."

As answers went, it wasn't the one she wanted to hear. But she'd long stopped wishing for alternative outcomes. More often than not, the answers to questions were simply what they were.

The truth.

Tate wrapped up his morning ride on Tot, the wet air going a long way toward making him miserable in the saddle. Normally, he'd be happy to ride in any weather. Time spent on a horse was better than time spent on the ground pretty much any day, regardless of the condition of the skies.

But today wasn't shaping up to be that day.

After checking on the cattle in the eastern pasture, he'd worked his way south again. He'd avoided traipsing over the same ground the cops had covered, but another week was fast blowing past them and he was sick of not having any answers. It was Wednesday, dammit. The body was discovered over two weeks ago and the department still hadn't caught the bastard.

Was it really that hard?

Even as he thought the question, he knew the answer. The Pass might not be large in population but it was vast on land. The Reynolds, Vasquez and Crown ranches made up the majority of the town proper before stretching on to cover vast swaths of the county, spiraling out in three separate directions. Reynolds Station had its own zip code, for heaven's sake. It wouldn't be all that hard to get lost in his little stretch of Texas.

Not hard at all.

Which was why they'd begun their own attempts at patrolling the property. Hoyt had mapped out a monitoring system, walking him and Ace through his quadrant analysis of the ranch. Hoyt had identified each of the areas Tris Bradshaw believed he'd seen depressions or changes in the fence line. Although she took modest interest in the workings of their business, even Arden had gotten into the discussion, pointing out various places that seemed like good hiding places. Yet even with a list of places to start a watch or pay closer attention, it was nearly impossible to manage any sort of real surveillance of the property.

Which left him aimlessly roaming the grounds, looking for anything that might lead to a killer.

Tate let out a low string of curses. This was such BS. He was a rancher, for heaven's sake, not a detective. He had plenty to do and none of it revolved around hunting for criminals who might be skulking over his property.

More mist slicked over his hat, dripping slowly off the brim and he let out a long, low sigh.

When had things gone so far off the rails?

He wasn't hardwired to feel sorry for himself, but he had to admit, this whole murder thing had blindsided him. It had taken them years to dig out of the trench the old man had put them in, but they'd done it. More than that, as a matter of fact. They'd expanded and their business now thrived.

Yet it felt like they'd fallen right back to square one.

The subject of town gossip and speculation. He'd heard the whispers himself and had felt the prying eyes every time he drove into town.

He and his brothers typically managed a breakfast in the Drop-In Diner on Mondays when they all went into town to do business. Bank, farm store, discussions with their lawyer if needed—it was a weekly ritual and they usually kicked off the day with a hearty breakfast, some light trash talk and a lot of shooting the breeze.

For the past two Mondays, all eyes in the diner had been on them. The quiet whispers. The casual attention as people stopped at their table to talk, pretending to keep it casual even as they were hoping for a crumb of information. Even their lawyer had gotten into the mix, his attention diverted from talk of an impending purchase on a head of cattle to discuss the sordid details of a dead body.

And underpinning all the confusion and chaos that had suddenly become his life was Belle. He'd done well avoiding her over the past decade, but with the discovery of the body, suddenly she was front and center in his life. He'd handle it—he knew that—but it didn't change the fact that she'd unsettled him as much, if not more, than the discovery of a dead man.

Which was an insult, but that didn't make it any less true. Nor could he deny another truth. He enjoyed her company.

Perhaps a bit too much.

Arden's crafty management of dinner—and the extension of an invitation before anyone could argue—had ended up okay. It was more than nice to look over and see Belle sitting there, laughing in his kitchen. He'd wanted to be mad at his sister, but the truth was he hadn't had such an enjoyable evening in far too long. Even if he had spent it with a raging hard-on and a deep desire to punch his older brother.

Ace had seemed to take extra enjoyment in hugging and touching Belle, making her laugh as often as possible. Even Hoyt—sullen, surly Hoyt—had gotten into the game by the end. His younger brother had used charm on the woman.

Charm!

From Hoyt.

Had the world gone mad? Or was it just his corner of it?

The walkie-talkie at his waist chirped just as he heard an engine puttering in the distance. He unclipped the heavy device at his waist. "Reynolds. Over."

"It's Ace. Belle's heading your way. You still in the east pasture?"

"Yep."

"Stay where you're at. She'll come to you."

"Got it." Tate re-holstered the walkie-talkie at his waist. He'd almost question the seeming ability to conjure Belle from thin air just by thinking about her, but he thought about her all the time and she'd been remarkably absent since Sunday. So his powers were probably just a bunch of BS.

And besides, he thought about her too much. That was the plain and simple truth of the matter.

Since the terrible time they'd broken up, she'd always played in the background of his thoughts. During those times when he'd dated other women, she had faded fully into the background—he wasn't particularly keen on using another woman to assuage an itch and he'd done his level best to truly put himself into those relationships with nothing but good intentions—but inevitably thoughts of Belle would creep in.

It would catch him off guard at first, a result of seeing her around town or hearing her name through an acquaintance or maybe Arden's mention of a girls' night out. That was usually all it took to remind him of her and to crash into whatever else was going on in his life. To remind him that she was the one who no one else, no matter how beautiful or charming or sexy, could ever live up to.

The freaking curse of his life.

The steady hum of an engine grew louder in the distance. Even through the rain, Tate heard the purr. Where he expected the typical eight cylinders that powered police vehicles, it was her smaller personal SUV that came into view.

Was she off duty? On a Wednesday?

The steady *putt-putt* continued and even without extra horsepower he had no doubt if Belle chose to put on the gas, that mild-mannered SUV creeping closer from the distance could haul ass.

One more reality of their situation.

Belle Granger knew how to hold her own. The fear he lived with—that she'd perish at the hands of a criminal with a gun—couldn't stave off the truth. The woman had gumption. She also had extensive training, both physical and mental, to handle the job she'd chosen. None of it made him feel better when he lay in his bed at night and imagined her facing down drug dealers or running down a back alley after a perp or, his most recent nightmare, discovering the grisly, tortured body of a dead man.

With those unpleasant images filling his mind, he

dismounted off Tot and left the horse to roam. Although it would be a pain to chase after him if Tot elected to go off running, the combination of cruddy weather, the warm stall that awaited him and the apples in Tate's coat pocket ensured the horse likely wouldn't roam far. Tate rubbed the horse's neck, running his hands through Tot's mane. "Take a load off, boy."

Tot's warm brown eyes, always so perceptive and open, seemed even more so as they flicked toward Belle. Tate avoided thinking too hard about what the horse saw and stepped back, giving him a light pat on his flanks. "Go enjoy for a few minutes."

"Were you talking to him?" A wry smile rode Belle's face as she closed the last few steps between them. The MPPD T-shirt and jeans she wore reinforced the idea that she was off duty.

"Always."

"Does he answer back?"

"In his own way."

She shook her head but the smile had turned reflective. "Tate Reynolds. Horse whisperer."

It was an old joke and one that had grown more pronounced years before when they'd caught a Robert Redford movie one Sunday afternoon. She'd been at his place, along with a few other kids from their study group, and the movie had come on after a Cowboys game. No one had paid much attention as they'd closed their books and, crazed on an afternoon of gummy bears, Cokes and cupcakes, tumbled out of the house and back home. It had only been Belle, having already completed her homework, who'd grown enraptured with the movie and Redford's steady "whispering" to the horse.

"You can do that."

"Do what?" He looked up from his stupid physics book, sick and tired of how the ideas made sense but describing them on tests didn't.

"That cowboy. There in the movie." Belle pointed toward the TV. "He talks to horses. Calms them. You can do that."

Something hot and warm settled under his chest before it crept up his neck. "No, I can't."

"But I've seen it. Animals love you. Especially horses."

It wasn't something he liked to talk about, but the horses did love him. And he loved them. All of them, even the ornery ones their foreman liked to take on from the rescue.

"I just know how to work with them. No whispering involved." He'd shot her a warm smile then, the one he'd been practicing. The one that seemed to get him out of trouble and make the girls smile and made his bus driver giggle.

The one that seemed surprisingly ineffective on Annabelle Granger.

"Why are you embarrassed about it?"

"It's hard to be embarrassed about something that doesn't exist."

Looking back on it now, it was one of the first—of many—conversations with Belle where she called him on his crap. She didn't take the easy smile and quick jokes at face value, but forced him to go deeper.

To look deeper.

The rub was, she was the only person he was willing to show what *was* deep within him.

Shaking off the weird old memory, he nodded in

Tot's direction. "You know as well as I do that animals communicate with us. Having a voice, more oft n than not, only fouls up our ability to communicate."

"I won't argue with you there."

"Finally." He shot her a grin, the one she had a near-legendary immunity to. "Something we agree on?"

"Maybe."

As compromises went it wasn't much, but he'd take it. "What brings you out on such an ugly spring day? And why aren't you at work?"

She shrugged but he didn't miss something dark flash briefly in her eyes while her mouth thinned into a flat line. "I had some comp time coming to me so I took it."

"So you came here? Seems like you could spend your free time in more interesting ways."

"I wanted to make another go of the fence line. See if there's anything we've missed. Look at those spots your ranch hand mentioned once more."

Whether he liked her job choices or not, he'd always admired hard work. He equally admired an ability to put the job aside every now and again.

Yet here she was.

"After two weeks and several bouts of rain?" He shook his head, pushing back even if he'd had thoughts of doing the same. "Darlin', it was a long shot you'd find something the day we found the body. Mother Nature's seen to it there's nothing left to find."

"It's more the fence line. I want to trace the killer's path. Where they went. Why they picked that place."

"Profilers have already been here. Have already taken enough photos to launch a magazine. Why not use those?"

She stilled, that smile still firmly pasted across her lips, even as any hint of humor vanished from the depths of her blue eyes. Tate's gaze roamed over that face—that heartbreakingly familiar face—and fought the urge to press a fingertip to the small divot in her chin.

Fought the urge to touch her.

Just like always, he held back the urges and the needs and the desperate desire that had driven him since before he fully understood what it was to want a woman.

"I get a better impression on my own. Seeing it with my own eyes, not the framing of a photograph. That's what I need."

"Even if any and all evidence is gone."

"It's not about evidence. It's about the scene. Why that place? Why that moment in time?" She rubbed at her cheeks, wiping away moisture that had gathered there. "Look. I only drove out here as a courtesy. So you'd know I was here."

"Okay. You're here."

"Fine. Then I'm going to go take a look around."

She turned to go and something in the finality of it all struck him as wrong.

Maybe it was the endless lightning that seemed to spark, darkening every conversation they attempted to have. Or maybe it was the lingering memory of having her in his kitchen, laughing over a glass of wine and a plate of pasta. Or maybe it was even the fact that she stood there, in the warm spring air, rain coating her hair and her face and her coat.

Maybe it was just Belle.

But before he could check the impulse, he had her

in his arms, dragging her close, his mouth descending on hers with all the fury of a spring storm and all the gentleness of a warm rain.

Belle had no idea what had happened. One moment she was talking murder scenes and profiler photos and thinking about tracing the steps of a killer and the next she was pressed tight against a large, warm body. She knew she should protest—had she been in uniform, decked out with her body camera she would have—but he felt too good.

And she wanted him way too much.

This had bad idea written all over it, but the combination of sexy man, warm rain and a very hot pair of lips made her ability to say no nonexistent. Belle wrapped her arms around Tate's neck, threading her fingers through the short hair at his nape. Her fingers tilted the back edge of his cowboy hat and she was tempted to throw it off, but knew it would land in the mud. She could hardly be responsible for soiling a cowboy's prized hat.

"Tate. We can't do this here."

"Car. Your car." His lips pressed against her neck, his voice muffled yet urgent.

"What about Tot?"

"He's fine. He likes the rain."

She giggled, especially with the realization that the horse could wind up halfway across the property by the time they were done, but figured Tate knew better. "Okay."

She put her hands at his waist and pulled him against her, stepping backward across the grass toward the car. He seemed to be everywhere all at once, his hands on her, his lips roaming over her skin and that warm breath driving her crazy everywhere it flowed over her sensitive nerve endings.

How many times had she imagined this? How many nights had she lain awake, remembering how good it was to be with him? Could she really walk away now?

Absolutely not.

She felt the door at her back and fumbled behind for the door release. The rain had continued to fall lightly and was just steady enough to coat their bodies with slick moisture. The moment they got the car door open and fell across the back seat, she could feel the heat rise off them, steaming the windows.

Belle had no idea what she was even doing here. After her earlier conversation with the chief, she realized that she simply needed a bit of time away and had taken an afternoon of comp time. She'd earned it fair and square. The excessive hours she'd put in lately granted her a free afternoon.

It was only once she'd gone home, her plan to relax on the couch with a romantic movie she'd DVR'd the prior week, that she realized her error. The opening credits had barely rolled when she'd grown tired of her own company. Instead, the case and her conversation with Chief Corden weighed heavily on her mind. In a matter of minutes, she was back in the car and headed over to Reynolds Station.

How had that turned into a wild make out session with Tate in the back seat of a car? And did she really think that was all they were going to do for a few minutes?

Although she knew without a doubt Tate would stop in an instant if she asked, Belle had no desire to.

No desire at all to walk away.

It might be a bad idea, but she wanted him desperately.

Her SUV was a lot less roomy than her work vehicle and she found between the size of the back seat and the length of Tate's body, they were half in and half out of the car. As she thought of an image of what the two of them must look like, she couldn't hold back a giggle.

He lifted his head from her neck. "What are you laughing at?"

"We look ridiculous. We don't even fit in here."

"You need a bigger car," he growled, returning his lips to her neck. His hat had fallen to the floor of the car when they'd tumbled in and his short hair stood up at spiky angles. Its softness brushed against her chin as his tongue did wicked things against her skin.

"At least it's not my work car," she said, her voice breathless. "Those in-dash cams are darn inconvenient when attempting a quickie."

The comment was enough to bring him back to the moment and he lifted his head once more. "Do you want to stop?"

"If you stop now, I may have to pull out my gun."

One of his smiles—one of those truly rare smiles that lit his face without any guile or artifice—captivated her. "We wouldn't want that now would we?"

"An officer has to give a reason for discharging their weapon. Bunch of messy paperwork."

"I can see where that would be awkward." He nodded and schooled his expression in mock solemnity. "What would one put down on the form in that instance?"

"Getting brains kissed out?" She laid a hand on his cheek. "Um, no. Kinda gory."

"It is a police report. No sugar-coating things."

"Scratched an itch, maybe?" She smiled at the imagined paperwork. "Or even better. Attempting to end long dry spell."

"A dry spell?"

She wanted to play it off. Pretend that she'd had plenty of experience since the last time they'd been together. But it would be a lie. Other than a few short-lived romances and some rather unsatisfying sex in both of them, she'd focused on her career. Now that she did the math, it was humbling to realize just how much time had passed. The dates she'd had since those relationships hadn't produced more than a few good-night kisses.

Which meant she had a choice. Tell Tate the truth or casually avoid any further mention of what had transpired since the last time they were together.

"Belle?"

In the end, the choice was easier than she thought it would be as she stared into his gentle gaze, something soft and achy settling in her chest. "Yes. It's been a long time."

And in that moment, she was glad she'd waited.

Chapter 12

Tate drowned himself in the feel of her. Warm skin. Lush curves. And a scent that was uniquely Belle. The faintest hints of hibiscus and vanilla that he always associated with her.

Memories and fantasy and reality all seemed to converge at once and Tate felt himself going under. How long had he dreamed about this? How long had the feel of her in his hands continued on, a powerful sense memory that he could still conjure after so many years apart?

And how was it, no matter how powerful those sense memories, that the feel of her against his skin could prove just how lacking they really were?

Belle hadn't been kidding—the space was much too small to accommodate both of them—but he wasn't giving up. Cradling her in his arms, he managed to twist them and turn them around so that he was laying on the back seat and she was perched above him. He wanted to strip her. Wanted to see her pale skin. Wanted to see her flesh in his hands. The need clawed at him, a living, breathing dragon inside of him.

Even with the need and all that clawing fire, he stilled, holding himself back.

"Are you really sure about this?"

Her eyes had grown drowsy, her dark pupils wide as they filled her light blue eyes. That sexy haze faded quickly at his words. "What was I just saying about my gun?"

But this wasn't just anyone. And he and Belle had been down this path before and it had done its lasting damage to both of them.

Wasn't he right to be cautious?

"It's not like we've done this in a while."

"Has the process changed?"

"No."

"You sure?" She pressed, the hint of a smile ghosting across her lips. "Because you seem very concerned all of a sudden."

His hands played at the hem of her T-shirt. "I'm sure."

"Good. Because you know, with all this talk, you're making me think I may need to seduce you."

Seduce him?

If she thought she had to seduce him then she hadn't been paying attention very well. Everything about Belle Granger seduced him. Her smile. Her mind. Even that damnable focus on work.

She seduced him in every way imaginable, and even

several he hadn't thought of yet. And he'd thought of quite a few.

"Seduce me?"

"I think so." Her mouth thinned to a straight line. She leaned over him, her breasts pressed to his chest, and whispered against his ear. Her lips skated lightly along his earlobe, the featherlight touches torture on his self-control.

"I'm not—" He broke off as she lightly bit the lobe. "I'm not reluctant."

He felt her answering smile in the way her lips spread over his ear. "So how are we going to do this?"

"Now who forgot the process?"

She readjusted herself over him, the move adding even more pressure to his groin. He winced at the sensitive contact, but wouldn't have changed it for anything.

"I'm actually talking about the space here in the back seat," she said, before adding, "And that small little matter of protection."

A mix of gratitude and embarrassment filled his veins, combining with all the finesse of cement. "I have something, but I'm afraid it might embarrass you."

"Embarrass me?" A funny light filled her eyes and Tate knew he was in imminent danger of overstepping.

"Yeah. Sort of."

"Well, yes? Or sort of?"

"Hoyt was ripping on me the other day when we were out working a stretch of fence. It was right after you were here for dinner. Before I could stop him, he shoved a few condoms in my back pocket."

"Why?"

"He told me they might come in handy."

"Handy for whom? Or with whom?"

"I'm looking at whom." He tapped a finger against the edge of her nose. "You."

"Oh."

"My brother might not say much, and he's usually a raging curmudgeon when he does, but every once in a while, he hits one out of the park."

"Hoyt actually prepped you to have sex with me?"

Since his brother had—and he was going to thank him with a sizeable bottle of whiskey later—Tate couldn't resist teasing Belle a bit more. "I guess it depends on how you look at it."

One lone eyebrow arched over that crystal blue. "How are you looking at it?"

"Maybe he was just prepping me so you could have your way with me?"

She didn't look convinced, but she didn't actually get off his lap either. "So where is this special gift from Hoyt?"

"My back pocket."

"I suppose you want me to do the work to go find it?"

"Well, you know," he said with a smile. "If you're headed that direction anyway."

"Oh, I'm headed that direction. But before I go." Belle lifted up slightly, her hands going to the hem of her T-shirt. Before he could even move to help her, she had the shirt over her head and her hands behind her back, unfastening her bra. The breasts that pressed against the cups were bared to his view as her bra and shirt fell to the floor of the car.

She was gorgeous.

The girl he'd remembered—and he'd remembered her well—had nothing on the woman on his lap. Her breasts were softly rounded, her nipples hard with need, and he knew he had never seen anything more beautiful. Unable to resist, he reached up, cupping that fullness in his palms, his thumbs playing over those tight peaks.

Her breasts had always been sensitive. He'd been fascinated at how responsive she was when they were together and he'd used that knowledge to torture himself, touching her over and over in his fantasies ever since.

And now she was here.

He kept up the steady pressure against her flesh, watching as that sensual haze once again clouded her eyes. He lifted up, replacing one of his hands with his mouth, a taut nipple firm against his tongue. Her high moan echoed off the confines of the car and he kept his hands against her waist, holding her still.

Urged on by her response, he suckled her harder, pulling her flesh deep into his mouth even as he lifted his body against the apex of her thighs. Need spiraled through him, his own body hard to nearly the point of breaking, and still he pushed them both on. Her moans grew more urgent, and they both grew more frantic as one moment tumbled into the next. He wanted to stretch this out. Wanted to relive every moment of every tortured fever dream he'd had for the past decade, but the reality of having her was too much.

When her hands dropped to his waist and she tugged his work shirt free of his jeans, he let her. And when they fumbled and wrestled their way over the back seat to get their pants down far enough so their skin could meet, and their flesh could join, he let the moment overtake him.

Overtake them both.

He wanted her and she wanted him. The reality of their mutual need was enough to overcome his own mental pressure to prolong things and his attempts to live out a heated fantasy.

All of it simply faded away in the joy of the moment.

True to her promise, she found the condoms Hoyt had pressed on him earlier that week. Her motions sure and steady, sheathing him before guiding him home, sinking over him in the warmest welcome he'd ever received. As he filled her, pressing past her tight warmth, a heavy sigh shuttered from his chest.

The situation was all wrong.

The location was practically impossible.

The circumstances that surrounded them were criminal.

But in that moment, his body intertwined with Belle's, everything was right.

The piece of trash lay on the plastic tarp, curled into the fetal position and weeping in low, steady tones. The drug runner had begged for mercy, first in his native Spanish and then in sporadic English, but all to no avail.

Justice was swift and uncompromising and it gave no pardon to the pleas of cowards.

Where was kindness and generosity when this man ran drugs back and forth over the border, ensuring they'd find their way into the veins and lungs of innocents? Where was his conscience and his weeping when money poured into his pocket and into that of his employer? Where was his devotion to God and the pleas for mercy when he did his drug lord's business, killing others for sport?

The work that had come before—first the test case in that dirty little hotel room in Juarez, then the work he'd completed in El Paso and then Jesse Abrogato right here in the Pass—had led him to this moment. Target after target, refinement after refinement.

And justice.

The endless thirst for righteousness had only just begun. He would see that it was not only served but that those to whom he meted it out knew the need to repent for their sins.

The thug in Juarez had been an opportunity he'd finally had the courage to take. He'd toyed with the idea, of course. Had conceived the vigilante approach as a way to finally make a real and tangible impact on those who had so little respect for human life. On those who'd taken everything from him with their careless greed.

But he hadn't known how to carry out his plans. The low-level scumbag had shown him the way.

How easy would it be to lure his prey? How much would they share about their colleagues? How much justice could he mete out before the body simply expired?

The work was slow and tiring, but it was satisfying.

And in the end, he'd found his calling. Justice had always been hard work. He'd spent his life in pursuit of what was right, with the law his moral compass. He'd made a career of it, one case at a time.

Now he could put all he'd learned to good use.

Now he would see the endless hours of frustrated anger and barely veiled hostility at a criminal's ability to slip through the system finally meet its due.

And now—finally—he could avenge his family.

The wait had been a long time coming. If only he'd

known how satisfying the work would be, he'd have started long before now.

And if he'd only known how freeing his actions would be, he could have begun to rid the world of its blight and pestilence so much sooner.

With an eye on the knife that he'd sharpened to a fine point, he walked back to the body on the tarp. And once again went to work.

Belle listened to the beat of Tate's heart beneath her ear and took comfort in the firm, steady thump. They were still sprawled across the back of her SUV, with his legs propped on the runner of the car and her body curled over the top of his. She'd managed to wedge her knees on either side of his hips and had used the position to anchor herself to him.

Warm air blew in through the open car door, as hot and muggy as it had been all day.

"I should probably move." Her voice had all the structure of a warm, thick cup of hot chocolate.

"I don't think I can move." His voice rumbled over the top of her head.

"Okay. We'll just stay here like this for a while."

Was it wrong she wanted to stay here forever?

Somewhere in the back of her mind, Belle kept waiting for the sense of guilt to kick in. For that little voice of censure, telling her that this was a bad idea.

Only it hadn't been.

It had been wonderful.

Even if it hadn't solved a thing.

"Do you think Tot is okay?"

"He knows his way around. And he particularly

loves the grass in this pasture. I doubt he went very far."

"That's good."

"He's a good horse. And he's attached enough that he rarely goes off too far."

As pillow talk went, their conversation wasn't and Belle tried to ignore the slight warning bells at the ease with which he shifted back to more mundane topics.

Or the way his heartbeat had picked up beneath her ear.

That steady, leisurely thump post-sex had grown thicker. More insistent. Like anxiety of the assured fight to come had already set in, even as his voice still carried the lethargic aftereffects.

"That's good. I'd hate to be responsible for having your horse end up clear on the other side of the ranch."

Silence descended once more, that feeling of awkwardness and their conversation growing more stilted. She wanted to remain just where they were, the real world still outside the car, but she could hardly deny that the back seat of her SUV was far from comfortable.

Nor did it make a particularly cozy love nest.

Especially when there were actual body parts hanging out the end of the bench seat, exposed to the elements.

"I guess you want to be getting to that fence line?" Tate said.

That feeling he was trying to shake her off grew and she lifted her head, nodding. "Sure. I can do that."

"Okay." His hands briefly tightened on her lower back, at odds with his acceptance, before he dropped them as close to his sides as he could in the confined space.

Belle lifted up, the twisted position of their legs, their half–pulled down jeans and their lack of shirts all combining to add to that feeling of awkwardness. What had, moments before, felt sexy and intimate now just felt ungainly and…well, naked. Like the story of Adam and Eve, she'd tasted the fruit and now she had self-awareness and embarrassment.

And the hard, cold reality of what she'd done.

Belle stretched her hand out and grabbed her T-shirt where it lay on the floor of the car. She took the extra moment to drag it on before attempting to disengage herself from Tate's body. She struggled to pull herself free, finally just giving up on the potential worry of being seen in the buff outside the car.

With modesty long gone, she wiggled herself out of the back seat, ass first. Belle ignored the misty rain drops that coated her skin and dragged her panties into place, then gave her jeans a quick tug back up over her hips. She diligently ignored how sensitive her skin suddenly felt, rubbing against the soft cotton. It would do no good to think of that. Or the man who'd put her in that condition in the first place.

Tate was already out of the car, his jeans zipped but still unbuttoned. She simply stopped and stared, watching as he dragged his shirt back on. She knew what he looked like. Empirically, she knew. Hell, a few moments before, she'd had all that glorious skin beneath her fingertips.

But it was something else to look at that naked chest, glistening with the misty rain, from a distance. Hard pecs defined his chest, firmed from years of tough, physical labor. Those gave way to thick stomach muscles, all of which bunched and moved beneath his motions as he put his shirt back on. A shot of something decidedly sharp and needy cratered in her stomach.

Despite their sudden awkwardness, she'd go for round two in a heartbeat.

Oh no. Oh no, no, no. The mental headshake repeated itself over and over in her thoughts. This had trouble written all over it.

Tate looked up after he buttoned his last button. "I'll get Tot and we'll hang out here a bit while you check the fence line."

"You don't need to do that. I don't want to keep you from your responsibilities today."

"I was already out in this field." He let out a whistle and Tot perked his head from where he stood grazing in the field about twenty yards away. "There's plenty to do."

"Fine."

The back door of her car still stood open, the interior light shining outward into the gray air. It was part beacon, part single exposed light bulb swinging over a jail cell.

Incriminating.

Telling.

Illuminating the scene of the crime.

What *had* she been thinking? Thinking, she admitted, was the problem. She hadn't been thinking at all. Instead, she allowed every heated memory, the close confines that had recently thrown them together and that ever-present desire for him take over her common sense.

With a slam on the back door, Belle crossed to the

trunk. She opened it and pulled out a few things. A large camera, already outfitted against the rain. A department-issued metal detector, on the off chance something might have fallen off either the dead man or his killer. And the poncho she kept in a back well, something to keep her dry in the elements.

Not like it mattered, she thought. But maybe a bit of rain would do her good. Would wash away the feeling of him. The scent of him that still lingered deliciously on her skin. Would erase the memory of that moment where she let her inhibitions go.

Tate fought the urge to go to her and wrap her back up in his arms. The back seat had been uncomfortable, sure, but he'd take it again in a heartbeat if it meant having Belle back against him, his arms wrapped around her lithe body.

What was he even thinking? He knew making love with her was a bad idea but had gone ahead and done it anyway. Knowledge didn't equate common sense in this case. No, instead, it was the knowledge locked in his memories that had created the desire to repeat the experience.

And then he'd gone and fouled it all up in the worst way.

Talking about his horse?

He loved Tot. He knew Belle knew that he loved Tot. But to talk about his horse in the throes of a postcoital glow? What a moron.

Hoyt and his damn big ideas, sticking those condoms in Tate's back pocket. If he hadn't had them, none of this would've happened. He and Belle would've simply stood here, in the east pasture, staring daggers at each other. Maybe tossing a few verbal barbs at each other. Their usual MO.

Instead, the feel of her body pressed against his would haunt him. The sensation of filling her, riding the waves of pleasure with her, would keep him steady company.

As ghosts went, he could think of worse. But dammit, this ghost had an awfully tight grip.

She hadn't said anything else since she walked back over to her car, and Tate gave her the distance. He watched as she struggled to pull a few things out of the trunk of the SUV and tamped down further on the gentlemanly urge to help her. It wouldn't kill him to walk the fence line with her. Nor would it be a complete waste of time.

The lack of information on Jesse Abrogato's killer still chafed. If there was something there, something to find, didn't he want to be part of that solution? The chance they'd find anything was beyond a long shot. Spring rains and the natural changeability of the land practically ensured it, but what if?

What if there was something that had been over-looked?

It would mean being close to her. It would mean breathing in the scent of her, and the memories of what it felt like having her over him, around him, surrounding him.

But between the large camera she carried, some long metal device she struggled to hold in another hand and the slick rain, she really did need his help.

And he was just a big enough idiot to step in and help her.

Chapter 13

Sex didn't solve anything. She knew that. She'd always known that. She'd lived with that knowledge for the past ten years. She and Tate had been as wildly compatible sexually as they'd been in other areas of their life.

And it still hadn't mattered. Not ten years ago and not today. But oh, had it felt good.

Whatever memories had lived in her mind for the past decade had paled in comparison to being in Tate's arms once again. The strength of his body. The firm lines that had only hardened into the thick, impressive frame of a man in his prime. The glory of giving herself up to him and shutting out the world for a while.

The world had come back—with a vengeance—but it had been amazing while it lasted.

Of course, now the two of them were back to opposite sides of their personal Grand Canyon; even the best, most mind-blowing sex couldn't change that.

She went to work on the fence line, following the methods Julio had taught her. She read the patterns in the land, using her eyes and her tools to see what she might find. What might be hidden in the earth.

Tate wasn't wrong. The approach was more than a long shot. It actually smacked of desperation, if she was honest with herself. But the complete inability to secure a lead on the case had her grasping for straws and more than willing to engage in meaningless work if for no other reason than to act.

She'd had a conversation once with a friend who'd complained over drinks about her office job. How all she did most days was sit in meetings or send emails and Belle had thought at the time that wasn't a job.

It wasn't action.

The conversation had only reinforced for her the choice she'd made to go into law enforcement. To go to work every day with purpose and focus.

With action.

Yet here she was, roaming Reynolds Station, basically doing the police equivalent of sending emails. Walking the fence line in the desperate hope something would show itself wasn't work. It was mindless effort meant to make her feel busy because there was nothing else to do. No leads to run down and not a single damn suspect to question.

Tate had kept his distance, walking Tot beside him on a lead. The horse seemed content enough, traipsing through the grass and mud, stopping to investigate as it suited him. The rain had stopped, but the air was still thick with humidity, when man and horse pulled up beside her.

"Anything I can do?"

"I'm good."

"You sure?"

She glanced down at the heavy camera hanging around her neck and the metal detector she still carried. "Here. You're on detector duty. Consider yourself deputized."

He took the metal detector without comment, his focus on the ground as he moved the machine in a light, even arc as he walked.

"We're looking for anything that stands out. Anything a killer might have left behind or anything the victim might have tossed to the ground, like a clue."

"Guy was in pretty bad shape. You think he managed to find a way to leave clues, too?"

"You never know."

He shrugged at her logic. "Fair enough."

Belle ignored how good it felt to walk with Tate beside her and kept her focus on the ground. Looking at him led to other ideas and she didn't need to dwell on the fact that a mere twenty minutes ago, they were naked—or mostly so—and having sex.

"You think this is the only murder?"

Well, that was certainly a way to end a good sex glow. Even if the two of them had done a pretty good job of ruining it without talk of murder.

"It's the one we're investigating." The retort was hollow on her tongue and she wished she could say more.

But Belle knew her orders. She was well aware of what the department expected of her and telling a civilian top secret information on a suspected serial killer wasn't the way to either advance or prove herself a valuable member of the team. Nor was it a way to make the citizens of Midnight Pass feel safe.

Even as she knew her responsibilities, it couldn't change just how badly she wanted to talk to him and tell him all they suspected. Wanted to have him as a confidant and as a supportive partner who she could talk to about her work.

"Sufficiently vague," he said, shooting her a sideways glance. "Is that the department line?"

As usual, Tate's intuition and ability to read her was more curse than gift and she struggled against the urge to tell him what they suspected. "The department is in the midst of a murder investigation. Surely you can understand it's not information that's shared broadly."

"Even if said murder happened on my property?"

"Even then."

They lapsed into silence once more, a decade's worth of anger and hostility fueling the quiet. She nearly called a halt to the search then, but it was only sheer, stubborn will that had her pressing on.

That and the sudden high-pitched wail from the metal detector.

He stared down at the face of the metal detector, its sudden screech splitting the air. Tot whinnied lightly and shied to the side, and Tate let out on his lead so the horse could move away from the insistent noise. He took a few more steps, the noise quieting, so he doubled back, sweeping over the ground to see what had set off the metal detector.

Belle rushed to his side, dropping to her knees as he homed in on the location that emitted the strongest signal. She was already pushing the machine away, her gaze eagerly roaming over the ground.

"Do you see anything?" Tate switched off the metal detector, the whine beginning to echo in his head.

"Not yet." She leaned farther forward, her nose practically in the dirt as she searched the wet grass.

He wanted to drop to the dirt as well but between Tot's lead and the heavy weight of the metal detector, he was stuck. So he watched Belle, her focus absolute. Where someone searching for a small object like keys or an earring would be pawing at the ground, she was methodical, her gaze roaming over the earth even as she touched nothing.

"There." The triumphant shake of her fist would have been funny if it weren't tied to something so serious, and in moments, she had her hands in her back pockets, digging out a pair of rubber surgical gloves, an evidence bag and a pair of industrial-sized tweezers.

"Where was that hidden?" The question came out before he could help it, the memories of her naked and draped over his body still far too fresh for comfort.

"I got them out of the back of the car. After…"

After they'd made love. And now she was back to business.

As if to prove his confusion on what should have come next, her attention was already back on the ground, her focus absolute and very clearly on her job.

Her dedication to her task gave him a moment to watch her and he was helpless to look away. The blond curls that had always captivated him had tightened up in the moisture and a few sprinkled over her cheeks as she worked, having fallen away from where she'd piled her hair in a haphazard twist high on her head. Her shoulders were slim and her body remarkably strong. The woman he'd made love to before she went into the police academy had grown stronger, her muscles long and lean, producing the woman he'd made love to today.

It had been amazing—a mix of what he'd always remembered, yet in some ways entirely new. It had been a long time since they were together and while his memories were strong, he had to admit some of the specifics had faded. He hadn't quite remembered, for instance, the pitch of those light moans that spilled from her throat as she expressed her pleasure. Nor had he remembered the exact weight of her breasts as they curved into his palm. Nor had he ever seen the tight muscles of her stomach and the clear strength that was an outward sign of her job.

All of it had fascinated him, the woman who he'd known practically a lifetime who could still surprise him. Who could still be new in so many ways.

"Oh, my God."

Her quiet utterance brought him back to the moment, his attention shifting quickly from the images of her delightfully curved backside to the misty gray day that surrounded them. "What is it?"

"This." Belle pointed toward something small where it lay, half in, half out of the mud.

"What is it?"

"I'm not entirely sure, but it's something. It has to be." She held a small item in her hand and scrubbed gently at the face with a gloved finger.

Tate was careful where he stepped, but moved closer. He'd already dropped Tot's reins, giving the horse the room to roam once more. Although he couldn't fully make out the definition of the item in her hands, it looked like a pendant or a charm someone would wear on a necklace. Had it fallen off the body?

Or the killer?

"It looks expensive."

"My guess is gold. It's a solid piece and it's very finely made. It looks like a religious symbol of some sort."

Tate leaned closer to take a look, only to catch her warm scent. Once more, images of lovemaking filled his thoughts, the woman standing before him wavering in and out with the images of her rising up over him in the car.

"Tate?"

He snapped to attention, refocusing on the small item in her hand. "It looks like a small gold piece of the Blessed Mother."

Belle rubbed her hand over the face of the pendant once more before nodding. "You're right. I don't want to remove too much in the event they can get a print on this, but it is a pendant of Mary."

The people who lived in the Pass were predominantly Catholic and it wouldn't be a surprise for anyone to have a piece of jewelry representative of their faith, but it was a surprise to find it on the land. While he didn't personally know the beliefs of his ranch hands, he'd spent enough time with all of them to know they didn't wear any personal jewelry when they worked.

"I don't think this came from any of my guys. I can ask if anyone's lost any jewelry, but I've never seen something like this on anyone."

"I didn't notice any jewelry on anyone I interviewed

either. And while several had tattoos, nothing seemed overtly religious."

Belle's observation caught him up. "You looked for that?"

"Hmm?" She glanced up from the pendant, her gaze refocusing on his face. "Looked for what?"

"My guys who you interviewed. You looked for jewelry and tattoos?"

"I looked for a lot of things. What they wore. What they said. How they acted. It's my job."

He hated what she did. Hated that it put her at daily risk from gunshots and madmen. But he respected her. And he respected what she was determined to do.

"You're a good cop."

A wariness settled in her eyes, one he knew was a direct result of his attitude over her professional choices. "I like to think so."

He gently laid the metal detector down before dropping into a crouch so they were on eye-level. "I know we sit on opposite sides of a very large chasm. And I know I'm a jerk about it most of the time. But you're a good cop."

That wariness softened. "Thank you."

"You're going to do right by the man who was killed here, even if he doesn't deserve it."

"Yes," she sighed as she stared down at the small pendant in her hands. "I am."

"There's something to be said for that. It's easy to stand for the people who deserve it. It's a lot harder to do it for the ones who don't."

The lingering vestiges of wariness vanished completely, replaced by something he couldn't quite define. He might have said satisfaction, but there wasn't anything there that suggested gloating or victory. Only a calm sort of acceptance.

He wanted to believe that counted for something.

He got back to his feet and extended a hand. When she clasped his, her fingers tight, Tate pulled her up. And fought the shudder that she possibly held in her hands the personal possession of a killer.

The scent of burgers and french fries filled the air as Belle and Tate walked into the Reynolds kitchen. A note lay on the table and Tate snagged it after they walked in.

"Arden left us dinner with her compliments."

"That was awfully nice of her." Belle glanced around the kitchen, the counters empty of the clutter that usually filled her own. Instead of clutter, there was a large bowl of mixed fruit on the center of the table.

Her friend might have fought against the notion, but Arden cared for her brothers. While Belle had no doubt Ace, Hoyt and Tate were well able to care for themselves, Arden saw to it that the house had just enough of a woman's touch to be both comforting and welcoming. She highly suspected none of the Reynolds boys would have thought to artfully display peaches and grapes nestled around a large grapefruit.

"Arden made Juicy Lucies."

"She made what?" Belle glanced up from the fruit.

"Only the best burger in the whole world. The cheese is inside the patty."

"Sounds delicious." And it did. If she were staying. "You enjoy. I'm going to head out."

"Why?"

"I'm cold and wet and I need to get into the station with the evidence."

"It's after six. Who's there to take it?"

"I can check it in. Lock it up."

"So go do that and come back."

"I—"

His gaze was direct, his voice even more so. "Come back."

Whether her emotional resistance was still low from their heated lovemaking in the back of her car or the fact that she just didn't want to be alone, Belle wasn't sure. But there was something about his offer that was irresistible.

"Okay." She nodded. "I also have a change of clothes in my locker, so there's an added benefit to running into the precinct quickly."

The heated look that filled those green depths suggested she didn't need clothes at all, but he didn't say anything and Belle hightailed it for her car before she could consider his reaction too closely.

Even if she was still considering it twenty minutes later when she walked into the evidence room at the precinct. One of her favorite deputies was there, looking bored as he played on an iPad.

"Hey, Ricky."

"Belle!" The guy looked up, his bright smile infectious. "Haven't seen you in a while."

"Been trying to keep busy."

"So I hear. This killer case has everyone running, but very few clues."

"That might have changed." She pulled the small evidence bag from her pocket. "I found something on

Reynolds land this afternoon. I think it may be tied to our killer."

Ricky's eyes widened and he muttered something under his breath in Spanish that sounded suspiciously like an impressed curse. "How'd you do that? They swept the site pretty well."

"I got lucky." *In more ways than one*, her conscience immediately leaped up to taunt her.

"Don't mistake hard work for luck." Oblivious to her thoughts, Ricky reached for the evidence bag, holding it up to the light. "Looks religious. My grandmother had something like this."

"Oh?"

"I loved to play with it when I was little and sitting on her lap." Ricky was careful as he shifted the pendant around beneath the plastic. "It's an image of Mary. Lots of people wear them. Captain wears one, I think."

"Captain Grantham?"

"Yep. He's a good man. I see him in church every week. He was in a bad way for a long time after his son died, but he seems like he's been doing better lately."

Ricky chattered on, his words echoing in her head and clanging with all the finesse of pots and pans being slammed together next to her ears.

Captain Grantham?

The second in command at the precinct behind Chief Corden.

The father of a young man who died from a drug overdose.

Was it possible?

Even as the questions and scenarios tripped over themselves for prominence in her mind, she willed herself to slow down. It was easy enough to check him out. If the man wore a similar necklace, then this couldn't be his. He was the captain, for heaven's sake.

Their leader.

"Um, Ricky. Can we keep this quiet for now? Log in the evidence so it's secure but would you mind not saying anything?"

That bright smile faded, his gaze going dark. Ricardo Suarez was a good cop and she saw that skill and talent rise to the fore immediately. "You okay?"

"Yeah. Sure." She nodded, hoping desperately her voice was light enough. Easy enough. "Feds have been all over this one and I want to make sure I talk to Chief Corden first. Give him the heads-up about what I found. See how he wants to handle this before everyone's beating a path to your desk to look at the evidence."

"Sure."

Belle waited, curious to see if Ricky would say anything else, but he only waited her out.

"Okay then," she sighed, her thoughts still roiling and bubbling like a witch's cauldron. "Lay that paperwork on me."

Tate saw the tension and the upset the moment Belle walked back in the door an hour later. She'd promised she'd come back but it was a relief to see her actually walk back in. "You okay?"

"Sure."

"Belle?" Before he could act, she was across the room and in his arms, her hug tight and absolute as she gripped his waist. "Belle? What is it?"

She didn't answer right away and he gave her the space, wrapping his arms around her back and simply holding her, giving the comfort she needed. He took a surprising amount of it in return.

While he was sorry she was upset, somewhere deep inside he reveled in the fact that she'd come to him with whatever it was that bothered her. That she took solace in him—in what was still between them.

He pulled back slightly, tilting her chin so she had to look up at him. "You want to talk about it?"

"No."

"Usually a good reason to talk, then."

She nodded, her eyes wide in her face. It was that look—that innate vulnerability that tugged at him—that had the warning bells going off. "What happened?"

"I can't—" She broke off, seeming to gather herself. "I can't tell you."

"Can't? Or won't?"

"I can't." She slipped from his arms, taking a few steps back to put some obvious distance between them. "You're a civilian."

"What does that have to do with it?"

"I can't. It's against procedure. And it's wrong."

He watched as she worked through it in her mind, each argument and personal frustration playing across her eyes, cheeks and lips in an emotional dance. He wanted to argue, telling her he had a right to know about anything that made her this upset, but some small instinct held him back. Whatever he *wanted* to do, now was the time for listening. And for putting into practice the fact that he did respect her and her ability to make decisions.

Even if it was killing him to stay quiet.

When those vivid and varied expressions finally

stilled, he sensed she'd come to a decision. "I'm under specific orders to say nothing on this subject."

"Okay."

"Which means I can't tell you."

"I believe that's the definition of saying nothing."

"Don't be a smartass."

Duly chastised but pleased to see her slight smirk, he pointed to a seat. "I'll get the coffee. You're going to tell me and I'm not going to say anything to anyone and we're going to figure this out. Together."

She took the seat so he figured that was good for something, but it was her words that caught him up short. "Your mother used to do that. Pour coffee to talk at her kitchen table. I think the first cup I ever had was in this kitchen."

His hand shook as he put the carafe back onto the warming plate, memories of his own conversations with his mother still some of his most comforting.

"Would those be the conversations when she told you her middle son was an ass?"

"Those came later." He whirled at that, surprised to see the smile on her face. "After you actually were an ass. I'm talking about before."

"Before what?"

"Before my mom died. Before I knew what to do about her and her moods and her addictions."

"You talked to her about that?" Tate set the mugs on the table, pushing one across the surface toward her.

"Yeah. I wasn't going to. I didn't want to talk to anyone about it but she had a way about her. A way of pulling things out."

"You called me the horse whisperer, but my mom was the people whisperer." It had worked on everyone but his father, which had an odd sort of irony to it. One he avoided thinking about all that often.

Shaking off the memories that always made him feel useless and more than a little sad, he shifted back to his concern for Belle. "She was a vault. I never knew she talked to you about your mom."

"I sort of figured she had. And after my mom died…"

"Well, she didn't. Ever."

Although he thought about his mother often, he hadn't thought about those kitchen conversations in quite some time. Either his own or the ones she invariably had with others who came to their home.

"Okay." She nodded.

"My mother was good with people and one of the reasons was because she respected who they were and what they needed to say."

"It helped to have someone to talk to. And she somehow understood that I'd had to play parent way too early."

While he'd always sensed there was even more to the story than Belle had told him, he knew her formative years with her mother had been difficult. "Isn't that is a rather kind description."

"Yeah, but it's true. She struggled, you know. My mom. And she loved me. I knew that, even if she had no way to show me."

"That doesn't make it any better."

"No. It doesn't. But as time has gone by, it's given me some measure of acceptance. Working with others. Seeing the situations I do in my job. Some people just aren't cut out for life. Or for what it throws at them."

"And that doesn't bother you?"

He thought about his own father. About the man's inability to rise to his responsibilities and duties with honor and trustworthiness. Those things still bothered him and he didn't believe there was any amount of conversation that would change that.

"It's not about if it bothers me or not. I hate that my memories of her are poor ones. That I think of her as a duty and responsibility instead of as a loving parent. That I have to live with the knowledge she drove my father away before I ever had a chance to know him or that she spent her life running from the demons that lived in her mind, chasing them with booze or whatever she could swindle a doctor into prescribing. But despite it all, that's just the way it is."

"Sounds awfully forgiving."

"Does accepting something mean you've forgiven it?" Her gaze was steady across the table and Tate suddenly realized they were no longer talking about her mother. "Or maybe a better question, does forgiveness mean you forget what happened?"

"I think it all depends on the person."

"How so?" Belle asked.

"I think there are people in this world who are more open-minded. More able to see the forest for the trees."

"You don't think you're one of them?"

"No. I don't."

Belle's gaze dropped to her coffee, her shoulders hunched over the mug. He'd known her practically his entire life and in all that time—even during the hard times with her mother as well as during their breakup—he'd never seen her look quite so bereft. In that hunch of her shoulders he could practically see the weight of the world resting there.

"What's wrong?"

"I have a suspicion about the killer. And it's a bad one."

Thoughts of her mother, his father and their shared past vanished in the face of what she'd discovered. "From the evidence today?"

"Yes."

"What do you think?"

"I think we have to accept it may be an inside job."

She walked him through her suspicions, matter-of-factly and with minimal inflection. The suspicions of her chief and the Feds that they were dealing with a serial killer. The job description of each of the victims. The matched wounds on each victim's heart.

Tate took it all in, but could hardly believe what he was hearing. It had all been bad enough when he believed a man had been killed on his land. But a serial killer? One who chose his victims from the underbelly of the drug trade?

"And there are three kills. That's what makes it a serial?"

She nodded. "It's the accepted wisdom and pattern behavior. And we have three we can connect."

"I want to believe that's all, but that's not why you came in here looking like you saw a ghost. You've known about this."

"I have."

Tate ignored that subtle thread of betrayal that she'd not told him about the case. It wasn't logical or right, but it was his land, dammit, and he'd had a right to know. It was him and Belle, for heaven's sake, and she hadn't told him. Instead, she'd put duty to her job before him. Again.

"So what else has you upset? You mentioned an inside job but nothing you've said indicates that."

"The jewelry I found. In the east pasture." She stilled, tracing her index finger over the rim of her mug. He let her go, giving her the time she needed. "I think it may belong to Captain Grantham."

"Russ?" When she only nodded, he added, "Russ Grantham?"

"Yes."

"But he's a cop. And a father. And a damn fine man."

"I know."

It was that acknowledgment—and the sheer misery that filled her eyes—that had Tate going silent, only one question rushing over and over through his mind.

Why?

Chapter 14

Her suspicions lay heavy between them, an emotional mess hovering in the air over the kitchen table. The tone of Tate's voice had continued to rise, question after question, until it all faded to silence, one question remaining.

"Why?"

"I don't know. Maybe it's about Jamie. Or because of Jamie."

"Russ has become a killer because his son died? That's awfully convenient. Or an awfully convenient place to drop blame."

"I'm not dropping blame."

He waved a hand, his face already as contrite as his words. "That was a low blow. But come on, Belle. Jamie had a problem. That doesn't make the rest of his family killers."

"Come on, Tate. Work it through with me. Is it really that far a stretch? Especially for someone with training and knowledge. Someone with access to police files and criminal records?"

Belle hesitated a moment, walking through it again in her mind. The questions she'd asked herself on the drive back to Reynolds Station. The memories of how badly Captain Grantham's family had suffered with Jamie's addiction. The missing piece of jewelry that could be the linchpin to all of it.

"Jamie's drug problem was legendary. The family struggled with it for years, their hope crashing each and every time he had a relapse."

She'd seen it, too. Had witnessed it all firsthand. The sadness she'd see in her friend, Reese, every time her brother got into trouble and later, once Belle had joined the force, the pain Russ carried. She'd remained silent, her own experiences with her mother too close to the surface, but she'd understood the pain. The soul-crushing disappointment when one of Jamie's dry spells ended and resulted in a bender that started the cycle all over again.

Fire lit Tate's gaze once again, his disbelief palpable. "But that doesn't make someone a killer. You saw the body. You know what we found. Can you honestly sit there and tell me you think Russ Grantham did that to another person?"

"I think I need to pursue that angle and the pendant I found earlier is a part of that."

"And you won't back down?"

"I can't. Don't you understand that?"

"What if it is Russ?"

"Then we'll prosecute him. Punish him just like any other criminal."

Tate let out a harsh bark, his heavy exhale dark and deep. "What a load of crap. You can sit there and talk to me about a man. A good man. One we've both known our whole lives. And you can sit there and tell me if he's guilty he should be prosecuted to the letter of the law as if it were no big deal?"

No big deal?

It was a *massive* deal. One that weighed on her as nothing in her life ever had. An hour ago, she'd been diligently pursuing a criminal. And now she had to accept that she might be on a manhunt for a friend.

Even with that stark truth—and the resulting chaos that would come after if she were correct—she had to move forward. Had to push on.

"If he's gone around killing people? Yes, I can."

"That's so typical." Tate slammed out of his chair, the heavy scraping of the legs over hardwood as jarring as his motions.

"Typical of what?"

"Of you. Your attitude. Your devotion to this notion of truth and justice. Add the American way on top of it and you're a damn freaking superhero, aren't you?"

"Insulting much?"

"Insulting?" He whirled around from where he stood at the counter. "You've just sat here and accused a good man of being a cold-blooded killer. How can you talk to me about insults?"

"And how can you stand there and lecture me like I don't know how terrible this is? How, if I'm right, I'm going to destroy a family? You think this is easy for me? You think finding justice in all this is a freaking walk in the park?"

Tate ran a hand through his hair, the edges sticking up along the path of his fingers. "Then what is your goal?"

"To do what's right. To stop a killer. To protect the citizens of this city."

"By worrying about someone taking down drug dealers? By blaming a friend for it?"

"And that's classic Tate Reynolds straight down the line. It doesn't fit your view of the world so it must be stopped or ignored or discarded."

Belle watched her direct hit land. Saw it spread as he keyed into her words and her innuendo.

And then she saw him dismiss it all to bulldog right through his point. "So now I'm supposed to feel bad for people who sell drugs? Or believe Russ Grantham suddenly decided he wanted vengeance and has gone on a killing spree?"

Argument after argument sprang to her lips and each felt hollower than the last as she thought of her family, superimposing her own mother's face over Jamie Grantham's. The days of sobriety, followed by a bender over whatever her mother couldn't handle. The pressure of the outside the world that reared up and forced her to return to the hollow emptiness she found in drugs.

She'd lived with the results of that and she understood how insidious the problem was.

"I lived with the same for the majority of my life. I understand the devastation and the pain. That doesn't change the facts."

"And what are those?"

"That once you justify one kill, it becomes way too damn easy to justify the next. And the one after that. And the one after that."

"That's a cop-out." The harsh slash of his mouth hadn't faded, but there was the slightest softening in his tone.

"Is it? Where does it stop? What happens once you go through the drug dealers? Is it that big a leap to go after the psychiatrist who couldn't help? The guidance counselor who didn't do enough? The friend who enabled?"

Tate bent and picked up his chair, righting it before gently pushing it into its place beneath the table. "You talk like Russ is an animal. Something to be put down."

"If he is the one doing this, then he needs to be stopped."

"And you're going to do it?"

"I'm certainly going to help get it done."

When Tate said nothing, Belle knew it was time to leave. Not only had she lost her appetite, but she'd also lost the desire to argue any longer.

Tate paced the kitchen, the lingering scent that was so uniquely Belle still hanging on the air. His family had stayed away from him—suspiciously so—and he wondered what Arden must have told Ace and Hoyt to keep them all out of the house on a Wednesday night.

It was probably a good thing they were gone. He wasn't fit for company anyway. The discussion with Belle—from the deeper understanding of her mother's addictions to the suspicions over Captain Grantham—had left him raw and uneasy.

Where does it stop?

Belle's question had run through his mind, over and over, an out-of-control hamster on a wheel.

Where did it stop? If Russ Grantham was guilty—and that was still an awfully huge *if* in Tate's mind—but if he was, what did that make his choices? A man who'd committed himself to finding justice and to upholding the law, reduced to a killer?

He hadn't known Jamie Grantham well, but he hadn't needed to. For a time, the young man's problems were all Midnight Pass had talked about. Oh, they'd whispered at first, but those voices had grown louder and louder as the problem became more and more profound. The drug benders that had ended in a car chase through the county, Jamie and another friend twisting his beat-up old truck around a tree. The fire that had swept through the chemistry lab the night Jamie had snuck in and tried using one of the Bunsen burners to melt heroin. Even prom the year he and Belle had gone hadn't been free of Jamie's drama.

All of it had piled on and piled on. On to Jamie. On to his sister Reese, bearing a huge brunt of that at school. And on to his parents.

Would it be that hard to imagine a parent's desire to mete out vengeance? To want to see the ones who'd ultimately enabled that behavior—and those like them—to pay for their choice?

Was he really one to judge? Especially because his own family's misery had been on full display for the entire town, as well? He knew what it was to be whispered about. For all your personal business to be out on display, like the latest episode of a TV drama.

Hadn't there been many a day when he'd wanted the

whispers to stop? When all he wanted was to go back to the days when things were normal. Right. Stable.

And when he didn't have a worry about anything.

Instead, he and his siblings had been forced to face the fact that their father was a cheat and a swindler, who'd treated their stock with illegal sustenance and had tried to pass all of it off as premium beef. Who'd defaulted on every loan he'd ever taken and who had done his level best to run Reynolds Station into the ground.

He, Ace, Hoyt and Arden had worked so hard to overcome that. To rebuild a business from the bottom up and to restore the family name into something that mattered. He knew the soul-searching and the sleepless nights and the seemingly endless days when it felt like you weren't making any progress at all, only beating your head against a very large, very hard wall.

Yet they'd done it. They'd come out the other side, stronger and more committed than ever before. They hadn't become killers. Instead, they'd survived.

Jamie Grantham hadn't.

Belle had survived, too, Tate admitted. She'd worked hard and had gotten past the sadness of her childhood and the poor example set by her parent. Even more than that, she had conviction and the belief that her actions had purpose.

Had he ever felt that way?

Certainly he wanted his family name to stand for something. And the work they'd all put into bringing the business back to a good, profitable place had taken a significant amount of purpose.

But to live with that conviction?

If what she suspected was true, her beliefs would bring down embarrassment on the leadership of the community. It would create discord and confusion for the Midnight Pass Police Department. And it would crater a family who'd suffered more than their fair share already.

Even with that knowledge, she was determined to do what was right.

Determined to push forward.

Why had he questioned that? More, why had he made her feel—after she'd gone to great pains to confide in him—that her choices were poor ones?

He believed in her. And he'd already seen how devoted and dedicated she was to doing what was right. He should be proud of that. Celebrating it. And instead, all he'd done was mock it and cause additional pain.

Whatever else they might be—and their afternoon in the back seat of her car still needed to be dealt with—they were also friends. Allies. And he was the one person on the entire planet she'd chosen to confide in.

It was about damn time he started acting like he deserved that confidence.

His gaze skipped to the counter, a fresh idea taking root.

Along with the potential to forge a truce.

Belle stared at the TV, the medical drama playing out before her nothing but empty noise. Other than the opening scene that had grabbed her with its intensity—and an ax sticking out of the head of an incoming ER patient—she'd managed to miss forty-five minutes of high adrenaline entertainment.

All because of the drama playing out in her own mind.

Thoughts of "How dare he?" and "I'll show him" had given way to her continued anxiety over how to handle Captain Grantham. There was still a possibility—a very large possibility—that the pendant she'd discovered wasn't his. It was a piece of jewelry, not a signed confession, after all.

So why did it feel like the truth? Like a real, tangible clue that pointed her toward the one responsible for such a heinous crime.

The questions had swirled, around and around, picking up steam but never seeming to land anywhere.

Her phone dinged with an incoming text message.

Are you home?

Tate.

She fought the stab of pleasure at seeing his name and quickly tapped out a reply.

Yes. Why?

Because I've been pounding on your front door for five minutes and you haven't answered.

Five minutes?

She leaped off the couch and headed for the front door, flipping on the porch lights. True to his word, he stood at the door with a bottle of wine in one hand and a few stacked plastic containers in the other.

"Hi."

"I've been knocking. Were you doing something?"

"Um, no. Must have had the TV on too loud."

If her comment was puzzling, he didn't show it; instead, he stepped into the house when she stood back to let him in.

Her house was small, one of the first single family homes built off one of the main streets running out of downtown Midnight Pass. It had been her mother's and she'd nearly given it up after her death, but in the end had swallowed the bad memories and figured that a paid-off house she could decorate to her liking was better than hunting for something new that came with a thirty-year mortgage.

The practicality had paid off, with a renovated kitchen, all new furniture and a look that had become decidedly hers.

"What are you doing here?"

"Aside from an apology?" Tate turned from his perusal of the entryway.

"Yes."

He held up the stacked containers he juggled in one hand. "I still owed you dinner."

"You don't owe me anything."

"Actually." He came closer, pressing a kiss to her cheek. "I do. It's horrifically unfair to dangle one of Arden Reynolds's hamburgers in front of a person and then not deliver."

"Oh." Belle knew his visit wasn't about a hamburger, but even with her lingering anger, she was so confused by his arrival she was willing to play along.

"Can I warm these up in your kitchen?"

"Of course." She pointed toward the back of the

house. "It may look different but I think you know the way."

Other than a strange look, he nodded and headed off, wending his way toward the back of the house and the waiting kitchen. "This looks amazing!" came winging back toward her the moment he stepped through the threshold.

"Thanks."

"When did you redo the place?"

She came into the kitchen, his gaze still roaming over the cherry cabinets and the dark marble she'd selected for the counters. "About five years ago. A few things had to wait and the spare room's still a massive work in progress, but it's mine."

"It's gorgeous."

Tate opened a few cabinet doors, hunting for plates. She should have told him where to look—should have made it easy on him—but something had her mesmerized as she watched that strong, solid back hunt through her cabinets. It looked natural. Normal. Domestic.

Had she ever had any of that?

Unbidden, her throat tightened around a lump of tears and she diligently pushed them back. Turning on her heel, she mumbled a quick excuse of needing to get more napkins out of the hall closet. If he was paying any attention at all, he'd have seen her reaction, but he appeared nonplussed when she walked back into the kitchen, both composed and bearing a package of napkins.

Even as a full basket of napkins taunted her from the countertop.

"Why'd you come back?" she asked.

He glanced up from where he pulled the burgers out of the microwave. "Because I owed you an apology."

"For what?"

"I'd say my all-around general assiness, but you already know that."

"'Assiness'?"

"It's a permanent state of being an ass."

The words were enough to break the tension, the laugher bubbling up in her throat. "I'll have to remember that."

"I owe you an apology for how I reacted to your news. You confided in me and I threw it back at you like you were the one who'd done something wrong."

"It's hard to think of someone we know and think well of acting in a way that doesn't mesh with that."

"I'm not sure murder meshes with anything."

She nodded, well aware he spoke the truth. "No, I suppose not."

Tate finished settling the burgers onto the plates and reached for a paper towel. "Ketchup? Mustard?"

"I'll get them."

Belle moved toward the fridge, her motions once again slow and dreamy. Was Tate Reynolds actually here in her kitchen? Arden had been over, of course. So had any number of other friends. But never Tate.

Although they managed cordial civility to each other, she'd never grown comfortable enough to include him in activities at her home. A Sunday afternoon football-watching party or a holiday tree trimming was hardly a venue for a serious conversation, but she'd avoided including him in the guest list. They were no longer a couple and no matter how many times she'd tried to convince herself they could stick to a casual relationship, something had stopped her in the end.

Because they weren't casual. They weren't just friends. And they sure as hell weren't acquaintances.

She loved him.

It was the great, glorious irony of her life. That the one man who was so compatible with her in every way possible stood on the opposite side of every other thing she wanted.

But she did love him. A decade of ignoring that fact hadn't made it go away. Nor had the determined scratching of an itch that afternoon. Neither had doing battle with him over the dead body on his property.

It was the terribly humbling fact that none of those things made a damn bit of difference. She loved him anyway.

Seemingly oblivious to her thoughts, he pointed to the table nestled in the back of the kitchen against the windows. "These go best with a Coke if you have it."

"I'll get a few." She retrieved the cold cans from the fridge and snagged a few napkins from that towering stack on the counter.

The satisfying pop and fizz of the sodas opening punctuated the silence and it was Belle who spoke first.

"I'm sorry I burdened you with my suspicions. I knew it wasn't right to tell anyone and now you're stuck with it, same as me."

Tate stopped, his burger halfway to his lips, and set it back down on his plate. "Why do you think that?"

"Because it's true. I have nothing but suspicion and I've now made you carry it. That stuff weighs heavy."

"You carry it."

"It's my job."

Tate glanced down at his burger. "Look. I realize I'm not the most sensitive guy in the world, but when did we stop being friends?"

"Don't start—"

Before she could even get out the rest of the thought, he held up a hand. "Hear me out. We were always friends. When did that part stop?"

Since the question struck so close to her earlier thoughts about Sunday afternoon football and holiday parties, she wasn't sure she was in the best frame of mind to answer, but Belle knew it wasn't a question to be ignored. "I wish I knew."

"So you feel it, too?"

"Feel it?" She nearly laughed at that one. "I feel it every day. We didn't just break up ten years ago. I lost my best friend. I lost my center of gravity. All because that friend didn't understand or support me. It hurt worse than losing the sex and believe me, that hurt pretty bad."

"It did?" His eyebrows wiggled, vintage Tate, and somehow in the midst of her outburst he managed to make her laugh.

Soul-deep laughter rumbled up from her belly and spilled out in a joyful noise. When she could finally speak, she choked out, "You really are an ass."

"At your service, ma'am."

The laughter was enough to break the tension she'd felt since he walked in and she picked up her burger, anxious to try one of Arden's world-famous concoctions. She took a bite and moaned around the mouthful. "Wow, that is good. How did I never know Arden made these?"

"It's a secret she hoards. I think she's really afraid

the Drop-In Diner will press her into service if they knew what wonders she could do with ground beef."

"I understand the fear."

They ate in companionable silence, broken only by a few errant sighs and possibly a small moan before Tate spoke. "I'm sorry. For the friend thing, too."

She glanced up from where she patted her lips with a napkin. "You are?"

"More than I can say."

"I'm sorry, too. If there's fault, we equally bear it there. I miss having you for a friend."

He nodded, but the acceptance didn't make it all the way to those bright green eyes. It was such a unique color—so vibrant and vivid—and one she hadn't ever seen on anyone beside the Reynolds boys. That color haunted her dreams and at odd moments, she'd connect it with a particular memory.

Staring into Tate's eyes the first time they made love.

The heated look that had filled his gaze when she'd stepped out of a clearing, naked as the day she was born, to go skinny-dipping at Town Lake out on the edge of Midnight Pass.

And the day they'd broken up, the heat rising in those depths, pushing out anything warm or welcoming or understanding.

It was that lingering memory that had her dropping her gaze back to her burger. They might equally bear fault for all that had come since, but he'd shut down during their relationship. Had refused to discuss what was between them or what other influences and factors in her life gave her dreams. Goals. Ambitions.

"I don't think we bear equal fault for the rest of it, though."

The words were quiet in her renovated kitchen, but they might have been said ten years before for all the presence they had in her heart. She'd carried them for a decade, angry and upset and frustrated at the injustice of it all.

If he hadn't loved her—if he'd not wanted to stay in the relationship because he didn't share her feelings—she could have moved on. But to leave her because he didn't support her dreams? Because he could say that he loved her and wanted her and wanted a future with her, if she'd only walk away from another piece of her heart.

That had left a raw, gaping wound and until that very moment, sitting in her new kitchen, a half-eaten burger in front of her, Belle hadn't realized just how much it hurt.

"What is that supposed to mean?"

"All that's come since?" She fought to keep the pain from her voice. Fought to keep things level and simple, like a recitation of facts.

Nothing but facts.

"I am equally responsible for all of it. But the reason we broke up in the first place? That's on you."

"Because I had a difference of opinion? Because you refused to see reason?"

How was it even possible that after a decade they still stood on opposite sides of such a huge chasm?

"I never asked you to become someone different. Not once. I understood what you needed. What you and your family were trying to do to restore the ranch. I supported you. Believed in you."

"And I'm somehow at fault because I didn't want to see you walk out the door every day, not knowing if you'd come home?" Tate shot back.

"Yes. You are."

"That's a cop-out. A raging cop-out. You ignored my feelings. No matter how many times I brought it up or talked to you about how I felt, you ignored it all, like you were giving me a little pat on the head. Poor Tate. I can take care of myself." He stood and paced the room. "You never listened to me. Never once gave me a chance to explain myself. All you did was placate me that you'd be fine."

"And I am fine!"

"Are you?" He whirled on her, his voice carrying across the kitchen from where he'd stopped at the doorway midpace. "Are you really? You come here to eat and sleep and little else. You work yourself to death. And you think your freaking captain is a murderer. Are you really okay? Is that even a life?"

His comments rained down on her like razors. "Is that what you think of me?"

"Think?" He shook his head, striding back toward her. "What's there to think? You are those things. Can you sit there and honestly tell me otherwise?"

"I'm doing my job. The job I'm called to. The life I'm called to. I'd expect my loved ones could support that. More than that, I expect they will support that. Why is that too much to ask?"

"And what have you gotten for it? Can you honestly sit there and tell me your life's better today than it was before you entered the academy? Can you tell me that bringing down the dregs of society is as satisfying as you thought it would be?"

On some level, she understood his point. She'd talked about it with her fellow officers and she'd done the job long enough that she knew it wasn't easy. That there were days where you not only felt as if you weren't making a difference, but when you actually felt as if you were going backward. Whatever internal charge of self-righteous goodness fueled you when you took a bad guy off the streets didn't last much past the booking because there was a new problem to solve.

A new bad guy—or girl—to chase after.

But at least you weren't leaving them on the streets to multiply. That was the solace she took in the moments when it all became too hard or overwhelming.

There was one less person out there to ruin others.

That was where she made a difference. Where she fought for some reason and ability to understand the ruin of her mother's life.

"I am satisfied," she finally said. "That's all that matters."

Tate still stood on the other side of her kitchen, but he might as well have been standing in Amarillo for all the distance that lay between them.

But only when he dropped his head, his gaze focused on the slate tile floor, did she have a small flicker of regret.

Regret she couldn't be someone different. And a stab of guilt that she wanted him to be the one to change.

He lifted his head, his gaze finding hers. "I won't claim to understand where you're coming from. Nor am I willing to tell you I've changed my mind when I haven't. But please answer me one question."

"What's that?"

"Do you honestly think I could go on if something happened to you?"

The sharp, distinct notes of her phone ringing prevented her from a response. Prevented her from delving too deeply into all he'd said—and didn't say.

Tate frowned at the interruption, but she already had her phone out of her pocket, his explanation over the fear of something happening to her needing to be enough. "That's the ringtone for dispatch. I'm sorry but I have to answer this.

"This is Belle Granger." Words spilled out of her earpiece like a hail of bullets and she did her level best to shift gears from the heart-wrenching conversation with Tate to focus on the incoming instructions.

New victim discovered.

Uniforms on-site believe the body was moved from the place of death.

Killer is on the loose.

She hung up, the reality of what she now faced had become something she'd confront alone. Looking up, she stared into those haunting green eyes. And said the words she knew encapsulated all the pain and anger and disappointment between them.

"I need to leave."

"Why?"

"They found another body. This one down in some overgrown brush along Town Lake."

Chapter 15

The two teenagers who'd found the body of one Eduardo Rivera were still green around the edges when Belle got to Town Lake. Whatever bravado and machismo had carried the boys to the park—and knowing teenage boys, there had been plenty—had shattered, leaving in its wake two scared children who'd never be the same.

One of the uniforms already identified by dispatch stayed with the boys, their shoulders covered by blankets as they sat on a picnic table about twenty yards from the body. Parents had been called and Belle recognized one of the mothers, now quietly weeping with her son, huddled at the table.

More lives affected by a killer. Even if indirectly so.

According to one of the uniforms, Chief Corden had arrived about ten minutes ahead of her and was already standing with a couple of Feds she recognized. A quick glance of the site didn't show Captain Grantham and she silently prayed it was a simple oversight.

That's all it is, Annabelle Marie. Get it together.

But her suspicions raged out of control all the same. Suspicions that went nuclear the moment she stepped close enough to assess the dead man that lay in the grass.

Rivera hadn't died easy. The bruises that visibly covered his body were evidence of that, along with the marks that scored his skin. The medical examiner would define the details, but she'd studied enough to know that the man who lay before her had been tortured before he was killed.

An involuntary shudder skated over her spine as Tate's recent words filled her mind.

Can you tell me that bringing down the dregs of society is as satisfying as you thought it would be?

"Granger." The chief gestured her over, inviting her into the small circle. Agent Noah Ross was already with him, along with a few of Ross's colleagues she recognized.

"Sir." She nodded to Chief Corden before quickly greeting each member of the huddled team. The fact she was invited in was a balm to the anger she'd carried with her from the fight with Tate and she resolved to push it to the back of her mind.

She had a killer to focus on.

An image of Russ Grantham haunted her thoughts and Belle resolutely pushed it away. She had a plan of action for dealing with her suspicions—including some basic detective work of looking to see if the man still wore his own religious medal around his neck—especially before she took them to anyone.

The fact she'd even mentioned such dark suspicions to Tate had been an error in judgment. A weak moment in a day full of them. Which was a poor excuse but she was going to hang on to it as long as she could. She did take solace in the knowledge that Tate would keep the information to himself. They might not agree on her career choices, but he was a good man and would never repeat what she'd told him.

It was odd to be that certain, yet she was.

Absolutely.

"We waited for you to get started." Ross gestured to the body. "We believe it's the same killer. Medical examiner has to weigh in, but it's a pretty sure bet."

Of course it was sure, Belle thought to herself. One killer on the loose was hard enough to imagine. Two would be unthinkable. But instead, all she said was, "The body was identified quickly."

"We had Rivera's prints on file," Ross confirmed. "And he's made quite a name for himself in *El Asesino's* business affairs. Agent Samson in the Corpus Christi office recognized the body the moment the photo scanned in. Had some trouble with Rivera a few years back."

"I thought *El Asesino's* men knew how to lay lower than that?" Belle asked.

"Normally they do. Rivera worked his way up in the organization, but he's a hothead. Caught a lot of trouble in his earlier years. The fact that he wasn't afraid to take on the messy jobs meant the big boss was willing to indulge him a bit."

Belle searched her mind for any memory of the victim and vaguely recalled that during her first few years out of the academy, the man was one of the thugs whispered about. Rivera had a reputation for cruelty and greed, a potent combination and, as Agent Ross had suggested, traits that had done him well in a criminal organization.

"Any gauge on time of death?"

"Again, the ME will weigh in, but we're thinking sometime yesterday based on the discoloration of the body and the state of the bruises."

Without planning to, she glanced back toward the boys seated at the picnic table. "A difficult find for anyone, but they're going to have a rough go for a while."

"They are."

The conversation turned to other matters as several more FBI team members came to photograph the body and the surrounding area. Rivera was covered as they worked, but Belle saw more than a few surreptitious glances head toward the site as they all worked. Her own gaze traveled there more than once, even as her thoughts winged out in a million different directions as she worked the crime scene.

Yet every time, they landed in the same exact place.

Was it possible a killer was closer than any of them ever imagined?

He made it to midnight.

Not bad, Tate thought to himself as he rolled out of bed and dragged on his jeans. If he'd been making a bet, he'd have given himself until one, but this was real life, not some stupid wager in his mind.

Nor was it a game.

The call Belle had received earlier had made that abundantly clear. Their dinner at an end, she'd raced out of the house, but not before tossing him a set of keys and asking him to lock up behind himself.

Such a strange juxtaposition.

They could barely carry on a civil conversation, yet she trusted him with the keys to her home. Had trusted him with the heavy weight of her suspicions over Russ Grantham. And had trusted him with her body.

But where did that leave them?

Back to the same damn point they always reached, he thought in disgust as he wrenched open the door to his truck and climbed in. At odds despite all the trust and compatibility that lived between them.

Do you honestly think I could go on if something happened to you?

He'd finally said the words out loud. He'd used a version of them a decade ago when they'd ended their relationship, but he'd never been that blunt. Nor had he ever voiced his fears so deliberately.

What if something did happen to her?

It wasn't like it wouldn't tear him up, whether they were in or out of a relationship. Belle Granger was the only woman who'd ever stolen his heart and it wasn't like he'd somehow gotten it back the day he pushed her out of his life. And best as he could tell, that same cold, bruised heart hadn't shown up anytime since, if he were honest with himself.

He flirted with women. Had dated more than a few. Took a few of them home when the itch got too great. And the rest of the time, he was sullen, broody and lonely. He hid it behind lazy smiles and dumb jokes, but none of those filled the holes.

Nothing fixed the emptiness since he'd sent her away.

And now she was on the hunt for a killer, doing her

job and standing for the dead. Why did that impress the hell out of him?

Maybe it was because it was hard enough to go into battle on behalf of those who did deserve it. But it was even more impressive when you placed justice over the reality of those who'd spent their lives as criminals. It was those very moments when justice must have seemed pointless, yet she fought for it anyway.

It was also in that battle that he saw his own. His father had ruined Reynolds Station, leaving a nearly dead entity in his wake. He hadn't seen the value in running a good business or treating his customers with the respect they deserved, and he certainly hadn't seen the value or the pride that went along with Reynolds beef.

But Tate had. He, Ace, Hoyt and Arden had all seen it. And they'd worked and sweated and *believed* until there was no other outcome possible but success.

Didn't Belle deserve the same?

The truck was cold, the coolness seeping through his jeans and Henley, and he hit the heater. The rain that week had seen to it that a few vestiges of winter were determined to hang on and he waited to warm up as he bumped down the driveway toward town.

Toward Belle.

She'd be home by now. And if she wasn't, he'd wait for her. But there was no way he was leaving things the way they were. No way at all.

Belle gave one of the on-scene techs a ride back to the precinct and followed him in to pick up a few items off her desk. It was a ruse, designed to give her a chance to look at Captain Grantham's office with fresh eyes, so it was a surprise to find him sitting in his chair, staring at his computer screen.

She'd worked out her plan through the long hours at the park. The information she'd lay on his desk, using the quick moments to assess the room. Not that she expected to find anything, but she wanted to use the time to see if anything looked different. Wanted to picture him in that seat so she could convince herself he wasn't capable of all she suspected. In her mind, that necklace was firmly in place around his neck.

It had to be.

It's just a piece of jewelry.

That had been her argument and, like a litany, it had looped through her mind since her conversation with Ricky Suarez outside the evidence room earlier.

Had it really only been a few hours?

The heaviness that had settled on her chest felt like it had been there forever. It gave credence to the fact that her suspicions were unfounded. Russ Grantham was a good cop and a good man. If he were the killer, wouldn't something like that weigh on him?

Drag him down to a dark and lonely place?

She'd worked with him for years and hadn't seen any evidence of that. In fact, she'd seen the opposite. To Ricky's point, of late Russ had seemed to have come out of the dark place that his son's death had left in his heart. There was a lightness about him. A renewed purpose. He'd spoken to the rookie class a few months back and had glowed about a career in law enforcement and what it meant to wear a badge.

Men like that simply didn't torture and kill other men.

"Belle! You're here late." Russ's smile went all the

way to his eyes, a reinforcement that he was healing and had moved past Jamie's death.

"I had to pick up a few things." She went into improvisation mode. "Saw your light on so I wanted to come say hi. I haven't seen you for a few days."

The words spilled out of their own accord and it was only after the casual greeting that she realized the truth of that. He *had* been missing for a few days. She'd chalked it up to the amount of time she'd spent in the field, but now that she thought about it, she hadn't seen him.

If the comment bothered him, it didn't show as he tapped on a stack at the edge of his desk. "Just wrapping up my stamp of approval on the paperwork on the Evans case."

"I heard Aames and Gonzalez closed that one."

"Yeah. Open and shut. And even better, Mrs. Evans has her heirloom jewelry back."

"Always nice when we do the job and return all that was lost," Belle said.

"It makes for happy customers."

"Mrs. Evans does love her jewelry. Claims it keeps her young."

Russ rolled his eyes at that. "I've heard she uses that line on her insurance underwriter, too. Each and every time she goes in to update her policy rider."

The talk of jewelry gave her an in and she weighed instinct over self-preservation. He hadn't seemed put off when she mentioned his days out so maybe this would go the same way.

"Had a breakthrough earlier on the Abrogato murder."

"Oh?"

"Something about the scene had been nagging at me, so I went back out to walk the grounds."

Russ's fatherly smile never wavered but his eyebrows did narrow at her comment. "I can't imagine you found much after the rain we've been having. Scene has to have been compromised by now."

"Rain actually worked in my favor, as a matter of fact."

"Is that so?"

"I wasn't looking for prints or blood. I wanted to see if anything was left behind. Mother Nature and some old-fashioned bloodhound work got me what I wanted."

"You found something?"

Her gaze deliberately shifted to Russ's empty neck before flicking back to meet his eyes once more. "A small piece of jewelry. The Reynolds family didn't recognize it so I think it's a sure bet it came off either our killer or our victim."

"You seem pretty sure about that."

"I am."

"You get it into evidence?"

The question was casual and if she hadn't been looking for it, she'd likely never have seen the calculation that flashed deep in his eyes.

"Yep. Followed protocol to the letter. Just like you taught me. Like you taught all of us."

"Good." He nodded, whatever she'd seen in his gaze vanishing as if it had never been. "Very good."

"I'd better get going. It's going to be a big day tomorrow."

"Why's that?"

The alarm bells that had rung since her conversation with Ricky silently blared in her ears, louder than a line of drummers as the opening she'd wanted fell right into her lap.

"Didn't you hear?"

"Hear what?"

"We caught another one. The murderer who's taking out drug runners. He killed another one."

Belle's blood still pumped double-time as she made the last turn onto her street. Captain Grantham hadn't said much more in their conversation, but she saw the obvious upset in his expression that he'd been left out of the loop on the case.

Saw it even more clearly as he tried to tap dance over the fact that dispatch had never called him to the scene.

Did Chief Corden know more than he'd let on? Agent Ross, too?

They'd taken her into their confidence on their concerns over the killer, but they'd never called the captain to the crime scene? That was a serious breach in protocol and command, even if the Chief was on-site already. Did they have their suspicions, too? She didn't want to get ahead of herself, but every instinct she possessed kept pointing at Grantham. It pained her, but not as much as it pained her to leave a killer on the loose, ready and able to wreck more havoc.

Her lights flashed over her driveway as she closed in on the house, a large truck filling the pavement.

Tate's truck.

What was it still doing here? She'd given him the keys to lock up and had assumed he'd follow her wishes. Had he stayed? Or had something happened and he'd had one of his siblings pick him up after she'd left?

She hit the button for her garage door and pulled up beside the truck, only to find Tate sitting in the driver's seat. His expression was somber and despite their fight before she'd left for the crime scene, she couldn't deny how good it was to see him. Or how her heart leaped in her chest at the sight of his solid strength and soft smile.

He was here.

In that moment, that was all that mattered.

She eased into the garage, her focus on parking the car, even as she itched to throw off her seat belt and race for Tate.

There was so much between them that still needed resolution, but all of it faded in the face of having him there. Of being able to take a few moments for herself, away from the pressure of the case and the confusion over Grantham and even the pain of their earlier fight.

He was here.

His car door slammed, echoing back to her from the driveway. Belle turned at the noise and the steady tread of footsteps. "Hi."

"Hi."

"How long have you been sitting there?"

He shrugged. "About a half hour. Figured you'd get home sooner or later."

"You had a key."

"Which you gave me to lock up. It seemed wrong to take it and let myself back in."

Belle considered him, standing there in the long-sleeved Henley she already knew would be soft to the touch and the hard set of his shoulders. She noticed the way his hands shoved into his pockets and his faded jeans hung low and hugged his hips. And she saw the need in his eyes and knew hers reflected the same.

And in that moment, something inside of her melted. Many things, actually. Her anger. Her pride. Her resistance.

In that moment, there was just the two of them and Belle knew she'd regret it the rest of her days if she didn't take what she knew without question would be offered.

"I'm really glad you came back."

"I'm really glad I came back, too."

Without checking the impulse or worrying about what the morning would bring, she raced into his arms.

And reveled in the fact that they were already open when their bodies met.

Tate hadn't understood what impulse had driven him back over to Belle's, but now that she was in his arms, he finally understood what his soul had instinctively known. She needed him.

And he needed her, too.

The weight of her case. The discovery of the body on Reynolds land. And the implications of both on a man he deeply respected had taken their toll.

He knew all of it, yet he fought to push it to the back of his mind as he focused on the woman in his arms. Her slim shoulders quivered under his hands as his mouth roamed over hers. Their mouths met, the kiss long and soulful and full of all the things he was unable to say.

How much he wanted her. Needed her.

And loved her.

No matter how he sliced it or ignored it or disregarded the feelings, they were there. They'd always been there, long before he even knew how to put a name to it all.

He loved her.

With all that he was, he loved Belle Granger. Hadn't he always?

Unable to wait a moment longer, he walked her backward toward the door, never breaking the contact of their bodies. She reached for the door handle behind her back while he reached up and hit the button for the garage door, the heavy rumbling confirming he'd hit his mark.

In moments, they'd moved through the small house. The interior might look different, updated in the latest fashion, but he'd remembered the layout from when they were kids, and he marched her on a path to her bedroom based on memory alone. They shed their clothes on the walk, finally tumbling onto her king-size bed, both laughing and naked.

"A king?" he asked the question as he nibbled a path down over her neck, flicking his tongue against her collarbone.

"I like space."

Tate lifted up on his elbows and gazed down at her. He couldn't hold back the wolfish grin. "And I plan to put every square inch of it to good use."

"Promises, promises."

"You bet they are."

With that, he moved down her body, determined to make good on every one of them.

The urgency that had gripped them that afternoon in her car was still there, but it had changed. Expanded, really. What had been a raging, out-of-control need was still…a raging, out-of-control need.

But it was layered with something more. The quiet surety of what lived between them.

Tate ran his tongue over her heated skin as his hands danced over her flesh. The scent he remembered so well—the hints of vanilla and sweet flowers—was complemented by the fresh traces of the outdoors that still lingered on her skin. It shouldn't have been so natural—especially for all the reasons she'd spent her evening outside—yet it was.

It was Belle.

And when his focus shifted to the warmth between her thighs, that banked urgency rose up, spiking high as her moans grew more fervent. Tate fought to hold on to the moment—to keep the pleasure building—but he knew how badly he wanted her.

Knew even more how desperately he needed her.

He pressed his lips to hers, capturing her cries with his mouth, and knew the moment she came apart. Seeing her through her pleasure, he held her close, drawing out every last drop of her response with his touch.

"Wow." The hands that had clutched tight to his shoulders throughout her release slackened as a loopy smile covered her face. "That's some welcome home."

Tate pressed a hard kiss to her lips, filled with pride at what they shared. At the pleasure he could pull from her. "I'm not done welcoming you yet."

"Perhaps we could share the load on that a bit more." Temptress that she was, her hand snaked down between their bodies, capturing him firmly in hand. "I'd like to do a bit of welcoming myself."

"Far be it from me to argue." The joy that lit up the bright blue of her eyes dimmed slightly but he saw it immediately. "What is it?"

"Nothing."

He reached between their bodies, taking her hand to rest it against his chest. "What is it?"

"I know it's been a while. And, well, I know we've been other places. But I'm on birth control. And I'd like things to be like they were before between us. No barriers."

His body was already in a state of razor's edge arousal and her words nearly tumbled the last of his self-control. "You want that?"

"I'm good. I don't—" She broke off, a light blush washing over her cheeks. "I've spent more of the past few years taking care of things all by myself than with anyone else. And, well, I'm good. Healthy."

"I am, too." He reached for her chin, tilting her head slightly so she had to meet his gaze. "And I haven't been all that prolific either."

"You haven't?"

He hadn't been celibate, but the past ten years had included more similarities to hers than he wanted to admit. His regular, healthy annual checkups had only reinforced that point. "I've dated a bit and I've had relationships. But no, I've not been running wild through south Texas."

"You haven't?"

He took a deep breath, hoping all he felt would actually come through. "None of them were you. They never were. After a while, it felt sort of pointless to try."

"Was Dove one of them?"

It was the oddest moment to laugh but he found he couldn't hold it back. "She got to you a few weeks ago, didn't she?"

"Am I a bad person if I say yes?" A small line

squinched up between Belle's eyes and Tate could only laugh harder.

"No, you're an honest person. And for the record, I think she was trying to get your goat that night over at Tabasco's."

"She succeeded."

"I think you and Dove, and me for that matter, have a lot more in common than you think."

"Tate Charles Reynolds, are you actually suggesting a threesome?"

He'd never been more strung out and aroused in his life, which made the rollicking laughter that kept bubbling up in his chest a decided contrast.

Damn, had he ever felt so good?

"I am not suggesting that, though you did put a rather exciting image in my head. What I'm suggesting is that I think the delectable Ms. Anthony talks a far more interesting game than she walks."

"You are actually lying here complimenting another woman while your hand is on my breast?"

"Yes, I am." He leaned in and pressed a kiss to the same spot. "I am who I am and I'm not going to change. But noticing another woman doesn't mean I think she's you."

"Keep up the sweet-talking and you might get yourself out of this yet."

"Maybe I don't want to get out of anything." To prove his point, he shifted his position, rolling so that he pressed into the warm, waiting entrance of her body. "Sweet talk or arguments or all the times that come in between, you have to know that you're the only girl for me, Annabelle Granger."

She shifted in kind, allowing him better access, and

teased him just so as she lifted her body against his. "No Belly?"

"I only call you that to get you fired up."

"And now?"

"Your cheeks are already flushed and warm for me."

Since every other part was flushed and warm as well, Tate didn't wait any longer. Especially when she shifted once more, taking him fully into her body.

As the moment overcame them both, hot and sweet and erotic and oh-so-familiar, Tate knew he'd never wanted her more. And as he began to move, he tried with everything he was to show her what she meant to him.

Chapter 16

"You cleaned up, too?" Belle asked as she looked around her sparkling kitchen.

Tate whirled around from the counter, morning sun streaming through the window to highlight his bare chest and feet, nothing but well-worn denim in between. "Cleaned what?"

"The kitchen after dinner last night. I was a horrible hostess who fought with you *and* ran out on you and yet you still stayed to clean up."

He poured her a cup of coffee and handed over the warm mug. She estimated she'd make it through no more than half the cup before the urge to leap on him and have sex on the kitchen floor did her in. If their discussion—and her apology—wasn't so important, she might have done so already.

"You weren't a horrible hostess." Tate took the seat next to her and set down his own steaming mug.

"You were here last night, weren't you?"

"Yes, I was here." He laid a hand on hers, linking their fingers on top of the table. "And if we're going for total honesty, I was a bad dinner guest who fought with you right back. I'm sorry."

"Me, too." Her gaze dipped toward the table before winging back up to him. "I'm truly sorry. I know we don't agree on a lot of things, but you came for dinner and instead I picked a fight with you."

Tate cocked his head, the motion also lifting one large, capable shoulder. "That's how you see it?"

"It's exactly what I did. We had hit a nice settled point in the conversation over burgers, which you were kind enough to bring over, and then I went and tossed ten years of anger back in your face."

She'd been reading his expressions for years, which made the inscrutable one that settled over his face that much more of a surprise. His gaze was serious, but not angry. His mouth was firm, but the lines showed no hints of frustration. And his eyes were wide open, even as she couldn't read a single thing in their depths.

It was unsettling and unnerving, but it was his comment that topped off the sense of unreality. "Maybe you and I need to start fresh."

"How do two people who've known each other their whole lives start fresh?"

He stood and moved closer, pulling her to her feet. Then he moved in, nestling her flush against him, his arms wrapping around her waist. She had no choice but to splay her hands across that broad, warm chest. "I think that's part of our problem, Belly."

"Back to that?"

"Old habits die hard."

She supposed they did and, if she were honest, she sort of loved the nickname. Unwilling to give him the satisfaction of knowing that, she focused instead on his bigger point. "Our problem?"

"Yep. *Our* problem."

She didn't miss the emphasis, or the way his arms tightened around her, both possessive and protective in equal measure.

"We've both been spending too much time in the past."

She was afraid of the question, but she'd never been any good at hiding things from him. And she certainly couldn't hide something this important. "Isn't that where we started? And isn't that why we keep ending up back in the same spot?"

"I suppose."

"That's awfully noncommittal."

"Maybe it's just a place. A starting point, if you will."

Whatever Tate was—and she knew he worked hard to project that practiced aloofness—Belle was well aware his waters ran far deeper than they appeared.

Before she could press him to explain, he continued. "I've been thinking about it. A lot. And I realized that I've spent so much time thinking about what happened a decade ago that I haven't taken a bit of time to look at what's happening now."

"What's happening now?"

"Two adults who might just have a second chance. Especially if they can grow up enough to push aside past hurts and maybe a bit of their pride."

"Do you think you can do that?"

A wry quirk tugged the corner of his lips. "Just me?"

"No." She shook her head. It wasn't just him. To be fair, it had never been just him. "Both of us. I'd like to try, but I'd like to know that you're willing to try, too."

"I'm willing to try. More than that, I want to. I want to live a different life than I've been living. And I'd like to do it with you."

"You're serious?" She hadn't doubted his sincerity, but there was something about hearing the actual words that stole her breath.

"Yes."

"And you don't care about my job."

She would have seen it anyway in the movement of his muscles, but his body tensed against her. "I care. A lot. And I'm not going to suddenly get over the danger or the worry. But I sort of realized that I was going to worry about you whether or not we were a couple."

"You did?"

Throughout their exchange a subtle gleam of teasing hovered in his eyes, so it was fascinating to watch as it vanished. "Always."

"But you've told me again and again that it's a wasted pursuit. That there's always another bad guy to catch."

"I still believe that."

If he still believed it, then what were they doing? For all his talk of forgetting the past, wasn't that the same place they'd been before? Was now any different? Or would they simply be putting a temporary bandage on things?

Because it sure as hell seemed like it.

"I can't go through that again."

"Through what?"

"Losing you. Feeling like I have to choose." She

slid from his arms, her steps backward insistent at the same time he instinctively tightened his hold. "I won't survive if I have to do that again."

"But that's what I'm trying to tell you. I'm okay with it."

"Okay?"

"Yes. I've realized what it means to live without you and I don't want to do it anymore."

She didn't want to fight. Didn't want to go back to that dark place where they both hovered in their respective corners, unwilling to hear the other out. But as one comment tumbled into the next, she struggled to see how he had really changed.

"So you want to be together but you still think my life's work is a waste? That I'd be better off doing something else?"

The lightness that had carried them through the night and on into morning faded, the air between them growing thick with a decade of resentment and anger. Oh, how she didn't want to go back to that place.

Yet how could she ignore it?

"I'm not entitled to my opinion?" Tate's tone was calm but it was impossible to miss the sparks of anger turning his gaze into a hard emerald. "I'm not holding you back and I'm through asking you to change. But that doesn't mean I have to like it. Doesn't mean I should suddenly feel good about seeing you stand over a dead body or a bloody crime scene."

"That rarely happens. Despite recent events, murder is an uncommon occurrence in the Pass."

"So you can stand there and tell me that the night you stood over Jamie Grantham's dead body, a wrecked-out shell decimated by drugs, you didn't stand over the specter of violent death? Or the car crashes you go to in the middle of the night, pulling lifeless bodies from the wreckage? Or the drug raids you go on with the Feds?"

"That's not all the time. Why are you making such a big deal about it?"

"Because it's you!" The anger that had built and brewed spewed forth with all the force of a geyser. "It's you, Belle! Every time you walk into one of those situations, it's eking out a piece of your soul. Every time you face one of those dark, desperate situations, you give up a part of your humanity for someone else's."

She'd believed herself immune to it. If she'd questioned herself even the day before, she'd have quickly assured anyone who asked that she'd long since gotten past this argument with Tate. Had gotten over the raw, ripping pain of standing on opposite sides of deep-running, emotional waters.

But she hadn't.

The deepest, darkest part of her lightened somehow when she went into those situations he disdained so much. In those moments, when she helped someone else at their darkest hour, she made some cosmic correction for her mother's life.

And he didn't understand a bit of it.

The man she loved—the one she'd love until the day she died—didn't understand the deepest part of her.

"No, Tate. You don't get it. I'm not giving up my humanity. When I go into those situations, I get it back."

Russ Grantham paced the small shed in his back-yard and focused on his next move. Sweet, wholesome Belle Granger had become his enemy. He had no idea how it had happened—and the reality had blindsided him as swiftly as a bullet to the brain—but it was true.

She suspected him. Suspected him for the murders of the trash that did their dirty work in the Pass and the areas beyond. Those suspicions had been subtle and more sly than he'd have expected, but they were there all the same.

He'd watched her for years. Watched how she'd come up in the department, working hard and growing in her skills. He'd had such pride in her, watching Reese's little friend grow into a fine policewoman.

He knew of her background, of course. Midnight Pass was small and even aside from the fact that his daughter was close with Belle, he was in a position to know everything about everyone. He knew her father had never been in the picture and that her mother had borne her own share of demons. He'd worried over that when she'd first joined the force, but had soon come to realize that up-and-coming Belle Granger was a natural for police work. A determined young woman, she'd taken that core ability and honed it through years of hard work and a willingness to put in the hours.

He'd had that drive once. That ambition. And that belief in the system that wrongs would be righted and the evil ones would be brought to justice.

How wrong he'd been.

How misguided.

And oh, how his eyes had been opened when he'd realized that he could right the wrongs on his own.

He reached for the medal at his neck, only to find nothing but his own flesh. That was bad luck, more than he could say. Abrogato had grabbed at it in a heated moment of struggle and torn it off. Russ had hunted for it once he'd ended the man's life, but the dark and the thickness of the grass had prevented him from finding it. In the end, he'd believed it would sink into the earth and, if ever found, would simply be ignored. A belief only reinforced by the heavy spring rains that had coated the Pass for a week.

Yet Belle had gone looking for clues and had found it.

It was a stroke of bad luck, but nothing he couldn't handle.

Nothing he couldn't overcome.

He could overcome anything. Hadn't he already proven that? Hadn't he put on a smile and gone back to his life and spent each and every miserable day since losing his son demonstrating that truth?

Only now he had to demonstrate a new truth. He believed in his cause and his calling. And while he hated to take an innocent life—one he genuinely cared for— he wouldn't stop his work.

His fingers ran to his neck once more, only this time, he tapped it against his chest, lost in thought. Losing the pendant was as much a stroke of bad luck as an emotional disappointment. He'd worn the gold image of Mary around his neck his whole life. He'd taken strength and comfort from her, believing that her mother's heart knew and understood his pain.

Yet now that pendant was a link in a deadly chain.

One that would have to end with Belle Granger's death.

His sister's woo-woo music floated out of the living room, something dreamy and full of strings, as Tate entered the kitchen. The door slammed behind him, a dark counterpoint to the music and the distinct odor of cloying flowers that she liked to put on from some weird-looking diffuser when she did her yoga.

The world was upside down and no amount of soothing music or smelly crap was going to make it better.

He prowled to the counter, dragged a mug out of the cabinet and then poured himself a cup of coffee. For all her spiritual ways and clean living, Arden was as much of a coffee fiend as the rest of them and the pot was full and hot.

Which would do as a fine stand-in until he could hit the whiskey bottle. He'd be surprised if he made it until three with the mood he was in.

Maybe two.

Damn it, what the hell had happened? He and Belle had come to an understanding last night. He'd nearly spilled out the fact that he loved her—had always loved her—over morning coffee and she'd blindsided him with all the talk of her job.

Why did that always get in the way?

And why was it so damned important to her that he was okay with it all?

He *was* okay, wasn't he? He wanted to be with her and he was fine if police work was her life's calling. And it really didn't matter if he was fine or not—he was well aware he had no say in the matter. He'd lived with that knowledge for ten years and wasn't interested in continuing to fight the battle.

She was a cop. A damn fine one. Couldn't he believe in her and love her and still hate that she did work that put her in the crosshairs of criminals?

He was halfway through his coffee when the air changed and his sister filled the doorway frame. "Scowl much?"

"Nosy much?" he shot back.

"You're the one stomping around in here like a grizzly bear. You interrupted my meditation."

"Meditate later."

"I was meditating now."

"Too bad."

"What is wrong with you?"

"You mean other than the fact that the house smells like a cheap whore's perfume and you're trying to put me to sleep with the music?"

Arden stomped across the kitchen, moving up so they were nose to nose. Or nose to chest as it were. Although his sister barely reached his shoulder, he had no doubt she could and would hold her own. "What crawled up your ass and died, Tate Reynolds?"

"Why does it have to be my problem? I walk in here to get a cup of coffee and this place has turned into a freaking yoga studio. There's no space. No air!"

In his anger, his arm swung wider than he intended, his fingers flying open as his mug flew loose, shattering on the floor. The coffee spilled out in an arc and Arden jumped back, out of its way. He wasn't so lucky, as half a mug of hot liquid poured over his jeans.

She went from virago to den mother in an instant. "Damn it, Tate. Hurry up and get those off."

The normal modesty he and his brothers maintained around Arden vanished at the evidence he was liable to get burns if he didn't shuck his jeans. In moments, he had them off, balled and tossed onto the floor. His sister had already taken off for the laundry room and was back in moments, a broom and dustpan in hand along with a pair of sweatpants folded from the laundry. "They're Ace's, so they'll be long but they'll do."

He took the offering, dragging on the cotton sweat-pants before taking the broom and pan from her. "I'll get it. You don't need to clean up after my stupidity or my temper."

As gestures went, it was small, but as those were usually the most meaningful, the set of Arden's shoulders visibly relaxed. While he cleaned up, she took his jeans and headed back to the laundry room. In moments, the shards had all been swept up along with the spilled coffee and the washing machine thundered from where it sat just off the kitchen.

Arden had two fresh mugs out of the cabinet, already full of coffee, when he dumped the last of the broken ceramic pieces into the garbage. "Now. Do you want to tell me what has you so upset?"

"No."

"Let me rephrase then. What has you so upset?"

"Just leave it—" He'd nearly brushed her off—was absolutely prepared to head out with his sucky attitude to spend time with Tot—when he stopped. And the moment he stood still, all the anger and hurt and resentment spilled out in a torrent.

"It's Belle."

"Of course it's Belle."

"What's that supposed to mean?"

The soft smile that ghosted across his sister's lips was matched by the mysterious twinkle that lit up her eyes. "It's always been Belle."

"That doesn't mean it's not the height of lunacy."

"I believe the quote goes something along the lines of 'love makes fools of us all.' Isn't that the one?"

"There's foolish and then there's madness. That's just the way of things between us."

"She's a levelheaded person. You're usually a levelheaded person. What happened? Maybe I can translate for you."

"What's there to translate? We came to an understanding."

"By understanding, I assume you mean sex?"

"I'm not discussing that with you."

"Oh, good." Arden rubbed her hands together. "When I finally start getting some again, I won't discuss that with you either."

He did just fine to avoid thinking about his baby sister in those terms, even as he accepted she was an adult. But did she have to go there? "Can't you cut me a break?"

"Why? This is fun. But now, back to our discussion." She picked up her mug. "You were about to tell me what you did to make Belle mad."

"I didn't say that."

"You implied it," she said, her words as tart as a lemon icebox pie.

"You're inferring it."

"And you're stalling. What'd you do?"

Clearly he had done something that morning, but to hell if he knew what it was. One minute he and Belle were having a moment, words of love dancing in his head like crazy cupids itching to break free, and the next she was slipping from his arms and accusing him of lacking understanding and support.

Of being the same damn jerk he was ten years ago.

The anger that had cooled when he dropped the mug roared back in full force.

"I didn't do anything."

"Then why is she upset?"

"How the hell should I know? And why are you taking her side? What about my anger? What about how I feel? She started in on me before I even knew what was happening and in moments I'm the bad guy. The dumb Neanderthal who can't accept her life's ambitions or goals."

Arden settled her mug and sat back, all humor and wry teasing vanishing in a heartbeat. "And now we're getting somewhere."

"What's that supposed to mean?"

"Exactly what it sounds like. What did you two actually discuss? Give me the Neanderthal parts and all."

When he said nothing, Arden leaned closer. "I'm on your side, Tate. Truly, I am. So tell me."

"I told her that I worried about her. That my biggest fear about how she put her life in danger trying to convict the scum of the universe was going to happen, whether we were together or not."

"And then what?"

"And then she was telling me how unsupportive I was and how she couldn't break up with me a second time. That she can't go through that again. Hell, Arden!" He pushed back his chair, unable to sit any longer. "I can't go through that again either. It damn near killed me the first time. The only thing that helped was I was so focused on cleaning up Dad's mess that I had something to pay attention to. A goal that needed my full focus. I don't know what the hell I'd do now."

"So you walked away."

"Yeah."

"Why?"

"Because she asked me to. Because she thinks I don't support her."

"Well, if we're going to set the record straight, you don't."

"Sure I do."

Arden crossed her arms, the gesture as familiar now as it was when they were kids. If she'd only had her hair in pigtails, he might have actually thought they'd transported back to twenty years earlier. "Then what did you say to her?"

Before he could claim ignorance, she added, "General gist. I should be able to translate from there."

"I already told you. It bothers me that she's in danger, but she's in danger anyway, so we might as well be together."

Arden's arms remained folded and he could have sworn she barely suppressed an eye roll but she said nothing other than, "And then what?"

"She goes off about how I think what she does is a waste. That there are always more bad guys to catch. More of the mess humans make of their life."

"Which, in your defense, isn't completely wrong," Arden said. "There *are* always more bad guys to catch. It doesn't mean choosing to catch them is a waste. I like feeling safe in my own home. I suspect the rest of the Pass feels the same way."

And right there—that simple point—knocked his anger down a few pegs. "And then I tossed a few examples in her face."

"Examples?"

"The bad situations that probably still haunt her."

"How'd that work out for you?"

"I'm here instead of in Belle Granger's shower. With her."

"Ewww." Arden held up a hand. "Stop. Please."

"Sorry. Low blow. Just needed to get back at you for the sex comment."

"Consider us even." Arden eyed him from her spot at the table, that blue gaze steely and raw. "Anything else?"

"I might have suggested she gives up her humanity for the dregs of society. Like a trade-off, her good for their bad."

"Oh, Tate."

He braced for censure, so the tenderness in her gaze and the soft smile that looked so like their mother's was enough to take a few more of those pegs out from beneath his feet.

"Don't you understand? That's exactly why she's so special. She doesn't give up her good. She shares it with others."

Blindsided and heartsick, Tate groped for the back of his chair and fell hard into the seat. "What?"

"She's not giving up the good. She's using what she has to make things better."

Like the proverbial hand his sister was always threatening to level across his head, she'd managed the same with only a few words.

Of course Belle's good made the bad better. Her good made everything better. Including him.

Always him.

Chapter 17

Belle had slogged through the past few days, still shell-shocked over what had transpired with Tate. After she'd put an end to their sexy coffee talk, she'd gotten ready and dragged herself to work and refused to think about what she'd given up.

Or, more to the point, what she'd sent away.

Love.

She loved Tate and no amount of self-righteous anger or frustration or worry that the future only held more heartache could change that fact. She'd considered heading over to the ranch more than once since Thursday morning. Had thought about what she'd say and how she'd try to make him see reason. Had even thought about telling him how she felt.

And each time, she stopped herself.

Hadn't they proven once before that love wasn't enough? Love wasn't their problem and never had been.

Which meant that she was right back to square zero, throwing herself into work and trying to run from her problems. And, she admitted, staring at her paper cup full of coffee that had long gone cold, spending yet another Saturday at work.

When she'd pulled into her driveway after leaving the Rivera crime scene, Tate was parked and waiting for her in his truck, and she'd believed they'd turned a corner. The hours that had followed in his arms had only reinforced that fact.

And then it had all vanished over coffee.

She hadn't been exaggerating when she'd told him that surviving their breakup had been the hardest experience of her life. Worse than growing up with an addict for a mother and the responsibility that came with that. And worse than the guilt that had haunted her after her mother had passed.

Could she have done enough?

Could she have tried harder?

Those questions had faded over time as she came to accept her mother's challenges, but oddly enough, they were the same questions that had haunted her over her relationship with Tate. With her mother, she'd finally accepted the truth—that she'd done all she could and had tried her best to help.

With Tate? She'd never been sure. Had there been an alternative to walking away from each other?

It had taken a long time, but over the past year, she'd finally begun to believe that things had simply worked out as they were meant to. That no matter how powerful their attraction to each other was, they were obviously supposed to move on in life separately.

And then Jesse Abrogato's murder had thrown them

right back together. Lovers unable to resist the lure of one another.

Since her own company held little solace and even fewer answers, she snagged her cup and opted for another hit of caffeine. It likely wouldn't remove the hamster wheel of her thoughts but it might give her just enough of a jolt to push through the last of her paperwork on the Rivera murder.

The chief had taken the lead on the overall report but had asked her to cover some of the interviews with park observers, Rivera's neighbors and his family. She'd wrapped up her list the day before and was now going through the tedious process of writing up her notes. Notes that had taken a back seat while she'd worked on the report of the evidence she'd discovered and logged on Reynolds property. Just that morning, Chief Corden's commendation of her strong police work had come winging back in her email along with a promise that he'd spend even more time with her report and also share it with Agent Ross.

She'd done all she could. And Monday, she'd share her suspicions about the gold pendant and see how her chief wanted to handle things.

Belle reran her interviews through her mind as she walked into the kitchen at the back of the precinct and put her cup into the brewing station. The contraption was large and overwrought and probably more than a bit of overkill for a single cup of coffee, but it had been a donation from one of the local restaurants a few months back when they'd remodeled and Belle loved everything about the hot water and freshly ground beans.

It also beat the swill they used to have by a country

mile—or more like a cross-country flight—and she was grateful for the thoughtful donation.

The brewer went to work, the distinct grinding of beans murmuring in the air as she mentally rewound one of her conversations from the day before. She was waiting on a callback from one of the Rivera interview subjects and had put an impromptu call in to Jesse Abrogato's sister in the meanwhile.

The discovery of the jewelry piece still bothered her, the implications to Captain Grantham significant. If it was his jewelry, obviously they had a far bigger problem on their hands than they could have ever imagined.

And if it wasn't…

Then they still had a clue toward finding a killer. Abrogato's sister confirmed that her brother didn't own any religious articles and that the gold pendant wasn't his. Whatever else he'd been in life, his sister's insisted that the man wasn't religious and had refused to pretend he was with external trappings. That had removed the suspicion that the piece was the victim's.

Tate had already confirmed the day she made the discovery that it didn't look like anything his men wore, which brought her right back to Russ.

There still wasn't concrete evidence on Captain Grantham, but she'd taken a bit of time to look at her email and call records from the timing of all the previous murders. Not only had he been out of the office this week when Rivera was killed, but Grantham had also been unaccounted for around the time of each of the three prior murders.

Funny how it hadn't seemed odd at the time, yet now seemed like a glaring, gaping hole. He was a man who communicated with his team regularly. Emails, texts and the daily requirements of leading a team of people ensured he was in close contact. Yet during those windows, it was as if he'd vanished.

The coffee maker sputtered out the last of her coffee, steam rising in its wake. She took the cup, careful to hold the hot paper by the rim. The station was quiet, a low hum of activity echoing from the front of the precinct where a few beat cops spoke in low tones. Belle hardly noticed it, the silence like a cocoon that allowed her to keep her focus and get her work done. Focus she sorely needed because her thoughts were so scattered. On Tate.

Just as they'd been for the past several days, her mind tormented her with what-ifs, tripping between Tate and the murders like an out of control roller coaster. Once more, the urge to drive over to Reynolds Station and hash it out with him again gripped her.

Would it make a difference? Or was it just another pointless exercise in hurting herself?

Even if they came to some sort of truce now, the hot sex and good behavior that were an inevitable part of a new relationship would fade. She'd still have her job and he'd still resent her for it.

And they'd be right back to where they started.

"Belle?"

The low, achy voice grabbed her immediately and she glanced up to see the object of half her tumbling thoughts standing in the doorway to the back entrance to the precinct, just beyond the kitchen. "Russ?"

He was doubled over at the waist, a look of sheer agony painting the tight lines of his face.

"I don't feel so good." The words came out slurred

and he stumbled forward a few steps, one hand clutching the wall while another covered his heart.

Sympathy roared through her, that ever-present need to help pushing her toward him. This was Reese's father. Her boss. And he was her friend. Whatever she suspected him of paled in comparison to seeing him struggle as if it was painful to even breathe.

In moments, she was at his side. She bobbled her cup of forgotten coffee when some of the liquid sloshed over the rim, burning the tips of her fingers and quickly righted it.

"Russ. Are you okay?"

"My heart." His words were thready as she placed her free hand on his back. Even through his uniform she could feel the heat rising off him. His pulse hammered beneath her palm and she fought to hold his weight as he wavered, his large frame toppling against her.

"Let's get you to your office. You can sit down. I'll call for help."

Those were the last words she got out before he twisted, that solid, still-strong body pinning her against the wall. One hand covered her mouth while the other gripped her arm. With shocking clarity, she recognized her mistake in trying to help him, especially out of sight of anyone in the squad room. Panic roared through her, ratcheting up her pulse and driving her into action.

The heat of her coffee registered through her adrenaline and fear. Going slack, she used that momentary shift in body position to hurl her coffee at him, the steaming liquid covering his face. He grunted, a low moan escaping his lips before his body slammed against hers even harder than before.

Belle wanted to fight. Wanted to protest and find a way out of the situation, but his renewed grip—now against her throat—was too tight. Each time she tried to kick out, the sheer size and strength of him and the extended reach of his arms held her in place.

The familiar walls of the precinct and the even more familiar face began to fade along with what was left of the air in her lungs and the edges of her vision grew murky.

When she thought about it later, she'd run through it all in her mind. How she could have defended herself differently. How she should have questioned his sudden illness. How the chief had deserved to know of her suspicions sooner so he could be aware of the situation.

But at that moment, she thought of none of it.

At that moment, all Belle could do was let the darkness take her.

Although he hadn't returned quite to raging jerkville with his family, Tate's conversation with Arden still lay heavy in his thoughts. He'd avoided spending too much time with any of them, instead choosing to spend the rest of the week and the better part of the weekend out on Tot, riding the property and thinking about his next steps.

He wanted a life with Belle. Nothing had changed that and nothing would. The past ten years had felt like a lifetime apart and he didn't want to do it anymore.

Nor could he shake the reality of his sister's words. *That's exactly why she's so special.*

She doesn't give up her good. She shares it with others.

She's using what she has to make things better.

Belle did make things better. She'd made him a better man, long before he'd even understood what that was or why it mattered. His own father had been absent much of his life, at first just missing and later distant as his bad business practices sprouted consequences. Ace had done his best to set a good example, bearing the brunt of responsibility as the oldest. His mother had filled in the gaps, her expectations of upstanding, honest behavior and compassion something she'd drilled into all of them.

But Belle had cemented it.

He'd walk her home from school or carry her things or hold the door for her. At first, it was because his mother had told him it was the right thing to do and later, it had just become natural. More than natural, he'd wanted to do things to help her.

She'd been a constant in his life—at school, after school, on the weekends. She was a part of his life and he couldn't remember a time when she wasn't there.

Until the day he'd sent her away.

He spurred Tot forward, their meander through the property taking them toward the west end, where they'd discovered the cut fence and then the dead body that had started this whole nightmare.

What if he hadn't headed out this way a few weeks ago? If the body had continued decomposing in the bottom of a ravine, subjected to the elements…

The discovery of Jesse Abrogato had started all of this. The hunt for a killer. The discovery of a second, connected body. And the return of his relationship with

Belle. He hadn't considered it through that lens, but now that he did, it was upsetting to realize that they'd come back together under the worst possible circumstances.

Against the backdrop of murder.

How hadn't he realized it before?

And how had he been so ignorant to understand how conflated her feelings were? Here she was helping him and his family and he'd denigrated all she worked for. And, by extension, who she was.

A lone figure, waving in the distance, caught his attention and he angled Tot toward the man. It didn't take long to see that it was Julio Bautista waving him over. Tot understood his impatience, running toward the man at a fast clip. In a matter of moments, they'd covered the ground between them.

"Julio. What can I do for you?"

"You don't know?" Julio's dark brown eyes narrowed as his wizened face tightened.

"Know what?"

"Bella? Is she here?"

The roiled emotions that had kept him company since the morning he walked out of Belle's house flared high, an irrational response to the older man's reference to Belle. "No, she's not here. Why?"

"She hasn't been seen since Saturday."

"What?" Tate struggled to take in Julio's words even as the implications were already dive-bombing his sense of calm. "Where is she?"

"We don't know." Julio shook his head. "I've been all over. Chief's been all over. We can't find her."

"When was the last time anyone saw her?"

"Annie on the dispatch desk said she left late on Friday night. Chief checked her computer and she had an email half drafted. Date on the start of it was late morning Saturday. That's the last we can figure."

And it was Monday.

The tension that gripped his stomach tightened with unholy fists.

Belle had been missing for two days and no one had known.

Belle came to on a sense of unreality. Her pulse pounded, the sound loud in her ears as she desperately fought for her bearings and her breath. Hard gasps accompanied the heavy thud in her veins and she struggled to get a sense of place through the raw, aching fear and swirling headache that blurred her vision.

Where was she now? And why?

Renewed awareness returned in full as her breathing slowed, that sense of unreality giving way to all she did know. Aside from the lingering headache, she was fine and she wasn't drugged any longer. And, as she wiggled her fingers, she realized she did have freedom of movement.

The dim lighting and lightly circulating air was a decided improvement over the small space Grantham had originally shoved her into and as her eyes adjusted to the light she could make out the edges of an air mattress that she lay on. Struggling against the headache, she sat up, rubbing at her wrists and the remembered ties that had held them together the first time she came to.

She *had* been moved.

The events at the precinct had haunted her in the initial hours after he'd taken her—the way he'd preyed on her sympathy and years of familiarity and friendship. What had happened to break him so badly? And when had the kindly father figure and mentor turned into a monster?

The cloying questions had only added to the tight space—best she could tell, he'd kept her in a small shed after taking her—and she'd finally given into the frustration and the sense of unreality with body-racking sobs.

Whatever she'd believed she knew about Russ Grantham, that man was gone. When the tears had finally cleared—the sobs both for herself as well as the grief over the loss of a friend—she found new strength. And the determination to keep focused. There could be no more sympathy or empathy for the shell of a man left behind after losing his son. To maintain either emotion would negate her ability to protect herself.

To do what had to be done to slay the monster.

That focus had fueled her as he'd ultimately transported her from the small space into this one. She had no sense of time or place, but she'd remained attentive through the fear and the blindfold he'd placed on her as he'd driven. She'd pictured Midnight Pass, using his home as the starting point for a mental map of the land. Had fought the urge to struggle as she lay in the back of a moving vehicle and instead used the time to think.

And considered how she might leave a similar clue as Jesse Abrogato had if everything went sideways.

The drive had been short—further credence that they were still in the Pass—and Belle had considered how to play things when she was removed from the car. Her plans were short-lived when he'd opened the trunk into bright sunlight, a gun pointed at her head even as his other hand came down over her mouth and nose.

For the second time, the world had gone black.

And now here she was.

Eyes fully adjusted, she looked around the room. Aside from the air mattress, there was a small, four-legged sink and a toilet. A plate of food sat on a drop-leaf table but there were no chairs. Nor could she find anything that could be used as a physical weapon. No other small furniture like an end table or a lamp. And, after a quick glance over the counters, not even any drawers that could be removed for their heft or cornered edges.

Russ Grantham was a cop and a good one, and he'd eliminated any ability for his prisoner to gain the upper hand.

Which only made her more determined to find one.

Tate ignored the steady, stoic stares of a team of Midnight Pass police officers led by Chief Corden and an equally stoic set of federal agents led by Agent Noah Ross and focused on what he knew. The intimidation tactics of a line of officers meant nothing to him. Their endless questions and probing for answers meant even less.

Belle was gone.

And he knew the man who'd taken her.

"Why did she suspect Russ?" Hayes Corden asked again, the same as they'd been asking for the past hour. Once again, Tate walked them all through the details she'd shared. Her suspicions over Grantham. The evidence she'd found on Reynolds property. And the grave concern that it had belonged to Russ.

"How well do you know Captain Grantham?" One of Ross's flunkies asked the question—for the third time, even though the phrasing had been changed up slightly—and Tate lost it.

"I've known Russ my whole life. So has Belle. So has most of the damn town. None of us thought this could happen and it tore her up. No one had any idea how his son's death affected him, but as she looked into this, she began to realize it was true."

"What was true?" Hayes pressed.

"That Russ had decided to take matters into his own hands."

"And you believe the captain of the Midnight Pass police force has Belle?" The same flunky asked that question and it was only the fear for Belle's safety— and the desperate desire that she come back to him safe—that kept him in his seat.

"Yes. Wherever Russ is. That's where you'll find Belle."

The raw panic that hadn't abated for a single second since he spotted Julio Bautista crested once more in his chest. Why were they sitting here talking about this when they should be out there looking for her?

The flunky spoke once more. "You realize this is a serious accusation, Mr. Reynolds?"

Strike three.

Tate pushed off the table, standing to his full height. He didn't miss the tense sets of eight pairs of shoulders or the subtle drift of hands in the direction of their weapons. Once again, he didn't care.

"She's out there. She's been taken, best as any of you can tell, off this property and you're all sitting here with your heads up your asses. Get out there! Go find her!"

It was Ross who finally spoke, his tone calm even as his eyes flashed a dark warning in the direction of his team. "We're trying to do that, but we don't know where to start."

"The lodge," Tate said, several memories from high school drifting back to mind. "The Granthams have a hunting lodge out on the edge of the Pass. He's got her there."

Eight sets of surprised eyes swung his direction, even as recognition dawned quickly in Hayes's. "Why there?"

"Why not there? It's quiet and isolated. Russ shut it down after Jamie died, but best I know he hasn't sold the property."

"He hasn't." Julio spoke up from the back of the room where he'd quietly been taking it all in. "And the lodge would make sense. It's isolated and he's owned it for so long we have to assume he's had more than enough time to set it up to his own needs."

Tate focused on Julio. "His needs?"

At the single, terse nod, panic turned to sheer terror. He'd seen one of Grantham's victims. And he understood what horrific needs now drove the man he'd once called a friend.

"Are you all right?"

Belle started at the intrusion from her perch on the air mattress. She jumped to her feet, surprised to see Russ Grantham in uniform, standing in the doorway. She hadn't heard any noise alerting her to his presence and then suddenly, he was there.

"I asked if you were all right."

"I'm not."

"I'm sorry for that. More than I can say." He'd left her alone and hadn't made any move to talk to her since he'd faked the heart attack at the station. He hadn't needed many words during her transport—his gun did more than enough talking—and her unconsciousness upon capture and then from the tranquilizer drugs at transport had ensured she wasn't asking him anything back.

Now was her chance.

"Why?"

"You know why."

"This isn't a way to help Jamie."

"This is all to help Jamie." Where she'd anticipated madness, she saw none. Only calm, cool control and, in an eerie counterpoint, the sweet, fatherly pride she'd always associated with him. "I lost my son, but I don't want others losing their children. I'm doing good."

"You're methodically torturing and murdering people."

"No. I'm dealing with the dregs of society. The animals who prey on others for greed and avarice."

Her gaze ran over his uniform, his captain's bars seeming to gleam in the muted light of the overhead. "But it's our job to deal with them. Lawfully."

A harsh laugh rumbled from his chest. Unlike anything she'd ever heard before, the sound was part sob, part cackle. It was the laugh of someone who'd lost everything and it echoed with empty, bone-deep despair.

"There's no law here anymore."

"Because you took it away."

"Because the criminals have overrun everything!

Because drugs run so rampant we've had to put officers on patrol around our elementary school. We have to put kids through metal detectors and purse searches at prom. And every month, we have more people who check into the Pass's drug programs and facilities. I've watched it. Studied it. And I finally found a way to end it."

Belle gave up her last, lingering belief that he'd mentally snapped. There was no sign of madness in his words. Only the harsh reality of someone who'd lost all hope.

Every time you face one of those dark, desperate situations, you give up a part of your humanity for someone else's.

Tate's words lingered in her mind. They hadn't been far from her thoughts since their fight on Thursday morning, but something in them suddenly fell into place. And all the heartache and anger she'd carried since then found its purpose.

She hadn't given up anything. It was the world around her that had lost its humanity and she was determined to give it back. To find some meaning and purpose and understanding inside the heart of darkness.

"I know how it hurts. How you want them to come back to you. How it should be so easy for them, to leave the next fix alone. If they only loved you enough. If you could only love them more, it would all go away."

Russ blinked before he wiped at the corners of his eyes. For the first moment since he'd pressed her against the wall of the precinct, she saw a flash of the old Russ. The man who'd mentored her and who'd always believed in her. "It doesn't go away."

"No. It doesn't. And they prove to you over and over that they can't just ignore that lure. The one only they can see. The one that takes them away for a while."

"He was a good boy." Russ's tears fell in earnest, even as he kept his distance on the other side of the room. "There was a time when he loved school and sports and music. He played with his sister. Fought with her, too, but he was her fiercest protector. He used to walk her to school to make sure she was okay. He used to kiss his mother every night on the cheek, then rub his nose to hers. He used to play football with me in the backyard."

"I know." And she did know. She remembered Jamie Grantham's sweet smile and happy-go-lucky personality.

"They took that. They took it all away."

The compassion that had carried her toward him in the precinct reared up once more and she went with instinct. With that steady determination that she wouldn't lose her humanity. Wouldn't lose what made her who she was.

She crossed the room, her gaze steady on his, her sole focus on getting to him and on helping him. His own gaze never wavered off from hers, nor did he refuse when she came close and pulled him toward her. "I'm sorry, Russ. More sorry for Jamie than I can ever say."

He pulled her to his side, accepting the hug with one arm. It was a move that registered a second too late.

With the speed they were taught at the academy and the subsequent decades of practice, he had his service pistol out of its holster, the butt of the weapon pointed at her. "I'm sorry, too."

* * *

Tate bumped over the Grantham property with Julio in his passenger seat. The police and the Feds had taken off as soon as he'd suggested the hunting lodge but it was Julio who had told him to come along.

"We will get to Bella. We will get to her because of you."

"What if I'm wrong?"

"Then we keep looking."

The response was simple and matter-of-fact and it did a surprising amount to calm the nerves that danced over his skin, his scalp tight and prickled with fear.

They had to be there. Where else would Russ have taken her? He was a well-known figure in Midnight Pass. It wasn't like he could drive anywhere in town without someone noticing him. That would go doubly true if he attempted to take someone. And until Belle had pinpointed his possible involvement, no one would have any reason to check out the hunting property.

No one would have any reason to believe it had become the lair of a murderer.

"Don't go to the house." Julio pointed toward the land that spread out as far as they could see. Several police cars were already at the small house Grantham had built on the property as well as the large barn they'd used for weekend parties. "Does he have a hunting blind?"

Tate had never been much of a hunter, but he had been out here several times in his life. He tried to think through the land and what he knew of Russ's love of the outdoors. "There are two blinds. One at either end. And there's a small cabin that had been on the property when he bought it."

"Go there." Julio pointed through the window. "Now."

Tate prayed the man was right as he continued bumping over uneven ground, pushing the work truck to its limits. The house faded in his rearview mirror and he prayed he was going the right way. Prayed they'd get there in time. It was only when a small structure came up on the horizon that Tate took his first hopeful breath. "There. Up on the right, around two o'clock."

"Park about three hundred yards away and cut the engine. We'll come in from—"

Julio broke off as the distinct silhouette of two people came into view in front of the house. The older man already had his gun out, his focus through the window as the couple came closer and closer into view. "Stop the truck. Now."

Tate pulled up short, the wheels spinning in some mud left over from the rains earlier in the week. He was out of the car before Julio could move to stop him, his own gun that he'd laid on the console between the seats already in hand.

It was foolish and risky, but he could only hope he'd be enough of a distraction to grab Russ's attention, giving Belle the needed leverage to take Russ's gun.

She was strong and capable and he knew she could do it. She'd been trained for this. Had been taught how to get out of dangerous situations. And he'd never believed in that training more than at this moment.

Belle marched from the small house next to Russ, his grip tight and his gun unwavering as he moved her forward. The moment they'd cleared the room where he'd held her, on toward the front door, she had a sense of where she was.

"This is your property."

"Yes."

Where he'd done his awful work. "So why drag the body to Reynolds Station? Or the other body to the park?"

"I needed a place. The cut fence over at Reynolds was a good distraction and it took the focus off of here."

Of course it had.

"Russ. Can't we—" She stopped as he pushed her through the door, on out into the bright spring day.

God, how had she been so wrong? How had she misjudged him so badly once again? She'd seen his tears. More, she'd seen how he'd broken at the memories of Jamie and she'd instinctively pushed toward that.

And was going to pay for it with her life.

The air was redolent with spring, the grass fresh and new. The scent seemed to surround her, brighter and more vivid than she'd ever remembered. She was heightened, all her senses on alert, like she wanted to take it all in for a few moments more.

If only she could turn it all back. Could have seen him for what he was sooner. Could have told someone sooner.

Aimless censure that had no place to land. She'd made her decisions and she couldn't go back.

Couldn't ever go back. Back to Tate. To her friends. To the job she'd once believed was so important. She loved him and she hadn't even told him. Her worst decision.

The heavy roar of a truck echoed in the distance, drawing her attention off her morbid, empty thoughts.

The sound caught Russ as well and his grip tightened even harder as he pushed her forward. "Move. We don't have much time."

Time.

More of it. Less of it. None of it. She refused to think about it. All she did know was that she was determined to stretch it out and use it to her advantage.

The truck traveled closer and closer over the ground before coming to a stop. It was that subtle shift that gave her the opening she needed and Belle moved into action.

With a technique she'd practiced in some of her self-defense classes, she made herself go limp, softening her body just enough that Russ had to shift to keep his one-armed hold on her. She had a small window—miniscule, really—in the momentum of his readjustment and she was determined to take it.

Russ shifted his hold and she used his body weight against him, sliding from beneath his arms as he over-rotated to keep his arm around her. The shift and the sudden distraction of the truck caused him to stumble and she pushed with all she had, sweeping out with her leg to cut him off at the knee. His hard grunt told her she hit her mark and the moment she felt his grip go slack, she ran.

Legs pumping, she pushed herself forward in a great zigzagging pattern, her only focus the truck.

The adrenaline that carried her forward and the hope of possible rescue shifted immediately as she saw the figure running toward her.

Tate.

He was here and he was in danger, his forward motion and focus on Russ. Shifting immediately, she went after him, screaming all the way. "Tate! No!"

Tate saw it all unfold before him, almost as if outside of himself. He saw Belle take her chance, kicking and getting away from Grantham. He heard the heavy wail of sirens in the distance as the police obviously realized the action wasn't at the ranch house. And he saw the gun in Russ Grantham's hand, lifting into the air in a deadly arc.

He saw it all. He heard Belle's screams. And then he heard the gunshot.

And watched as the man he'd known nearly a lifetime crumpled before him, his uniformed body falling to the ground as the hand that held the gun dropped to his side.

Belle stopped, the ground hard beneath her feet as she skidded to a halt. The determined run toward the truck had shifted into a sprint directly for Tate, fear and panic spurring her on.

Only she hadn't expected the ending.

Hadn't ever considered Russ Grantham would take his own life.

The tears. The gun. The walk outside. None of it had been for her. It was his.

In his last moments, Russ had found his own version of repentance and, ultimately, the freedom he'd never have found in a cage.

Belle hadn't even fully registered she'd stopped until Tate ran toward her. Arms open, his expression was naked and raw, his eyes wild with the moment. She ran forward, pulling him close, taking his comfort in return.

His mouth was on her, his words mindless in her ear as he kissed her cheek, her head, her temple. Moved on to her mouth before his arms pulled her tight against his chest. "Belle."

"Tate." She held him close, her hand at the back of his head, her lips pressing against his neck. "Oh, Tate."

"I thought I wouldn't get to you. That we wouldn't find you. I'm sorry. So sorry for all of it."

"No sorry. No apologies. You're here." She held him tighter, unable to do anything but hold on. "You're here and I love you."

"I love you, too." More kisses rained down on her as sirens wailed behind them and police cars skidded to heavy stops in the thick grass.

Belle heard the noise. She knew what they were there to do and she knew all that would come next. None of it mattered.

All that mattered at that moment was that she was with Tate. She loved him and he loved her.

"Belly?"

"What?" she whispered against his ear before he lifted his head, pulling back to stare down at her.

"I'm sorry I didn't believe in you."

"You didn't say—"

"Please let me finish."

She nodded.

"I believe in you. I've always believed in you. I didn't believe in my ability to love you enough to see past my fear."

"And now?"

"Now I do."

It was so simple. So easy.

He pressed on. "I've spent my entire life up to now in love with you and other than six weeks when we were young, I've never had you in my life. I'm done waiting. And I'm done letting fear dictate my happiness."

"What took you so long?"

"Remember that assiness I told you about?"

Even with all that had happened, he could still make her smile. "That state of being an ass you seem perpetually stuck in?"

"That's the one." He pressed a hard kiss to her lips. "It's gotten in my way and I'm not going to say it won't again. But please tell me you love me anyway."

"I love you, Tate Reynolds. All of you."

"Then I guess that's all there is to it. You're stuck with me."

"As long as it's forever, that's all I care about."

He pressed his lips to hers, sure and true and full of all the love that had always run between them. And as she kissed him back, under a gorgeous Texas spring day, she didn't really care any longer about how long it had taken them to get there.

He was here, they were together and that was all that mattered.

* * * * *

Don't miss the next installment of Addison Fox's
Midnight Pass Texas *series, coming soon*
from Harlequin Romantic Suspense!

Get 4 FREE REWARDS!

We'll send you 2 FREE Books
plus 2 FREE Mystery Gifts.

Harlequin® Romantic Suspense books feature heart-racing sensuality and the promise of a sweeping romance set against the backdrop of suspense.

FREE
Value Over
$20

SPECIAL EXCERPT FROM

⊕ **HARLEQUIN**®

ROMANTIC suspense

Ian Wallace has spent years obsessively pursuing an international crime kingpin, but when his ex, Petra Sloane, is framed for a murder the man committed, he realizes that keeping her safe is his true passion.

Read on for a sneak preview of the next book in the Rocky Mountain Justice miniseries,
Rocky Mountain Valor
by Jennifer D. Bokal.

Ian heard Petra's scream and his blood turned cold. He leaped from the floor and sprinted out the door.

The walkway was empty. Petra was gone—vanished. The echo of her shriek had already faded.

He turned in a quick circle, his eyes taking in everything at once. He saw them—a set of hands clutching the bottom rung of the railing. Petra. Her knuckles were white.

He dived forward and grasped her wrists. "I've got you," he said. "But don't let go."

Petra stared up at him. Her face was chalky and her skin was damp with perspiration. His hands slid. He clasped tighter, his fingers biting into her arm. One shoe slipped from her foot, silently somersaulting through the air before landing with a thump in the courtyard below.

"Ian," she gasped. Her hands slid until just her fingers were hooked over the metal rung. "I can't hold on much longer."

A sharp crack broke the afternoon quiet. It registered as a gunshot and Ian flattened completely.

Just as quickly, he realized that the noise hadn't come from a firearm, but someplace just as deadly. One of three bolts that held the section of railing in place had cracked.

HRSEXP0818

If one of the other bolts broke, the whole section would topple, sending Petra to the courtyard twenty feet below. Then again, maybe that was the best way to save her life.

"Look at me," Ian said to her. She lifted her wide eyes to his. "I have an idea. It's a long shot, but the only shot I have."

Her face went gray. "Okay," she said. "I trust you."

"I'm going to let go of your arms," he said.

Petra began to shake her head. "No, Ian. Don't. This railing's weak. It could fall at any minute."

He ignored the fear in her voice and the dread in her expression. "That's what I'm counting on. I'm going to kick the other bolts loose."

"You're going to what?"

"You have to hold on to the railing and I'll lower it down. At the end, you'll have to drop, but it'll only be a few feet."

"What if you can't hold on to the railing?"

That was the real question, wasn't it? Ian refused to fail. The alternative would be devastating to Petra—to him. "I won't let you get hurt," he vowed.

Petra bit her bottom lip. Their eyes met. "There's no other way, is there?"

Ian shook his head. "Hold on," he warned, "and don't let go until I tell you."

"Got it," she said.

Ian paused, his hands on her wrists. He wanted to tell her more, say something. But what? The moment was too important to waste on words.

"Don't let go," he said again.

Find out if Petra falls in
Rocky Mountain Valor *by Jennifer D. Bokal,*
available September 2018 wherever
Harlequin® Romantic Suspense books
and ebooks are sold.

www.Harlequin.com